Recommen

"Sachs keeps the story moving full-steam-ahead, balancing his fleshed-out portraits of memorable characters with visceral action scenes... ...An engaging and ultimately devastating disaster novel."

-Kirkus Reviews

*

"The Flood is an epic thriller and a remarkable work of art — you'll read it fast, but think (and dream) about it for a long time."

-Matthew Mather, bestselling author of CyberStorm

More Early Praise for *The Flood*

"I feel honored to have been a beta-reader. *The Flood* was unlike anything I've ever read before."

-Victoria L.

*

"Intriguing thrill-ride that never stops until the last page"

-Tia S.

*

"Master storyteller"

"You wind up changing who you're rooting for.... You see yourself in these characters. It's an action book and a psychological thriller at the same time, written with intelligence and courage."

-Joe M.

www.davidsachs.com

THE FLOOD

DAVID SACHS

Cover image by Martin Gomez

Published by benChaim

Author photo by Suzanne Ng, Sweet Pea Photography

ISBN 978-0-9940102-1-6

www.davidsachs.com

The end of the world came
And we no longer asked, who to die by fire and who by sword
We all died by water.

-Gerry Adamson

1

A man leaned over a power auger, listening to the motor echo over the snow. Behind him, a fragile tent stood out on the wide white landscape. Inside the shelter, the two scientists examined ice samples. They searched for clues in a 65-million-year-old puzzle, the great die-off of dinosaurs and half the species on earth.

One day, the ground shook.

The table in the scientists' shelter vibrated and slid towards the wall. The lamps swung from the roof. There was a booming noise from outside.

The world began to lean, until the table danced across to the opposite wall. Then the world flipped, the lights went out, and the sound of tearing filled the tumbling shelter.

They were the first to die.

2

It was a different world to wake to.

Travis Cooke was a paramedic and when he slept, coming off a long night shift, he still heard the ambulance siren in dreams. It confused him to be awakened by the noise. Sirens of all types, coming from all sides. His blurry eyes set on the bottle of sleeping pills and found their focus.

The clock on the nightstand said 7:15 a.m. He looked out the window and thought of zero hour. The streets of Brooklyn were filled with men, women and children running and cars almost at a standstill, horns honking in desperation. The end of the world. Terror. Terrorists, he thought.

Stressful and high-intensity events were his work. The reaction from his body should have been immediate. Instead, he was sluggish from the pills, uncoordinated. He fell from the bed. He thought of his son and ex-wife as he came to his feet. He turned on the TV as he began to dress. Before he could change the channel to the news station, he heard the president's voice.

"...urge you to move inland..."

The picture came a moment after the sound. President Crawford was in an unfamiliar room. His seal was on the floor, and a flag stood next to the desk, but it was not the Oval Office.

"...as far as possible. This is a national emergency, an

international emergency. The tsunami will be reaching Florida in under four hours, and will reach New York City by late this afternoon, before five o'clock, according to the best estimates we have right now. This will not be a survivable event. The National Guard will be directing transport airships to major hospitals. We ask all of those with cars to leave the coast immediately. We have asked that all transit companies, buses, trains, and airlines cancel all scheduled routes to assist in the evacuation process. We face a dark period in the next twenty-four hours."

The pause seemed to last for hours. The president was saying something he knew would cause panic, possibly worldwide. That was the first thought that came to Travis.

"In other countries, tens of thousands may already have been killed. Only by acting quickly can we avoid losing hundreds of thousands."

Travis tried phoning his ex-wife.

"The network is busy right now, please try again later."

He grabbed his jacket.

Travis Cooke ran out of his apartment wondering if it would be the last time he'd see it.

3

Some felt safest in cars, others were headed for New Jersey by foot. The stampedes into each subway station that morning crushed dozens of the first New Yorkers to die.

Travis Cooke ran down broad Flatbush, the solid lanes of cars bounded by humans moving much more quickly on the sidewalks. He found himself funneled through the streets, all the current now flowing to the Manhattan Bridge. The strangers looked at each other as they ran, confirming that this was really happening.

From Brooklyn to Manhattan and from there to New Jersey, a solid sweep of cars and bodies. The strange hush of the movement punctuated by honking horns, kids crying, and random shouts. It was a nightmare marathon, all jarring for position. Travis saw individuals and small groups huddled in the crowd's eddy spaces, sobbing, giving up already or simply unable to act.

There was a teenage girl he saw sitting on a bench, as if she were waiting for a bus. She stared at the rush of people. He thought about stopping.

At the Manhattan Bridge, the bottleneck of escapees impeded his progress. Bodies pressed into Travis's, a hundred voices grunting, crying, shouting in his ears. His world shrunk to those bodies immediately around him. The drugs in his body still made him dizzy, but running straight was easy and his body was waking up quickly from the emotional and physical stress.

Crossing the river took close to ten minutes, then they poured out into the streets of Manhattan, across Chinatown, where buses filled up and forced their exit through crowds, horns honking. He ran up Chrystie to 2nd Ave, his feet heavy, sweat pouring from his temples. Everyone was running now in their own direction, to tunnels, bridges, trains, buses.

He ran uptown for twenty minutes, the tempo of his footfalls searing themselves into his mind, blocking out any thoughts of the equally frantic humans he passed by.

"Travis!" he heard, and he stopped to look around.

His eyes couldn't focus on the shape approaching him. He tried to squint, but the sweat dripped and burned, making him shut his eyes. He felt his knees trembling with weakness and he leaned over, hyperventilating.

A hand was on his shoulder.

"Travis, where are you going?"

The voice was one he hadn't heard in a while, a drinking buddy from midtown days.

"Corrina and Darren," Travis managed.

"Travis, listen to me."

The hand held him more firmly then or he would have fallen over.

"Get cross-town to the piers. They're bringing in every goddamn ship on the sea to get people out. I just spoke with someone at Grand Central and it's no use. They'll be running trains out till we're under water and they won't get all those people out. But I got my cell phone, I was able to get on the Internet. The bridges and tunnels are jammed. People have started abandoning their cars, and they're blocking everything. The president has mobilized the Navy, private ships, everything, and they're all going to the piers. That's the last hope, Travis. I gotta go."

Travis's head was down by his knees. He reached into his pocket although he knew he wouldn't find his inhaler. His fingers dug into the palm of his hand as his chest burned with each asthma-constricted breath. How many minutes was he wasting? He forced himself upright and blinked his eyes clear. He put one leg in front of the other and began jogging again. After a few hundred yards he crossed 2nd. The security door of the building was broken, the lobby was quiet.

Both elevators waited on the ground floor. He pressed the button and got in.

In the elevator, the quiet scared him. He wondered if the doors would open, and everyone outside would be dead. Finally the elevator stopped and opened. He ran down the hall and banged the door of 1115.

"Jesus, it's you," a tall, thin man said, opening the door.

Travis pushed through him.

"Where's Darren?"

"Dad!"

The boy swept into his arms and Travis closed his eyes, forgetting about the man standing over him, as he held his son so tight he knew he was hurting him but he couldn't stop. He tried to slow his breathing down and heard his own heartbeat in his head. He released his son and stood up.

Corrina Adamson stared at him from the bedroom door.

Travis looked from her to the man and said, "I tried to call but the network was overloaded."

"We've been trying to get a line too, trying to find a way out," the man said.

His name was Gerry Adamson. He stood half a foot taller than stocky Travis. "The highways are jammed. I was able to get a text to my cousin and he's been stuck for two hours on the Turnpike. But now I can't get anything else, the Internet connection keeps going out. We were about to get the car and take the Tappan Zee."

"The West side piers," Travis said. "I ran into someone coming up here, he told me the only option left is by sea. They're evacuating from the West side."

"By sea?" Corrina said. "How can we escape a tsunami by sea?"

"I don't know, Corrina, but if the president is ordering ships to pick up refugees, I would think they know what they're doing."

Gerry rejected the idea. They had a car. They didn't have to risk everything on a desperation play.

"We don't have time to argue," Travis said. "You should be gone. Obviously you didn't like any of your options too much. The bridges are a mess, people are leaving their cars. Let's get the Hell out of here. If the piers plan doesn't work out, we can find a way to Jersey from there."

"I think we should go to the piers," Darren said.

The three adults stopped and looked down at him. At six years old, he held his face in an aping of serious adult concentration.

"Okay, let's go," Corrina said.

"What if there's no way out from there?" Gerry asked.

"It's just a few blocks," Corrina said. "We can go there and still have time to try something else."

She smiled at Darren, and he smiled.

Travis picked up his son's backpack, a cartoon design covering the back of it. "Is this all your luggage, Darren?"

"Yeah," Darren said.

"Let's go."

He picked up his boy. Corrina and Gerry each grabbed a large travel bag from a matching set.

By the elevator they waited, Travis glancing at Corrina and Gerry clutching their wheeled luggage by the extended handles. Travis had nothing save the jeans and sneakers, the sweat-soaked long-sleeved t-shirt and his light jacket. He didn't think of that, though. He thought only that he had Darren, which was then the only thing he cared to keep in this world.

4

November 19, Manhattan's citizens gave up their hold on the levers of the earth. The stock exchanges, the banks, the boardrooms and media centers, all were empty. The action was on the street, and in the homes. The flood was an event that cut across all life stories. Everyone was doing something when it came.

The current in the streets flowed west, to the ships. To the last way out. There were faces looking out windows above them all, resigned to their fate, or skeptical of the gravity of the situation, or who just hadn't heard and didn't know how to ask and didn't get what was going on at all.

Jogging straight up 51st St., Travis felt disembodied looking up and seeing the faces above. Another day, he might have been throwing himself through fire to rescue those people. Today, he hurried past, leaving them to death. For a reason he wasn't sure of, he was leaving them now.

He had worked abroad as a paramedic with the Red Cross in Sudan and Haiti. He'd faced massive damage to the population and had worked knowing he could only save a few of the many, but he'd worked to save that few. Why not here? His son was on his back as they jogged. That was why. He was no hero. When it was expected of him in his work to help, he did so. When fleeing was called for, he fled.

All he had in his understanding of what was behind all this was the one word spoken by President Crawford: tsunami. Millions of New Yorkers fleeing their city, and he imagined few had even taken the time to discuss what was happening, how this could be possible, whether it were all somehow a mistake.

He was aware of keeping together with Gerry and Corrina as they ran, their talk clipped by expressions of disbelief, but Travis's mind followed the buildings and street corners he passed, cutting across the heart of town past Rockefeller Center and Radio City Music Hall, Manhattan's studded body of concrete and steel, ancient masonry and mirrored glass.

As he voiced assurances to Darren, he thought that the stage his life had been played on might be destroyed forever. His would be the last generation to inherit four hundred years of Manhattan. Scenes of his New York life passed through his head. The Park. The school on Delancey and dad's shop just down the street, the bar on Bleecker, the University, the hospitals, the rugby pitches, the nights out, Woody Allen and the Godfather movies, and Sasha's party in Little Italy where the most beautiful girl in New York gave him her number. On this stage, his son's life had begun, too. The set designers had something new in mind for this next generation.

At 11th Ave, the crowds were dense, blocking the view of the Hudson River a block away, but the concrete canopy of the Manhattan Cruise Terminal could be seen framed by the sky. Travis spotted several National Guardsmen watching with hands on rifles, doing their jobs while he fled without even his pager. The crowds were moving forward, pouring into the terminal buildings by the thousands. There were cruise ships visible beyond the terminals. Looking south, Travis saw a mismatched array of large and small craft docking and disembarking from Pier 86.

It was like this at the dozens of piers down the West Side, around New York, down the East Coast. Many ships were freightliners, and the crews were frantically removing the massive cargo containers to make space while armed Guardsmen held the crowds back. The White House had learned from hurricanes Katrina and Sandy and had mobilized as aggressively as the most powerful nation on earth could. From New Jersey's naval station Earle came the AOE supply ships that were now filling their holds with New Yorkers — the USS Arctic, USS Supply, and USS Seattle.

The ships were manned with skeleton crews, and hurried from the dock with unprecedented and unpracticed urgency.

Over the heads of the crowd, Travis could see the towers of a cargo frigate pulling away.

"This way," Gerry said. "I think there's more movement by that terminal."

A fight erupted to their left, four men tearing at each other while a woman screamed. A Guardsman fired his weapon into the air, shocking the fighting men into passivity, but the effect on the crowd was to finalize the impression of chaos in America, that weapon fire was now necessary to maintain control. There was a surge forward under the strength of this new panic. Travis and his group were well into the crowd now, and he held

Darren in his arms. Gerry held his bag with the pull-handle by his side. Corrina still pushed hers on the ground, keeping it in front of her feet. As they held themselves close, they said only with eye contact, Stick together!

"Don't worry, Darren," Corrina said. "Don't worry, Darren."

They were within fifty yards of one of the terminal entrances, and soon they were inside the vast hall. The flow of the crowd now was bounded by the building, and differentiated into streams to each stairway to the embarkation levels. There was terrific screaming, echoing in the huge room as groups argued over which ship on each side of the terminal to try for, which stairwell was flowing best. The flow had its own natural course, and individual choices were rendered meaningless by the brute power of it.

Upstairs, security had been turned inside out: doors everywhere were open, and security screening sections and metal detectors abandoned. National Guardsmen waited on the building's exterior apron, maintaining order as Travis and the others emerged again to the open air. The ship itself loomed over them now, filling their vision, a great bulk of white and blue steel and circular windows, belted by lifeboats midway up, and capped by decorative spikes and curves of the top deck satellite globes, radar trees, the bridge, the logo-painted smokestack and other towers, just showing above the top.

A gangway rose up from the dock to an opening one floor up, and a human stream poured up and into the ship's belly, emptying NY and filling the boat. Ships fit for thousands emptying a city of millions. Travis thought of a mosquito on an elephant.

There was a surge from the left, hitting Travis and Darren first, pushing them into Gerry and Corrina. A large circle in the surge began to fall, and in the tight space, the group was all pulled down together in the mass. Men and women were climbing over each other to get up.

"Darren! Darren!" Travis heard Corrina amid the screams.

"I've got him," Travis shouted. With Darren still in his arms, he was sinking while the other bodies were pushing up around him. There were seconds until the crowd would surge again and he and his son would be under it.

A pair of black hands stretched down to him out of overcoat sleeves and white shirt cuffs. The hands grabbed his arms and pulled him upwards. Travis could see the man tensing his body to resist the pressure from behind him. He was in his fifties, dressed in a suit and overcoat, the tie gone. With his help, Travis was able to turn himself and pull himself upright behind Corrina.

Darren bawled, and Travis could just give him little squeezes on his back to calm him.

"Thanks," Travis said without being able to see the man behind him then, feeling him pressed into his back.

"Soft spot for kids," the man said.

Travis turned his head and just caught the forced smile that lit up the man's furrowed face.

He saw that Gerry and Corrina's suitcases were gone.

They could see armed National Guardsmen in the space between the stairs and the ship's hull. The

Guardsmen themselves had a desperate look; they were there to protect these people. How would they act if the people became the danger? Travis could see another ship beginning to pull away. He couldn't see the crowd beneath that ship. He heard gunfire, and then screaming filled the air. Pushing Corrina ahead of him, with the stranger pushing him from behind, he was on the gangway stairs. The move up was halting, but manageable.

There was shouting around him now distinct above the other screams.

"This way, this way!"

"Matthew! Matthew!"

"Don't lose me!"

"This way! Please follow the crew!"

This was a voice with authority. The voice assured Travis, and he felt the tension around him ease, too, with the voice. Looking out at the Hudson, he saw another cruise ship on its way down river, following closely behind a freighter whose deck was packed with escapees.

Travis heard all the voices around him going up the stairs. It was a habit he could not break. He was an observer of people and a listener, and he always heard the voices around him.

"I have to go back!"

"Oh God, help me!"

"This way, through here!"

"Please, I have to go back!"

"My leg is broken! Please help me!"

"Follow the crew!"

"Please, I have to go back!"

Corrina was suddenly gone ahead of him, and Travis was pulled off the gangway through the opening into a great hall by white-sleeved arms. He was shoved to the left. He was aware of soft light and colors around him, weird on this dark day.

"This way! Follow the crew inside!"

"Please, I have to go back!" he heard one last time from behind him.

5

He had seen fear before, in places of conflict and famine, where the worst things happen and life is carried out in unceasing desperation. The low ground, he called that state of living in his own private lexicon. So many millions of people around the world had lived there in the last twenty, fifty or hundred years — yet it was a completely alien place to most Americans. The low ground had followed him home. The low ground had found his son.

These Americans, Travis thought, have never considered death this way: announcing itself to each of them at once, for their families and friends and neighbors. He wondered what showed in his own face, how the possibility of losing everything was displayed in his eyes.

They were shuffled down the hallway by staff standing alongside another opening in the wall, from which a bright glow lit those turning and disappearing into it.

"Head to the light," the staff called.

There was no need for the direction, the pump was primed and the flow set. The group turned into the light, a wide white-on-white staircase leading only down. After the first flight, the staircase walls gave way to banisters and railings and the open belly of the vessel. Travis saw the vast area of the ship's Grand Atrium, a football field space with the feel of a Roman plaza, 70 foot gold-foil columns and drapes piercing the great hall vertically, the floor level marked by fountains, flower boxes, food counters and bars, lined by shop-fronts on all sides. The central fountain featured a great marble statue of a thin, broadly-finned fish, its angular impressionistic form curled into a violent surface dive through the array of water sprays. There were several of these staircases, and all those on the port side funneled the refugees in here. The space was already crowding.

Dark wood-paneled columns arose at the sides of the Atrium, supporting the many tiers of balconies above. The tourists, those paying passengers who had departed Key West on their 21-day cruise only the day before, lined the railings on each level. The floors themselves, cutting off at the edge of the Atrium airspace, were front-lit a bright emerald green, while the open staircases, Travis now saw, were alight with bright green paneling as well. From the railings, the rows of tourists looked down in silence at the refugees filling their ship. The line slowed on the stairs, but here there was not the pressure of bodies stacked against each other.

Travis wondered if this could be real. Had he finally taken too many pills to sleep? Was this a dream? Had he died, and this was something else? It was as though the drugs had returned to his blood. He felt as though he was stumbling through a liquid.

"We'll find out if the president's an idiot or not," Corrina said.

As their own group reached the Atrium floor, Travis thought back to high school dances in the gym: that was his standard for crowd estimation, a full high school gym to him meant 800 or so heads. He guessed there were already two thousand in this room alone. He looked up to the crystal roof a great distance above, passing over the faces of the tourists on the radiating balconies. It seemed like a scene from the Wizard of Oz. He realized how much quieter it had become. Individuals crying out for lost loved ones or sobbing over their thoughts could be heard. There was a release of tension at getting where they were going, to a place that promised safety. Their brains now raced through what could happen on this ship. They desperately hoped to feel the ship move.

Travis noticed Corrina and Gerry holding each other tight, and he saw tears flowing down his ex-wife's cheeks and over her smile. He kissed Darren on the forehead. He'd saved his son. Oh God, it was a terrifying and wonderful feeling.

"Come on," Travis said. "Let's push in. Darren, do you have to pee?"

Darren shook his head, no. He had stopped crying; his eyes were red and his nose dripped, but he was trying not to look scared anymore.

"Don't worry, Daddy," he said. "I can swim if we fall in. I can swim by myself now in the deep end."

"That's great, champ," Travis said. "We're not going to go in the water, though."

They shuffled on together, tightening in the crowd as the city's deserters continued to stream in from the several staircases. Huddled together, they simply stared, losing track of time. Travis noticed the on-board shops closed and deserted. After twenty minutes, or perhaps half an hour, they felt the vibrations of the engines coming to life. Soon, there was the sound of the ship's whistle. Nothing else from outside could be heard, and Travis imagined the scene of desperation outside, as the ship freed from the pier.

With the last arrivals still pouring into the room, they felt the escape begin. The ship separated from port and from the unlucky still behind. From the desperation they'd been in moments ago, it was bizarre and jarring for the refugees now to find themselves surrounded by such exaggerated, fantastical luxury.

By the bottoms of the staircases, Travis noticed white uniformed men. Ship's security, he presumed. This conveyed a real and specific sense of safety. The men were unarmed. Another statement of safety.

"Have you made your pick who'll be first to piss in the fountains?" a voice near Travis said.

The speaker was the stranger from the pier, his arm outstretched. Travis shook his hand.

"I got that old rummy by the calla lilies," the man said.

"Thanks for your help," Travis said.

"No problem, no problem," the man had a deep, rich and rough voice. "Got a granddaughter about his age. I'm Claude Bettman."

"Travis Cooke. This is my son Darren."

"Hi," Darren said.

Claude Bettman crouched like a baseball catcher. "Hi Buddy. Not so scary in here, huh?"

Darren shook his head. Claude stood up straight.

"This is---- Corrina. And Gerry." Travis turned to include them. "Claude helped us out after the crowd collapsed. I'm really in your debt, Claude, I mean that."

Claude grinned. His lips were slightly purple, and he

had an aristocrat's smile. "I think this is the kind of event that cancels all debts."

"Did you hear anything about how the evacuation was working?" Corrina asked.

Claude shook his head slowly. "I heard ships would head out to sea to ride out the wavefront. That was from a military guy on TV."

"I don't have the slightest clue what this actually IS," Travis said. "I just woke up and all hell was breaking loose."

"An earthquake," Gerry said. "It split a huge shelf off the Antarctic. They kept changing the story. Whether the earthquake caused the tsunami, or whether one earthquake caused a split of the ice shelf that caused another earthquake, or what. But they say we're going to have higher water levels. Once the wave comes in, the water may not be going back out. The whole East coast might be under."

As a few outside the group listened in, Gerry pulled out his cell phone for a more current update. He couldn't connect.

"Networks overloaded," Claude said. "Every cell phone owner in America is trying to use it right now."

Corrina had Darren in her arms now, and they rubbed noses and smiled eye to eye.

Nothing stops her, Travis thought, and he felt the familiar craving, wishing he could just join that embrace.

There was an electric sound as speakers around the ship came to life.

"This is Captain London. To all our new guests, welcome aboard the Festival of the Waves. An unfortunate name for this very difficult time, but this is a good safe ship."

It was the voice Travis had heard coming up the gangway, the strong voice that first pierced the terror. It had been the captain himself pulling the refugees on board.

"We have an excellent crew that will keep us all comfortable as best we can. We will be making 15 knots out to open sea, and should be rendezvousing with that bump in several hours. That's all it will be. A tsunami in the open sea is just a wave, you'll hardly feel it. For safety reasons, I ask that all the newcomers please remain indoors whether in the Atrium or Royal Theater, and that our other guests please remain in their rooms. I will be giving a warning prior to meeting the waves. I know that this is a devastating day for all of you right now. But we're safe here. Be grateful for that. Breathe."

6

Lee Golding stood on the Penthouse forward deck, cupping his hands to light a cigarette in the wind. This was the top deck housing cabins, and the level had an extended lip at the bow, an outside deck at the far forward reach of the ship.

Lee Golding, the Mighty Lee Golding, the Alabama Assassin. The biggest name and most-hated-bad-guy of professional wrestling (once upon a time), was on board as a celebrity guest. The cruise line had planned a screening of his greatest matches followed by a Q-and-A. Over the three-week cruise he was booked to do a talk, sit at the Captain's Table, and provide color commentary for a kids' water polo game. Two of his films were supposed to be shown on the Festival's big screen, the new comedy and one of the action ones. Probably not anymore.

His massive frame had not swollen with fat in his retirement from the ring like many of his comrades'. Not quite that much, anyway. His blonde hair receded slightly around his reddish temples, and hung long to his shoulders. He still had the trademark goatee, dyed silver. His face was neither ugly nor especially attractive. It was heavy and pleasant. He made friends easily.

Around him on deck were several other of the booked tourists, mostly keeping to themselves, enjoying the air that the ship's captain had just asked them to forsake. There was no social convener to introduce them to each other. The ship's security was more than engaged in handling the load of refugees in the ship's belly and didn't worry themselves with keeping the paying guests off the decks, at least for now. When the crowd below was under control, perhaps they would sweep the decks. For now, the captain's voice on the loudspeakers was the deterrent. Lee Golding was undeterred.

He'd stayed in his room with his wife Jessica until the ship had left the pier. Then he'd left her there to watch the ship make it out to sea, and to watch what New York looked like being left behind to die.

Lee was out on deck passing by 15th Street and Pier 57. He saw industrial freighters, top heavy with loading cranes. There were still many ships loading, and the crowd remaining did not seem to him hopelessly large. He imagined he could still hear their screams over the sound of the many ships coming and going. As he saw one ship pull away from the dock, he heard shots fired. He thought of New Orleans, how the desperate had shot at helicopters in a gambit for attention. It was more likely the police, he thought. There's no way you could wait at the back of the crowd. There was no way people would do that peacefully, unless a cop was there with a gun.

He wondered how it would go when the cops left. It would have been so much better for the ones left behind if there'd been no warning. They'll die just the same, but first they have to go through this. If. If anyone gets left behind. If there really is a tsunami at all.

There were small ships in the water, heading in the opposite direction, up the Hudson and inland towards Albany. The little boats bobbed in the headwind. All those little guys going one way, and this big ship splitting the herd in the other direction. Lee thought of the tsunami in Southeast Asia, the stories of animals sensing disaster and heading to safety while fishermen marched to the docks like any other day.

The Empire State Building stood out above the island's skyline. The Festival of the Waves rounded Battery Park at the south end of town. The rough dark waters of Upper Bay opened up before her. The Statue of Liberty came closer. The few there on the deck made towards the starboard rail to watch the Statue pass. It was the reverse trip of refugees of other eras, past the statue, past Ellis Island, Brooklyn to one side, Staten Island to the other, then under the Verrazano Bridge, to leave the outpost of America behind.

"Not quite the same feeling as when we pulled out from Key West, is it?" came a voice.

Lee came out of his daydreaming and smiled as he turned to the man a few feet away along the railing.

"No," Lee agreed. "The cruise has definitely lost some je-ne-sais-pas." Lee's voice was louder than necessary, deep and amiable. Not quite his stage voice, but bigger than mortal.

"I'm Rick," the smaller man said, a Texas accent. "Rick Dumas. I saw your wife and you a couple times on the ship, I'm just down the hall from you. You're Golding, right? The Mighty Lee Golding."

"Yeah," Lee replied as they shook hands. "You don't have to say 'The Mighty' every time, though."

He sized Rick Dumas up as they stood together. His ship-neighbor was small, and had a pleasant but nervous face, as if he didn't know when anyone might turn on him.

"I was a huge fan," Rick said. "Really, your feud with Sinbad was phenomenal. Can you do your shtick for me? Come on. Do your shtick."

Lee smiled. His face bulged out red, his eyes popping from his head like eggs, as he laughed devilishly. His fingers went to his lips in a V and he wagged his bendy tongue through the V.

"Golding gonna getcha!" he hissed.

His face softened and he laughed, and Rick laughed, and the Alabama Assassin slapped him on the back.

"Give my regards to Broadway, huh?" Rick said. "So long 42nd Street. Take a deep breath, 40' latitude, 74' longitude. That's central Manhattan. I have one of those GPSs and I try to remember important places. When did you come up and start watching?"

"Just after the pick-up, when we left," Lee replied.

"I came out when we were coming in. Man, you should have seen the air traffic. So many helicopters."

"All going to United Nations, I bet."

"There's no shortage of people in Manhattan who can afford a helicopter ride," Rick said. "I bet there were a lot of rooftop landings. Say, could I have a smoke? I don't usually smoke, but what the hell. How often does the East Coast get destroyed?"

Lee reached for the pack in his windbreaker pocket, contorting his girth. Rick lit his smoke with difficulty, Lee again using his hands as a wind screen, holding the lighter, too.

"You don't seem nervous," Lee said. "You worried

about this or what?"

"No, no. These ships, they're really the greatest feats of engineering of our time. I mean, just turn around, turn around."

Rick spun his finger and the two turned to face the majesty of the Festival of the Waves, towers of decks, of gleaming white steel and glass above them.

"A city under its own power at sea. A 90,000-ton traveling island of amusements and indulgence for 2,400 paying guests and 930 crew. It's our era's Great Pyramids. But they were for kings only."

"Yeah, but they had to be dead first."

"Listen, this is as heavy duty as ships come," Rick continued. "Do you ever hear of a cruise ship going down? OK, there was that one off Greece but the captain was drunk. I mean, they put hundreds of millions of dollars into these. If any company ever lost a ship, they'd be ruined. Just think of the lawsuits."

"Ever hear of the Titanic?" Lee asked.

"Come on, that hit an iceberg. And that was over a hundred years ago! That's not even relevant, not to me, anyway."

"When the captain announced the plan, he said the risk was minimal," Lee reasoned aloud. "That even if we weren't picking up the refugees we'd be riding out the wave. So I guess it must be safe."

"Hey, look at that dude," Rick said. "He looks like Man Mountain McTavish!"

Lee turned and saw a man standing alone. How had he not noticed this passenger yet? The man was more mountain even than Man Mountain McTavish, who'd always been soft in the ring. The stranger stood close to seven feet tall, and was broad shouldered. He had grey hair down to the bottom of his neck, and a thick beard. His arms came out of his short sleeves like a bear's, the hairy flesh flexed as the man held the railing.

He stared ahead and was oblivious to the two men who watched him.

"Looking for whales?" Rick called, and Lee laughed.

The man-mountain did not respond immediately. As if some unseen intervening agent passed on the message, he turned after a moment.

"Call me Ishmael," the man-mountain shouted back.

Lee smiled. That was from Moby Dick. He'd listened to that book on the road from one stadium to the next. It was about a guy who wouldn't take "no" for an answer. And a whale. Lee felt an instinctive connection with this other giant.

The bulk of land receding behind them became more indistinct in its details. By the time the security guards asked them to return to their rooms, the United States appeared as only a thickening of the horizon.

"Please stay in your rooms until you hear from the captain," one of the white-uniformed guards said. "It will just be a few hours. We really need to rely on everyone's cooperation to stay safe and get through this without any tragedies."

The grey-haired man-mountain walked in past the Mighty Lee Golding and Rick Dumas with a friendly glance to include them, so that they could experience with him the shared thrill of this event. The two smiled back. The giant's facial expressions were so intense Rick and

Lee could not help but smile back, but he quickly lost his inclusive cast, turning to his own thoughts. The giant looked away and went on inside.

His name was Adam Melville.

He was a man who looked and planned for special moments. That's the way he travelled; he was a moment collector. Even with his planned cruise interrupted, he couldn't shake that habit. An event of this importance made him feel important watching it. And no one knew what was on the other side.

A long-time tech entrepreneur, he had a big imagination, and he was trying to imagine what he could see in the event that others didn't. As he returned to his room, Adam thought again through the clues: the news reports, the early devastation, the unparalleled evacuation, the reported projections. He was a man who'd always thought of big ideas, and how the big ideas touched his life.

We know a great deal of the world's history, he thought. From the time of each civilization's adoption of the written word, we know of all their major events: 5000 years of history among the Sumerians in modern Iraq and in Egypt, 3300 years in China, 2600 years in Mexico. As the written word spread across Europe and the Indian subcontinent, so did our knowledge of history gain over wider swaths of the earth.

This event was beyond all that history's telling, but that was not our only knowledge. Written history goes back 5000 years, but humanity goes back 7 million years, a much longer period of witnessing. This event had precursors within the collective memory of man. Our myths were older yet than our histories, and they told of such things.

7

Captain London spent more time on the bridge than most in his position. Many captains on large cruise ships split their time between paperwork and social activities; the running of the ship was left to subordinates. This was not so with Captain London in routine times. It was certainly not so now.

He relegated the first officers to the sidelines as he managed the evacuation and embarkation from New York himself. In fact, the extraordinary traffic in the river and out to sea demanded Captain London stay on deck and he would no doubt remain to ride out the wave. There was no pilot ship to lead them out from harbor this time. Distance required between ships was compressed, and his maximum speed in the harbor had been raised, among the many regulations and laws London had been ordered to break.

London was not particularly troubled that Homeland Security had ordered such safety standards to be ignored, to get as many people out alive as possible. What he didn't like was the lack of security in letting the refugees aboard. He liked to be in control, and that seemed to allow an element he couldn't control. Even his security crew was weaponless, but who knew what was coming aboard now?

It was not, however, a situation in which debate or questioning was an option.

The senior officers all wore black suits. One could tell who the captain was without seeing the rank on their shoulders. The captain was at the helm, and the officers orbited around him.

London was not born to lead; he was made so by his own hand. He came from a small town, middle class background, and had understood from an early age that the drive to succeed was a race won not by speed, but by early start. He wasted no time. He had, through years in the Navy, university and various sports teams, cultivated not only the work ethic to rise, but the social connections as well. He hadn't gained his advantages directly through those connections; rather, by embedding himself among groups accustomed to leadership, he grew to understand it as the expected outcome given the application of his qualities. Here he was, the undisputed chief of a hundred million dollar enterprise, a crew of near a thousand under him. Yet those aggrandizing details were less important to him as a sailor than the more basic fact that he was master of his ship.

Captain London was of average height, with a bearing and a voice weighted by his own gravity. He had a healthy weathered face and thin gray hair, and looked like a club golf pro.

He liked this bridge. It was old school. Out of all the ships on which he'd served in his career, this, with its long curved banks of windows, controls and monitoring equipment below, was coolest. At the center was his chair, a rotating throne he found embarrassingly comfortable.

The Festival was a decades old ship that had

undergone major refurbishments twice. She was, to London, a beautiful and messy mix of new and old.

"Get Harrington in here," he said. "Let's learn what there is to learn."

Minutes later, the Chief Radio Officer was on the bridge. He was a young man, fat and always sweaty in his black suit.

"Just the headlines," Captain London said.

"At 15 knots, the wavefront is not more than five hours sailing."

"We'll make better speed when we get out. Go on."

"Right now the waves are under ten feet but they will be considerably larger after passing onto the continental shelf. However, the troughs are currently long and the waves smooth. Coast Guard pilots have scouted and confirmed that it should be no danger to our vessel. We're to ride it out and wait. Homeland Security is running the show, and they still don't know where they're going to direct returning ships and seagoing refugees. I… got the impression they just don't now what the coast is going to look like after. Not to mention they've been as busy evacuating themselves as planning for everyone else."

"Your editorial commentary is still unappreciated," London said.

"So, we're just supposed to ride it out and wait?" first officer Van der Hoeven asked.

"Yeah," Harrington said. "Radar shows other ships heading out the same way."

"Have you heard from the company?" London said.

"They're satisfied with your decision and urge you to

aid in any way, sir, so long as the guests are not put in any danger."

"Meaning the ship, of course," an officer said.

"What's the latest on the event itself?" London said.

"It's muddled. And what's clear, is probably wrong."

"Harrington," London said.

"Sorry, sir."

The Communications Officer recited the same outline of events all on the bridge knew already. He had a few extra details: the fault was along the mid-Atlantic ridge; that there had been a major calving of glaciers off the Antarctic ice shelves on one end, and Greenland on the other, seemingly a result of the earthquake; and satellite images and measurements of the rising water levels indicated a major change to the ocean floor topography itself.

"In other news," Harrington continued, "Washington, or at least our fearless leaders, have been evacuated. President Crawford is in Colorado at a NORAD base. The White House and Pentagon are empty, guarded by Air Force cover."

There were murmurs of astonishment and excitement from some.

"What's the refugee situation?" London asked.

"Here or more generally?" Harrington asked.

"In general, first," London said

"It's going to be the worst natural disaster in history," the Communications Officer said, losing his humor for the first time. "Rio has been wiped out, Miami may be underwater as we speak. There's all this chatter of lessons learned from New Orleans, how they've mobilized immense resources so quickly and are directing efforts at hospitals and old age homes. It seems almost useless, sir. In a disaster of this magnitude."

"Those are lives being saved," London said. "The actions of our crew are part of an effort that will mean hundreds of thousands saved. The scope may be far larger, but we can still save lives. Thanks for your report. I imagine it will be a while before we receive new orders. In the meantime, Harrington, scan the news. But keep it to yourself. I don't need the crew distracted with worries of their families. Now, what of OUR refugees, Bausch?"

"Sir, there's more," Harrington said.

The others held their breath. London was not often interrupted.

"Go on, Harrington," the captain said.

"There's a Navy supply ship that's lost contact. It was being used in the rescue, and they've lost radio contact and the on-board tracking has been shut down. They sent a search jet to its last coordinates, but it's not on course. It's disappeared, sir. They're seeking reports of any sightings at sea."

"Don't let your imagination get carried away," London said. "There are going to be issues as the flood breaks down communications systems. Cell networks have been going out all day. For a while, everyone will be a bit in the dark. Now, Bausch, what of our refugees, please?"

"Twenty-three hundred aboard, all in the Grand Atrium and the Royal Theater. Everything as planned," said Bausch, the Chief Security Officer. "Birnbaum is out managing the situation right now."

In extraordinary times, responsibilities were less than

clear. Captain London trusted Staff Captain Birnbaum, and had put the new passengers under his management. Captain London had also put the massive resources of the hotel manager at the use of Birnbaum, meaning the restaurants, the wait staff, the housekeepers, the pursers; all could be drafted into the effort.

"They're double-shifting galley staff to feed the new and old guests," the Security Officer continued. "My men have swept the decks and have good confidence that the guests have all returned to their rooms. Still… another announcement wouldn't hurt. There were quite a few out for a look, and with the resources required managing the refugees, we haven't the numbers to maintain constant watches at all sections of the decks."

"Have Birnbaum pull the staff together, in groups if he has to, and give them an update of the situation. It's critical that the staff understand that things are under control and still being managed as tightly as before. Have them told that this is an opportunity and a responsibility to help in a crisis. If the staff maintain composure, the guests will remain at ease and under control."

"Vince Lombardi it is, sir."

"Sir, we haven't handled emergency planning given the new realities on the Festival," a First Officer said. "Our prior emergency drills have, I think, been rendered obsolete."

"This is the reality," London responded. "We are not up to SOLAS standards. I accept my personal culpability for this. Somehow I expect it to be overlooked. We are drastically short on lifeboats, and the Atrium and Theater couldn't be evacuated in a reasonable, let alone legally mandated, time in any case. So, gentlemen, let's keep this ship afloat."

The skies had cleared in the afternoon; the visibility was excellent. Making 25 knots now as it emerged from Lower Bay into open sea, the vessel barely rumbled. The sun was behind them, so that the ship chased its own shadow. The First Officer on duty was left at the helm. The captain stood to watch as other great vessels passed it by to take their turn evacuating the docks.

No external circumstances could take away the beauty of the ocean.

In thirty-three years at sea, London had seen its immense power unleashed many times. He knew that the manifestation of this tsunami at sea would be minor; over the deep water the waves would be minimized. As it approached shore, the wave's energy would be directed upward by the rising floor, and the series of waves would run into each other and add their amplitudes. Then would it become the monstrous force that just might change the world.

They were hours out to open sea as their rendezvous with the waves approached, the senior officers crowding the bridge. Finally, Captain London sent them below, keeping only a bare crew, and imagining them away as he looked out over the sea.

8

"Ladies and gentlemen, may I have your attention please," a black-jacketed officer called out to the crowded Grand Atrium from halfway up a staircase. "My name is Antonio Dipietro, and I'm the Festival's Hotel Manager. We thank you for your patience and cooperation. First of all, if you look around for the signs, you will find our restrooms. You don't even need to see the signs actually. Just look for the line-ups. I apologize for this inconvenience, but I'm sure these lines will go down soon. We will be able to keep you comfortable here until we learn when we can return to port. We are going to be bringing food out for you all. We'd like to ask for your patience, it will be about forty-five minutes longer and you will be able to eat. I will be back soon for the food service."

Service doors which had been locked prior to the rescue were opened and an army of personnel came through, bearing tables which they set up all around the perimeter of the great hall.

Seeing the effort being made to keep them comfortable had a palpable effect on the crowd. They were not forgotten, and this was a competently run enterprise. Since the ship had left New York, the sadness of the refugees was quieted by the twin spirits, shock and fear. With the action of the crew, the spell seemed to break. There were smiles of relief, as well as long pent-up sobs.

Travis noticed the lines at the bathroom did shorten quickly, and soon the hotel manager appeared again on the staircase.

"Ladies and gentlemen," he called out. "I would like to ask you to wait just a few minutes more while our crew gets the food set up. When that is done, there will be an announcement to please come in an orderly fashion, line up for the buffet and help yourselves. We'll have pizzas, hot dogs and hamburgers, as well as water and juice. We aren't quite sure when we'll next have food ready to bring down as we have our regular guests to take care of as well, so please come and get your fill. Just wait till the signal. Thanks."

The food came in, a grand procession of staff passing gleaming chafer dishes and trays to other staff already waiting to serve.

When the hotel manager called on the refugees to begin lining up, Travis's group didn't rush, while many others did. It was a long wait, but there was lots of food. There were stacks of pizzas at the end of each table, with several open boxes at a time. There were large trays piled with hamburgers and hot dogs, and coolers of juice and water.

"What'll you have, champ?" Travis asked Darren.

"Hot dogs, please," the boy said.

The four of them found a spot on the floor and sat down to eat. The marble was cold. Darren studied the metallic and crystalline lines in the tiles. The hot dogs were hot and good and made them feel better. A bit of strength came into each of them. Corrina looked up at the gem-cut skylight decks and decks above, and the tourists watching down from the railings, all the way up.

Corrina Adamson was a strikingly attractive woman, but only from close up. From afar, everything about her seemed average. She dressed and did her hair so that her beauty could not be seen but up close. She had long, light-brown hair, curling down across her forehead and cheek so that one did not see her face except directly from the front. You had to take the time to look at her to know her beauty.

She came from small town South Carolina and had swung between tomboy and girly-girl as a child. Even in high school she had been a multi-sport athlete, an adventurous and tough "guy's girl" who loved putting on party dresses and make-up. As an adult, she had subtly hidden her looks, a bit of idiosyncratic defiance. Her ever-present smile and good humor, her raspy voice and rolling accent, and her fierce (and equally hidden) intelligence had bewitched both Travis and Gerry, and a few before them.

She had a temper, but had long ago begun to feel sorry for Travis more than angry.

After many of the refugees had gone back for seconds, the staff returned to clear off and remove the tables.

The intercom again came to life.

"This is Captain London. We are about to run the waves. We are in no danger, but I suggest you all prepare for a bumpy ride."

There was a murmur of excitement in the crowd as individuals returned from wherever they were to rejoin their families or other groups. Travis and his group stayed together on the floor, Darren squeezing in between his mother and Gerry.

Without noise or warning, the floor gently rolled, and they all leaned a bit to stern. It lasted several heartbeats, and one held breath. A few things fell over and crashed, as well as a few people. Some fell from sitting. It calmed for a moment, and then there was a second wave, and they held their breath up and exhaled down. A third smaller roll and then a fourth. The voice came back on the intercom.

"This is Captain London. It may seem hard to believe, but that was the tsunami. The danger has passed-"

The crowd erupted into cheers, so that the rest of the captain's message could not be heard. It was only the audible click of the intercom shutting off that forced that realization and quieted the crowd. Then they looked dumbly around wondering what they'd missed.

"That was it," Gerry said. "I can't believe it. All that fear of the tsunami, and we were completely safe."

"You were right," Corrina said to Travis.

"I'm sorry," Gerry said. "You were right."

"Can we take a nap, Momma?" Darren asked. "I'm tired."

He had been kept excited all day, and with the passing of this fear of the tidal wave, he suddenly was very tired and his eyes drooped.

"Me too, sweetie. Let's lie down."

Gerry removed his jacket and lay it over his wife and her son in her arms. The two closed their eyes.

A new voice came over the crowd, a woman's voice.

"-all those in unaffected areas to donate canned goods,

blankets and especially cash to your local Red Cross office."

The twelve-foot wood columns supporting the open walkways of the decks above fringed the Atrium like a Roman courtyard. Televisions bolted to several of them around the Atrium had come on, showing a news anchor at his desk, his eyes down at the papers in his hands. It was an unknown face, from a local station news-desk far from the East coast. The familiar network studios were missing from the broadcast.

Corrina and Darren sat back up.

"The reports we're getting are devastating. We're — I'm sorry, there are just so many reports coming in, it's very hard to keep on top of this, but we're doing the best we can. We've been told that the first warnings of the disaster came from over a dozen earthquake monitoring stations. One on Antarctica recorded this as a 9.6 on the Richter scale, which would make this the largest earthquake ever recorded. We still do not understand if the earthquake along the mid-Atlantic ridge caused the calving of the ice shelf, or if that event triggered the earthquake. We have reports of major tsunami waves all along the coast of South America this morning. We hope to have footage of that for you shortly."

The news anchor looked distracted for a moment.

"Now this: we are getting eyewitness reports that the Staten Island Ferry has been hijacked during its evacuation efforts. There have been shots fired; it's unclear if anyone has been hurt. It's unclear where the ferry is being taken, or why. And we've just gotten the latest report from the meteorological center in

Colorado..."

The anchor gave the next news all but stunned, satellite images big and colorful on the wall behind him. The Florida Keys were gone, as was much of the southern panhandle. Miami, Fort Lauderdale, Palm Beach, Jacksonville all were severely flooded. Disney World was flooded. It continued along the Gulf coast, Tampa, St. Petersburg, Fort Myers and Tallahassee.

The Florida panhandle filled the screen, but it was not the Florida anyone would have recognized.

In the crowd, noise began to rise. A few cried loudly, others hushed to hear more.

"We have just received a bulletin from the Department of Homeland Security, there is an update on refugee centers, we'll be putting that on the screen in just a moment. We're now being told that there are twelve American deaths so far, from a bus crash in Virginia. That's twelve tsunami deaths so far… this is obviously outdated, we know those numbers will be much higher. At the top of the hour we'll be reviewing what we know from South America and that will give us some idea of what to expect in the coming hours.

"The devastation, particularly in Brazil with its enormous coastal population, has been unprecedented. We are looking at satellite images of South America and it is incredible, you can see Tierra del Fuego is gone and miles of shoreline have just disappeared. We have reports now from New York — helicopter reports are saying that the highways are moving again, traffic is at a snail's pace in the tunnels, but it is moving. It seems the peak of traffic is over, and we believe that most of the city has been evacuated, incredible in the short time we've had. The Tappan Zee is still stopped, there is a major accident on the 87 they are trying to clear, they only have half an hour to get that bridge clear, and traffic is blocked well back into Yonkers."

"How are they going to get off the bridge?" Darren said.

"I don't know, honey," Travis said. "Please be quiet for a moment."

"I'm sorry," the newscaster continued, "this is very difficult, these horrible reports keep coming in."

Darren tugged at his father, "No, but Daddy, how are they going to get off the bridge?"

"I don't know, honey."

His arm went around the boy's shoulder and he gave it a squeeze as the news went on.

"We believe the tsunami is just minutes away from Washington, D.C. and we can only imagine the damage this will cause our great monuments. Let's take a look at Twitter reaction to this now, obviously this is *the* topic. We have dozens of celebrities stuck in evacuation, tweeting their situation and thoughts."

Those who connected the images and words with themselves or their families cried. Those who kept their minds closed to those connections just tried to hold the information in, to make sense of it.

The news went on for forty minutes, mostly looping through the same summaries of events over and over and then the screens went black and Captain London's voice came over the speakers.

"I'd like to first thank you for your patience. I have

gotten reports from the staff, and we experienced no damage from the emergency docking or the tsunami. We have received notice from the Coast Guard that the tsunami has not yet hit New York, and it may be hours or longer before they can gather information on where they would like us to come in. I will update you as information comes in but for now, we will remain at sea. We are again opening the ship to our guests. For our booked passengers, restaurant service has again begun. Feel free to leave your cabins. For our evacuees, we have a wonderful staff who will do their best to take care of you. We encourage you to go above on deck and relax. There is a medical center on board, please ask any of our staff for directions if you need aid. Our facilities are at your disposal, and I guarantee the air on deck will help you recover some strength. We ask only that you do not use the interior restaurants, as we do not have the capacity. Dinner will again be brought to the Atrium and Theater between eight and nine this evening."

The captain looked out over the ocean, one and eternal, filling all he could see. Here, events and people on land always seemed distant, as if a story he'd been told about someone else. He'd sailed many types of vessels, and even on a cruise ship, the feeling out on the ocean didn't change. Whatever happened, this thing never changed. London knew he could ever only understand its surface.

9

Many in the crowd followed the captain's advice. They were spreading back up onto the stairways and lining up around the see-through elevators when the last cell phones still getting signals went out. The realization spread through the bulk of the crowd within just seconds, but in pockets they did not understand and reacted to the exclamations by asking strangers, "What happened?"

Some spoke their worst fears aloud, while others shrugged it off as expected given what they'd seen on the screen. Before any mood could prevail, the captain's voice was back.

"As many of you probably know, we've lost cell phones. I just want to let you all know that we still have a satellite link with the folks back home. The cell networks are down. Well, it doesn't take much to do that in the best of times. The ship is still able to receive information and instructions, and to communicate our position. So please, once again, enjoy the Festival."

The refugees and the paying guests mixed on the upper Sky Deck among the deck chairs, around the bar and pool, and by the railing. You could still tell them apart, somehow. The refugees had been in life and death panic just hours before. For the guests, the whole thing was still theoretical. It was too big to be real. Many had traveled from inland for the cruise, and imagined their own homes and families safe. For the refugees, it was much easier to believe that they were the lucky ones, that their friends had not escaped.

The guests were still on the ship, the refugees were still on the shore.

Around the ship, the near thousand-strong crew was made stalwart by their ship's master. There were tasks that continued, and tasks that were stopped. The staff captain and hotel manager made these decisions, so live entertainment programs were cancelled, the casino and shops stayed closed, while babysitting stayed open, along with the basketball court and golf simulators. The library and movie theater were open, and housekeeping went on in the cabins and public areas.

The off-duty crew too were pressed into service to the refugees: supporting the galleys in their massive new responsibilities, carrying the tables and foodstuffs, the jugs of water and juice, and an improvised responsibility that many picked up: mingling on deck. The staff were there to serve, and they felt it, even if that meant bringing some better cheer.

Travis rested in a deck chair, watching his ex-wife at the railing with his son and Gerry Adamson. That threesome peered off the rear deck, at the sun setting behind them. It was a glorious sunset, flowing its spectrum over the low clouds in the distance. Travis felt their moving away from the light.

It was funny, looking around: the running track, the swimming pool and climbing wall, the tiki bar, water slides, and the basketball court in the distance. That was different from the refugee camps he'd been in. No goats. The guests seemed embarrassed by the ship's facilities now, a little ashamed of the opulence and frivolity of their home to the poverty-and-disaster-stricken guests. Still, some kids played basketball and others swam, their parents trying to maintain normalcy and smiles in their children.

While a few of the ship-guests jogged grim-faced on the track, most of the adults had no stomach to enjoy themselves.

Travis's head was turned and he stared hypnotized at the basketball court and the three-on-three game being played by teenagers. The ball was dribbled and Travis nodded to the rhythm of it from the boy's palm to the court. He had his boy, and he was happy. The world could be ending, but he felt lucky.

Most of those on the Festival were trying to keep away thoughts of the overwhelming whole. Travis tried to focus back on the smallest pieces of the present. To his left, he watched an attractive woman consoling a man who was sobbing silently, as though his grief had taken away his sound. His head was tucked into her breast and she stroked his hair while tears very slowly lined her cheeks.

The man looked about forty, his black hair streaked with grey. His body shuddered as regularly or irregularly as a heartbeat, and it shook her each time. She was younger, in her late twenties, and Travis saw in her face that she was a refugee too. There was something she'd left behind, her own thoughts were not on the man.

Travis got up and walked to the tiki bar. Only as he came right under the overhanging palm-leaf roof did he hear the reggae music playing shyly from the bar stereo.

He sat at a bolted down bar stool and ordered a beer. Beside him, a small man smiled and nodded hello. The bartender opened a bottle and passed it to Travis with a frosted mug.

"How much?" Travis asked the bartender.

"Well, this ship is all inclusive sir, so you just enjoy and relax."

"Welcome aboard," the man at the next stool said, watching Travis's face to judge his willingness to converse. "I'm Rick Dumas."

The man was about fifty. His still-blonde hair was thinning and cut short so that his scalp showed through.

"Travis Cooke," he answered. "You were a guest aboard?"

"Yeah. Trans-Atlantic special, they only do it once a year to get the ship from the Caribbean to Europe for the summer. Twenty-one day cruise. You know what day we're on? Two. We were supposed to go to Boston today, then do the crossing. Christ, we left from Key West, I wonder if it even exists any more. Sorry, I don't know if you have any people there. You from New York I guess?"

"Yes. You?"

"Dallas. Four hundred sixty three feet elevation."

The man had distracted Travis enough that he didn't notice he was halfway through his beer.

"Sounds like a nice place to be, right about now."

"I'm in real estate. The market is gonna explode. Every few years when there's a flood bad enough in the south, Alabama, Louisiana, Mississippi, we always get a little burp in the market. This will be off the charts — the entire East coast is gonna be homeless."

Rick saw the discomfort in Travis's face.

"We were on the Great Cities of Northern Europe tour," Rick said. "Boston, Dublin, Oslo, Copenhagen, Gdansk, Riga, Stockholm, Helsinki, St. Petersburg. Quite an itinerary, huh? I was in the Captain's Club too, that gets you special cocktail parties, complimentary massages, Egyptian cotton towels, champagne, the works."

"I'm glad Boston was on that list or you might be halfway across the ocean right now and we'd still be on the dock. Wet."

"Hey, do you see that?" Rick said, pointing out to sea. "Is that another ship? Hey, maybe you guys can hitch a ride back with them and we can get on with our cruise."

He paused, then smiled gently. "Just kidding, guy. Seriously though, I mean, if the damage isn't too bad, I wonder if we'll get back out when we drop you off. I mean, they haven't told us that yet. We'd only be one day behind."

Travis looked out at the other ship. At least they weren't the only ones to follow this plan.

The sun was dipping below the horizon behind them, and the shadows were long all around them, those of the closed umbrellas looking like an array of spears.

By the railing, Corrina stood with her hand on Darren's shoulder. In her young life she had enjoyed all the advantages of a beautiful girl, but she'd eventually begun to feel disadvantages, too. As she looked out on the open water, she wondered at the feelings she'd had as a child, when everyone was so nice to her that the world seemed a kind place, and her opportunities, the possible spread of her future life, seemed as wide as this ocean.

The world had not been always kind or open in the course of her years, but she had treasured life and discarded fears.

Now, she thought of her mom and sister, down in South Carolina. The Carolinas would have been hit sooner, with less warning than New York. She thought of her coworkers at the temp office, and all the resumes she'd filed each day and who they belonged to. She thought of her friend Sasha, who she had known since kindergarten, who had eaten a caterpillar in grade three on a dare, who she had moved to NY with, and who had introduced her to Travis, and eleven years later, to Gerry.

One in four were dead, Corrina decided, and those faces came by, with her other friends, her neighbors, the kids in Darren's class and his teachers and the parents. One in four were dead, and the faces died in that ratio in her mind.

This was happening all over the Sky Deck, where many refugees and tourists had been drawn, and more and more conversations dried up as individuals were imagining who was dead and who spared. Each man, woman and child played God, deciding whom the flood had taken.

Corrina realized Darren was no longer next to her. She turned in a split-second panic and saw Claude Bettman sitting with Darren on a lounge chair, a little travel chess board set up between them. He was showing Darren how the pieces moved, Gerry watching.

Looking back out over the railing, Corrina felt that childhood excitement for the open space and the possibilities it contained, as a ghost of a memory passing through her. It made her shiver.

10

"The ship is not replying, sir," Chief Radio Officer Harrington said.

"Jameson, have you got her numbers yet?"

"Not yet," the First Officer answered, binoculars at his eyes. "But she's Navy. Looks like a supply ship. It must be the missing vessel. But it should have a large crew, and there's no one on deck. Perhaps she sailed without her full compliment for the evacuation."

"That doesn't explain why she can't respond."

"If there were a comms malfunction, sir," Harrington said, "it might explain how she lost contact to begin with."

"Let's get in closer," London said. "They may have need of our comms system. Wait till we get a positive ID before we call it in."

On the Sky Deck, many of the guests and refugees were watching the ship as well, the first they'd seen since the mainland had been left out of sight.

Walking away from the bar, Travis recognized the military look of the vessel and felt reassured at its presence.

The sound of the ship's booming gun pierced the air and that thought.

Travis sprinted to his family.

A line of smoke cut across the sky between the ships, and the command bridge exploded. The Festival shook.

Travis was nearly thrown to the ground. He paused on his feet and looked back. Fifty-foot flames were in the space the bridge had been. An alarm rang.

The Festival continued to close the gap towards the other ship, and now that ship began to move as well. The Sky Deck was overcrowded already in the sitting areas; now the pathways were chaos, bodies bumping off bodies, jostling to get somewhere. Travis met Corrina coming towards him with Gerry and Darren. Tears were streaming down the boy's face, but he was so scared he had no breath for noise. Gerry had pointed the bridge out earlier, where the captain was sailing the ship.

There was screaming everywhere as the other ship closed in. An alarm rang in the air.

"Where should we go?" Corrina asked.

Gerry looked at the faces in his circle, wide-eyed, thinking.

"I want to see what that ship is going to do before we go anywhere."

"Yeah," Travis said, still fixed on the coming ship.

They braced themselves in a nook against the wall.

There were no more explosions. The Festival was closing on the other ship now, and they could see a small group up on the other's deck, all in orange uniforms.

On their own ship, a fire crew was already at work up on the bridge.

"They're coming right at us," Corrina said.

The Festival did not slow down, did not change course. All on deck paused to see how the two ships' directions would line up. The chaos sprang back into loud action as the collision became probable.

"That ship is coming right at us," Corrina said again.

The Festival was angling away, but still might not cross the other's path before impact. As the Festival crossed the bow of the approaching ship, the potential point of impact moved from the middle of the Festival, the swimming pool and crystal pyramid above the Atrium, towards the stern: the waterslides, the communications tower, and the smokestacks.

"Go forward, guys," Gerry said.

"Yeah," Travis said. They began to walk quickly forward along the jogging track.

The Festival continued to pass in front of the smaller ship, but the space between the ship's nose and the Festival's beam was shrinking fast.

"Run," Travis said.

Travis grabbed Darren into his arms and they began to run. He felt his chest tighten slightly, but not enough to slow him. The other ship was so close now, the bow was coming right at them as they ran forward, the Festival's forward motion added to theirs in taking them away from the point of impact.

All were running away from the Festival's stern. The Festival seemed to have the speed to escape the collision; the Navy ship on track to cross the Festival's wake safely behind her. That was the last impression Travis had from a backward glance sprinting away, seeing the coming ship's bow disappear below the sight line from the Sky Deck. Then the collision.

The Festival rocked to starboard and the air was filled with the sound of metal twisting. Travis was thrown, tumbling to protect Darren from hitting the floor. Other bodies were flying around them, along with deck chairs and small tables. The deck angled hard. The Festival's body was bending around the other ship's prow. There was another sound right above them. Travis looked up and saw the massive water slides tipping to port, leaning more than the ship's deck.

"Come on!" Gerry said, grabbing Travis by the arm and running hard.

The supports buckled. Tons of hard molded plastic came crashing down, unleashing a torrent of water. The flood exploded after them. They felt the water catch the backs of their legs, and they went tumbling to the deck from its force.

Darren was clutched tightly in Travis's arms as his body was pulled forward by the water before it passed, leaving them soaked but unbruised on the angled deck. Shooting along the water's flow on the deck, he saw another tower coming down, and a young girl standing right in its path. Something blocked his view and he heard the crash of the tower slide as he and Darren slowed on the deck.

"JOHN!" a woman screamed nearby.

"You alright?' he asked Darren.

"Uh huh."

Travis came to his feet, pulling Darren up with him.

A man came running by, carrying the little girl Travis had thought crushed by the falling tower. A young woman ran behind them, shrieking in terror.

"Go, go!" the man yelled at Travis. He slowed in his stride to slap Travis's shoulder as he passed, the girl held tight in his other arm.

Looking back, they couldn't see the orange men on the other ship now, they were all hidden by the higher vantage point of the Sky Deck. Then they heard automatic gunfire. Screams of terror erupted anew. A second volley of gunfire sounded, this time mixed with the ping of impact against the steel of the rear towers.

11

Passengers were getting off the deck fast, filling the Festival's interior. Many had stayed out through the explosion and collision, to see if and where the collision came. The gunfire was enough to influence these stragglers to get inside. The enclosed stairwells leading down to the Grand Atrium echoed with footsteps and screams. Those who had remained indoors heard the explosion and felt the crash, but had only their urgent imagination to guess at what was happening. Some stood waiting for instructions to come, while others joined the panicked escapees from the outer decks, who were themselves hardly more certain where they were going. Many guests at least had their rooms to run to, but the guests with their rooms to stern of the collision were newly homeless.

Screams delivered the key facts well: the ship had been attacked. The attackers had guns. They were coming aboard. Travis's mind was clear and practical under the threat, while still racing with the questions who? and why?

Guests locked themselves in their rooms. Some pulled refugees in with them.

As Travis's group came down a second flight of stairs, they rushed out an open door to a ballustraded walkway with a view of the open Atrium. There was the sound of automatic gunfire, and Travis looked at the Atrium filling below him.

"We can't go down there," he said. It was the most vulnerable, open position to attack. He held Darren to his chest with one arm, and with the other, grabbed Gerry. "This way."

They were several decks above the Atrium floor, running the enclosed hallway.

Stateroom doors were all shut. Corrina began banging on one.

"Please!" Corrina screamed at the door. "I have a child, please let me in, they have guns!"

There was no response. She banged more, and shook fiercely at the door handle.

"Come on," Gerry said with his hand on her shoulder. "We'll try again."

Near the end of the hall the doors were spaced further apart. Again Corrina stopped, repeating her cries and banging on a door. Again there was no response.

Another burst of gunfire, but the sound was different. It was echoing in the open cavity of the ship's belly rather than muffled through her walls. Travis kicked the door in with a powerful stroke, splintering the doorframe around the deadbolt.

The group pushed through the doorway.

The door was still on its hinges, and Travis shut it behind them, pulling a chair up to hold it in place. The cries of the hallway and from the Atrium were shut out almost completely. They all slowed their breathing without speaking.

The four were in a small foyer and turned left to walk out into the main room of the cabin. An elderly couple stood in the corner, by the closed drapes of a balcony.

The man held the woman tightly and they stared at Travis and the others behind him.

"I'm sorry," Travis said. "We have a child and they have guns, we need to hide."

The cabin was a large luxury berth. Tan leather easy chairs and a matching couch faced a flat-screen TV at the far left. A round table was circled by high-backed blue cushioned chairs, all sitting on white and blue ceramic tiles. To their right was a gleaming black grand piano and a wet bar, behind that an open door showed the bedroom.

Gerry introduced the group.

Darren remained quiet. Still the fire alarm rang.

"What's going on?" the old man said.

"We've been attacked," Gerry said, speaking quickly. "A military ship blew up the bridge, they rammed us, and then the men came on board with guns. They were in some kind of uniforms."

The old women made an exclamation.

"Military uniforms?" the old man said.

"No," Travis said, and then he thought of what those orange suits were. "No, like prison uniforms. They must've taken control of their ship during the rescue."

"Please," the old man said, "sit down. The kid, does he need anything? We have food and drinks in the fridge behind the bar. My name is Norman, this is my wife Vera."

Travis deposited Darren on a bar stool.

Norman and Vera came away from the wall, and Vera collapsed into a chair at the round table. There was another volley of gunfire, and a horrible scream.

"What's going to happen?" Darren said.

Nobody answered.

"They blew up the bridge?" Norman asked.

Gerry nodded.

"So who's driving the ship?"

"They're all dead," Gerry said. "They rammed us in the rear. I can't imagine our engines could work."

"What about the captain?"

Gerry shrugged.

"What do we do?" Norman asked.

"We wait," Travis said. "We wait and hope nobody bugs us and that ship leaves."

Nobody spoke. Norman got a glass of orange juice for Darren. There were occasional screams from outside, some nearer, some farther.

Another blast of gunfire, from a handgun. It was followed by an angry voice.

"Get on the floor!" they heard from close by.

Quiet again from outside, quiet in the cabin. There was no noise for some time.

"How will we know when they're gone?" Corrina asked.

"I'll look," Gerry said. "But not yet."

They heard their cabin door pushed open, the chair falling over. Two men in orange jumpsuits walked in from the small foyer, one holding a pistol, the other a knife. They wore bandanas Travis recognized as gang colors. He'd seen them at work, around knife and bullet wounds.

"Against the wall," the one with the gun said.

"Where's your money?" the second one said. "Just

hand it to us and nobody dies in this room."

Corrina was squeezing Darren's face into her breast and they moved towards the wall.

"We don't have anything," Travis said. "We were rescued by this ship from New York, we don't have any bags or anything."

"New York's dead, and you will be too if you don't show us the money."

"You're from Rikers," Corrina said.

"What? Sing Sing, bitch," the man with the gun said.

"That ship was rescuing you," Travis said. "And you killed them?"

"Rescued?" the man with the gun laughed. "Taking us from one cage to another? We were the last ship out. A last-minute ship and not enough crew. So we're not going back to the cage. Now this is somebody's money pad, so I want to see some."

"I have a wallet," Norman said.

He went to the table behind him and held it to the prisoners. The man with the knife took it and opened it.

"Oh man," he said as he fanned the full sheath of bills. "The millionaire. The millionaire and his wife."

He began singing the Gilligan's Island theme. "*Just sit right back and you'll hear a tale, a tale of a fateful trip.*"

"Every moment you waste here," Corrina said, "your chance to get away shrinks. That's a Navy ship! How long do you think before they find you? What good will this money do you? You need to get off this ship or you'll go back to the cage."

"I will shoot you if you don't shut up," the man with the gun said.

Travis and Gerry closed their shoulders together in front of her.

"This is going to cost you your freedom," she said.

"Man, what do you know? This is the free-est I have ever been. We ain't going back! And whatever is left after all this, we'll want money."

"Alright, millionaire," the one with the knife said, "what about your wife? Let's see Mrs. Howell's jewels."

"My wife has a purse," Norman said. "It's in the bedroom."

"She can show us," the one with the knife said. He grabbed Vera.

"She won't know where it is, let me," Norman said.

"Stay there!" the man pulled on Vera and dragged her a step.

"Norman?" Vera said. "What's happening?"

She stalled to look back and the man tugged her hard.

"No!" Norman shouted, pushing between them.

The man with the gun fired, and the explosive sound rung in all their ears until all they heard was Norman squealing as he fell to the floor. The gun was already pointed at Travis's chest. It was done. The nice old man was still on the floor and the BANG of the shot still rang in Travis's ear.

"Now get me the damn money and the damn jewels, Mrs. Howell," the man with the gun said.

Vera began crying, her legs buckled, the man with the knife held her up and yanked her forward.

"Norman," she said.

Darren was held tight to Corrina's breast. He closed his eyes and just trusted in her arms around him.

"Bastards," Gerry said.

"You want some too? I told you how to keep from dying," the man with the gun said. "He didn't do it."

Travis was on his knees, holding Norman's head up. Norman's eyes were closed and he wheezed in jerks.

"Just let him go and stand up," the gun still pointed at Travis.

"You're sub-human. Filth!" Travis said.

"Sub-human," the man with the gun repeated. He spoke like his tongue was swollen. "Yeah, sub-human. Might as well drown in the cage. We was always sub-human… and you never cared if we killed each other, if we grew up with crackpipes on the ground and bullets in the air," the man held Travis eyes-to-eyes and continued. "They told us New York was gone, man. Washington, gone. Miami, Boston, gone. They ain't coming to stop us. So we sub-humans should play nice now we're free?

"People like you have nightmares about the world burning. People like me fantasize about it. And there's a lot of people like me. You all shouldn't have made us so angry."

The man fired again. Norman fell forward into his own blood on the floor. Vera screamed.

The man with the knife was holding her with both hands but she was strong and almost broke away.

"Animals!"

The man took one hand off and punched her in the stomach, holding her with the other hand so she couldn't fall. With each move, Travis and Gerry's bodies stuttered as if to leap, but their eyes never left that gun.

"The money," the man with the knife said.

The knife man took Vera and disappeared into the bedroom, but Travis could still hear her sobbing breathing. He felt impotent, as when the waterslide flood had grabbed him. He could risk nothing while Darren was there. Perhaps they might all be back mopping up their wet homes in New York tomorrow, but Norman was irreversibly dead, like the Captain and officers on the bridge.

"Now give me your wallets," the man with the gun said, staring at Travis.

Travis reached into his pocket and pulled his wallet out, but left the cash he knew was in his pants. He threw it on the table, as did Gerry.

The man opened Travis's wallet. There was no money in it.

"Boy, you are down on your luck," the gunman laughed. "Paramedic, eh? You'll have your work cut out for you."

He took the credit cards. "You never know."

He opened Gerry's wallet and took several twenties out.

The knife-man came out, pushing Vera ahead of him.

"Millionaire's wife came through," knifeman said. "Real cash. And diamonds and pearls. Good room."

He threw Vera onto the floor in front of the bar.

"Let's go."

The gunman stared at Travis. He lifted the gun level with Travis's face and fired.

The window behind Travis shattered.

"Better luck next vacation."

The two left.

Corrina loosened her grip and Darren finally looked at the room again. He saw Norman dead at his father's feet, and instantly burrowed his head back into his mother. Vera sobbed, face down on the floor.

"*No phone, no lights, no motor cars,*" the men sang as they left through the front hall, "*Not a single luxury. Like Robinson Crusoe, as primitive as can be.*"

12

A broken man lay on the Sky Deck in a burnt black suit. His face was black from the explosion, except for the red lines of blood. His hair had burnt away.

His body was twisted over some piece of furniture he'd landed on. He was broken and could not move. He saw things happening around him, and remained silent as the Festival refugees and guests ran past. When the others in the orange suits began to pass, he mustered the energy and accepted the pain for one last shout.

"Hey!"

It got someone's attention. Two men came and stood above him. One had a gun.

"I'm Captain," Captain London said with great difficulty. "Where's yours?"

The two men looked at each other.

"Haggard's gone below," one said. "Let's get the Commander."

They left.

London had seen the puff of smoke from the Navy ship. He'd yelled "Dive!" as the BOOM reached them, and he threw himself behind an equipment bank. He wondered if any of the others on the bridge had survived. Probably not. He wondered that he had. He imagined that when it was all said and done, he wouldn't. As he dived behind the equipment bank, he realized that the Navy ship had been hijacked during evacuations. Seeing the jumpsuits now, he knew the hijackers had been prisoners.

They had no guns aboard the Festival. They were completely vulnerable. Six officers probably dead on the bridge.

In time, the man he waited for, the Commander, appeared standing above him, the other two who had found him hovering behind.

"You're the captain?" the Commander said. Like the others, he was in an orange prison jumpsuit. He had a big round head and a stolen Navy officer's cap and spoke slowly.

Captain London nodded. There was the sound of gunfire from below decks, and London could now see both refugees and attackers running here and there, looking for cover or looking for each other.

"Go back to your ship," London said. "Surrender."

The Commander stomped his foot down on London's leg.

"Uniforms are all the same," the Commander said. "But we don't take orders now."

London rumbled with a rough laugh.

"Can't hurt me," he managed.

"Is that a challenge?" the Commander said. "Huh. You Navy?"

"Once," London said.

"You look like one. Even with a broken spine you got a rod up your ass. I was Navy. I hate uniforms. Navy. Cops. Guards. You don't get to give orders anymore, Captain. We killed a lot of uniforms today. You can watch us kill more. That'll hurt, won't it?"

"I'll be dead," London said.

The man sounded educated, London thought. He'd probably been an officer himself; he had that look, if not as much as London did. How could this help?

The Commander hated this beaten man who still acted like he was in charge.

"You're right," the Commander said.

He shot Captain London twice in the chest and watched him take his last breath.

13

Travis and Gerry pulled Norman's body into the bedroom, into the walk-in closet, while Corrina sat with Vera at the table. In the closet, they tossed aside the precisely placed men's and women's shoes to lay the body. Crisp ironed pants and shirts hung above Norman.

"He knew," Vera said. "He knew what they'd do. But he would not stand by while they touched me. He was a real man, a man of honor."

She had a Russian accent, dimmed from many years in America, socializing little with other immigrants. When Travis and Gerry came back into the living room, she was already staring at them.

Occasionally they heard screams from outside, gunshots. They sat around the table and did not talk. Corrina tried to hold Darren close but he pushed away and sat upright in his chair. The windows and patio doors showed night had fallen. The room was dark, only the chandelier above the table created a circle of light that they sat in. They each had retreated into themselves.

There had been a day during his mission in Sudan when Travis had led a Red Cross unit to set up a new refugee camp by a small village. By the time they arrived, the village had been wiped out by raiders. There were only bodies, dozens of bodies lying scattered between the thatch huts as flies licked at them and dust blew over them.

The bodies had to be cleared out before the camp could be set up. The message had already been sent across the countryside that this village would be the location of the camp, so they cleared the bodies and cleaned the site. He looked across at Darren and wished that the son would never see with his eyes what his father dreamt of.

"It was my first time returning home," Vera said, breaking the silence. "I was born in St. Petersburg. Leningrad. I have not been home since I was a child. Norman was my only family now. He was taking me to visit my home. But I have no home now. I hardly exist, I suppose."

"We'll take care of you," Corrina said. "We're going to get through this. I'm sure the ship has radioed for help."

Vera looked at her with contempt, tears still wet on her face. She spoke slowly: "Do you really think anyone will come for us? With half the world in chaos? You think they'll worry about us?"

"There are other ships out here," Gerry said. "Dozens of ships from New York alone, and they'll be nearby because they would probably all be following the same instructions as the Festival. Someone will help us. Even if those ships for some reason can't help us, there're thousands of people on this ship. Each one of them has friends and relatives looking for them. There will be help, Vera. Eventually."

"You are a fool," Vera said. "Where is Norman?"

"The closet," Gerry said.

"What? What are you talking about? Where is he? Norman!"

"Vera," Travis said. "Vera, Norman is dead."

Vera did not answer. She turned and fought the tears.

Travis nodded at Corrina. Vera had some form of dementia. Norman had been scared she would forget where the purse was. That's why he tried to go.

"It's okay, Vera," Corrina said. "We'll take care of you."

The lights went out. The alarm stopped.

There was screaming from all around them, no gunfire then, only screaming.

"I'll open the drapes, maybe there will be some light from outside," Travis said.

He stumbled to the balcony doors and pulled the floor length drapes back. Only the most vague outline of the sliding door was visible. Travis struggled to find the latch and slide the glass pane back. It was a dark night; the clouds above stood out as a dull grey glow in the blackness.

Even that tiny amount of light helped, and Travis could begin to make out shapes in the cabin as his eyes adjusted and he looked back in.

"The lights are out all over the ship. I can see a few emergency lights way above us, but that's it. I can make out the Navy ship, they have a few lights on. I can only see the very back of it. We'd better pass the night here," Travis said.

14

The ship had several theaters. The largest, the Royal Theater, boasted 800 luxury seats and a 1500-square foot stage, fronted by a small orchestra pit. This was the second destination Captain London had herded the refugees from the West Side pier in New York. The Goldings were among the last flooding through the six double doors at the top of the Theater.

When the Navy ship had borne upon the Festival, Lee and Jessica Golding had been on the deck. In the chaos that followed, their cabin was not an option for escape. It lay just stern of the intersection of the two ships. They could see from the crash that they were homeless. Lee had watched that ship come in right up until it tore through, and the men came over the sides.

As the torrent of refugees returning tapered off, individuals or small groups still continued to join them in the Theater. When the gunshots became louder, closer, and more frequent, Jessica Golding shut the door nearest her. Lee followed her lead and looked around for something to barricade the doors with. The seats were permanently installed, but there were drapes on the walls, hanging from six-foot wrought-iron rods. He grabbed at a drape and pulled hard, snapping the fixture holding the rod. The rod came loose, and Lee quickly slid the drape off. He brought the rod to the door. It fit through the double door handles but with its length it was difficult to angle it in. Lee Golding's action and intensity began building a panic in the room. Others came and helped, wedging the rod against the wall, forcing it into the depression the door was set in. Around the upper ring of the Theater and down in the lower corners, the struggle was repeated as groups of three or four men frantically pushed and struggled to fit the rods across the door handles.

Lee ran onto the stage to lock the door that led out through the backstage area and dressing rooms. In the hall there he saw the man-mountain with whom he had shared the escape from New York. The grey giant was alone in the hall, still searching for a place to hide.

"My room is gone," Adam Melville said.

"Come in here, you'll be safe," Lee said. "I need to lock this door."

They walked back out to the stage. When they emerged, the room was quiet. Jessica walked to the front and sat with Lee on the stage stairs. Adam found himself a seat near the front row. The seats were enormous luxury loungers, but he was still wedged between the armrests.

They waited.

It had been just hours ago that they'd watched New York recede, feeling that though the world was ending, they were safe. Safest seats in the house. When Adam had left the deck that afternoon, he'd had a flash about that wrestler, Lee Golding. A bad feeling. He had been troubled by this thought, and determined that he would keep an eye out for the other big man. And now Lee Golding had saved him.

It was not long before there was a noise at the door to stage right.

The wave of absolute quiet spread through the room, pushed on by the noise of the shaking and banging of that door.

Lee rose from his seat and stood by the side aisle, peering around the end of the stage.

Gunfire tore through the door, tearing into the angled floor of the aisle. Those by that side of the Theater screamed and rushed out of the path. The door shook from the other side. The curtain rod, it could be seen by all, was only just barely wedged across the two handles. The five and a half feet of rod to one side of the handles was loose, and drooped to the floor. The doors shook, and then one handle snapped free of the curtain rod and the door swung open.

Enter the pirates: two men in orange prison jumpsuits.

Lee stepped back, blocking Jessica Golding behind him as the two men came into view of the full Theater. One of the men had a rifle: a Navy M16A3, demonstrated in fully-automatic mode by the gun bursts at the door. He wore a tactical vest over his jumpsuit and a Navy officer's cap, tipped awkwardly.

"Well, well," the man without the gun said. "the motherload of the mothership."

"You got money. We got bullets," the gunman said to the room. "Let's make a deal."

"This could take a while," the man without the gun said, surveying the hundreds of faces.

"OK. We need a volunteer."

Lee Golding stepped forward.

"What do you want?"

"Wait, I know you," the man with the gun said. "Wow. I'm gonna make the Mighty Lee Golding my butler."

Lee was pressed into service as their surrogate mugger. The gunman and the gunman's partner would follow him up the aisle, and Lee would collect the money. For his collection, they quickly took the largest handbag from a woman near the front and dumped its contents. Lee took the bag, with the men behind him, and started his tour with Adam Melville.

"How did you ever get that ship?" Adam asked the invaders as he stood, and put his hands to his pockets.

The man without the gun's face went queer, his eyes opened wide.

"God, man, God! The guards and staff bolted early, so by the time that ship with no crew came for us, there was just the last few sucker-guards. God set it all up!"

The man spoke so flamboyantly, he was like a man possessed, or it seemed to Lee, like a pro wrestler challenging him in an arena somewhere.

"Then," he continued, "we had our own Navy guy to drive the boat: that's God's hand! And now the Mighty Lee Golding is my valet. Well, we're getting years of bad karma reversed today."

They had known, even in Sing Sing, what was happening around them. They knew that when the main body of guards evacuated, they were almost surely to drown in their cells. When the evacuation of prisoners finally came, the unexpected success of their uprising and of stealing the ship had driven them into a frenzy. Killing the guards and all but a few of the ship's crew had set a new tone for all of them in this very new world. If they were violent before, they were free now.

Adam took his wallet out and passed it to Lee. Lee looked back at the men.

"Just the cash and cards," the gunman said.

"You all been living the high life too long," the ranting man continued, "and your own chickens are coming home to roost. Today is the Day of Big Payback, when ying becomes yang, and the hardest luck crew gets dealt a flush."

He was high, Lee thought, and he found himself wondering how they got drugs in prison, and what drugs they had. Lee took out money and three credit cards and dropped them in the bag.

"Now frisk him," the man with the gun said.

"What?" Lee said.

"Frisk him!" the man with the gun said, straightening the gun towards Lee and Adam.

"What for?" Lee said.

"'Cause it's funny to me," the man without the gun said.

The Mighty Lee Golding turned and put his arms around Adam Melville. He began to pat him around, like in the movies. His arms struggled to reach around the bulk of the other.

"Don't forget his crotch, check it."

Lee patted down Adam's crotch, the insides of his thighs. His huge paws with the class ring and wedding ring went up patting Adam 's chest, and under his armpits which were wet, and the shirt dark, with sweat.

"He's clean," Lee said. He looked at Adam with a little

nervous laugh.

"Next."

Lee took money, jewelry and credit cards up the line. There were hundreds of refugees to rob, and they passed their things quickly through Lee Golding's hands.

Two thirds of the way up the first aisle, Lee saw the muzzle of the gun close by his head, moving loosely. He turned and grabbed the gunman's arm. The two crashed into the wall. The second of the pair was a few steps below on the aisle, and was immediately up the stairs onto Lee's back. Lee had an iron grip on the wrist below which the gun was held, and he cracked it against the wall while pressing his weight right into the man. He scarcely noticed the second on his back, before Adam tore the gunman from Lee with one hand, pulling the gun away from him with the other. The Mighty Lee Golding, the Alabama Assassin, shook his man like a rag doll, cracking the gunless man's back on the railing along the wall. The other swung away from Adam and began to run towards the door he'd come through. Adam lifted the gun with both hands and fired several rounds in one quick squeeze. The sound shocked his ears. The man in the orange jumpsuit fell to the floor.

Lee had his man on the floor and was throwing his enormous fist into the gunman's face until the gunman was no threat. Lee caught his breath and came to his feet.

Adam stood before him in the aisle, staring at the dead man, the arm with the gun limp by his side. Lee came to him and took the gun, and Adam didn't respond. Lee pointed it at the groaning, broken man on the floor and fired.

The echo dissipated from the air, and the quiet now in the Theater, whose acoustics were renowned, was such that the panting of Lee and Adam could be heard across the room. Lee put his hand on Adam's shoulder. Adam walked away from him, past the dead man, and collapsed in a seat.

Lee held the gun in the air. The rush, the adrenaline, heartbeat, serotonin, and all the eyes on him, were something he'd not felt in so many years since he'd left the ring. He was high with the rush. He leaned back and laughed his stage laugh. He made a V with his fingers and wagged his tongue through it.

"Golding gonna getcha!" he yelled.

The crowd roared in a cheer. He looked at Jessica and winked.

Lee left the handbag he'd used on the floor for those robbed to reclaim their things. Only Adam stayed in his seat.

Lee was down on the dead man, checking his tactical vest.

"Motherload from the mothership," he said.

The whole Theater must be able to hear his heart beat, he thought. Let 'em.

The pockets were full, all of them, with ammo clips. Eight 30-round magazines in all. Lee unclipped the vest from the dead man, blood and all, and threw it on over one shoulder. For a moment he tried getting the other arm through, but it needed adjusting to fit so he left it hanging from the one shoulder and returned to the front, to Jessica.

Adam tried to keep himself from vomiting. The

sudden threat taken suddenly away, he felt disgust from the sick opportunism of the prisoners, the fear, the roar of the gunfire, the bloody death. He killed a man.

The main lights went out. The alarm stopped. Only the emergency lights along the floor were visible, twinkling like stars below them, and they were above heaven.

15

Some length of time after the lights went out, the ship moved. It began as a shudder, then the floors shifted beneath them in Vera and Norman's luxury berth, and they felt the ship tilt to one side. The floor came up at a tremendous angle, and they all tumbled off their chairs, rolling over each other into the wall.

"The Navy ship's separating," Gerry said.

They stayed pressed against the wall, and then felt the room begin to spin slowly, as the Navy ship tried to reverse away, and the Festival clung to it.

"Momma?" Darren called in the dark.

"I'm here," she said.

With a shudder, it stopped. There was an echo of metal tearing, and the ship began to right herself. It stopped short of coming back to level, but straightened enough that they could stand.

"They're gone," Gerry said. "They must be gone."

"Will the lights come back?" Darren asked.

"I'm sure they have a back-up system," Travis said. "They'll fix it. And we'll be off this ship soon anyways, li'l bud, we'll be off soon."

Travis went out on the balcony and verified that the Navy ship had separated, still visible but moving away. He could now hardly make out the dark stern of the Festival, but he could see that its lines were bent and broken.

"I'll take a look down the hall," Gerry said, "and see if there're lights anywhere."

Gerry walked towards the cabin foyer, bouncing off the wall, and then tripping over a chair. Finally, the group heard the door as Gerry exited. They felt, each of them, that there were no guarantees of return when someone left a room.

The hallway was dark except for a dim track of emergency lighting along the wall, an inch above the floor. Gerry heard crying from many places. He began to walk forward. He didn't know what he was hoping to find, other than light.

Gerry Adamson was a strong man with a soft personality. He'd grown up poor in New York, his mom a single mother in and out of jobs, in and out of drunken uselessness. Gerry had raised himself. He'd raised himself to be mean, until a teacher took the time to explain where his road was leading.

Young Gerry was smart and mature out of necessity, so he listened. It was a surprise to those who knew him back then that he went on to become a teacher; a surprise that he'd had the inclination and a surprise that he'd had the discipline and ability. At the same time, those who knew him as an adult, as a lover of poetry and a gentle man, good with kids, would not have guessed at his rough boyhood.

He was soft spoken, although not quiet — he loved to talk, about art and ideas.

Poetry was one of the links between the two Gerry Adamsons — it was poetry that had allowed him to escape meanness and find meaning. His own first book of poetry had sold well in New York. But it could never make a career for him.

As it was a teacher who had brought the idea to him, it had been natural for him to become a teacher himself, to inspire kids to look beyond where they were.

His whole life, it seemed, he'd been trying to find a light in the darkness.

Travis took the others out onto the balcony to wait. The deck chairs had toppled against the railings, but they straightened them out and could make out each other's faces in the cloud-dimmed starlight. It was cold, but being able to see each other seemed a greater comfort than the warmth of the cabin.

Vera lay in one chair silently. Corrina sat in the other, holding Darren. Travis sat on the floor, his back against the railing. There was only blackness filling the space he had earlier been able to make out the Navy ship in.

Gerry felt like a space walker moving through darkness, following the thin glittering line on the wall. The sound of crying around him, and nothing else, scared him.

"Is there anybody there?" he said.

There was no answer. He imagined others as terrified as his family behind each door.

His hand was along the railing, and he passed an obstruction so that the cavity of the Atrium opened to his left. There were two emergency lights on the walls and he could make out movement down below him. Darkness moving inside darkness, and still the only sound he heard was crying. He looked down at what he guessed were scores of people below him, whimpering. He went back to the room.

3257 was the number on the door. When he knew he was near it, he felt the doors to find the number. At 3257 he opened the door and went inside.

"It's me," he said.

"We're here," Corrina's voice came back to him.

He joined the others.

"There's nothing for us out there," he said. "At least not yet. There's no one in charge, no order, no lights. Just guests locked in their rooms and refugees crying in the Atrium. We should wait here till morning."

"What if the ship sinks?" Darren asked.

"We shouldn't be in any danger, honey," Corrina said. "These big ships have watertight compartments to seal off any leaks. And if anything does happen, there are lifeboats."

"Oh."

Vera insisted Darren and Corrina sleep in the bed. She found extra blankets and made a bed for herself on the couch. They watched her carefully, but she seemed completely composed, and never again mentioned Norman. Travis and Gerry stayed out on the balcony, uncovered on the lounge chairs in the cold. There was a break in the clouds and the moon showed through. That bare obtrusion of light made the sea sparkle and showed just how alone they were.

The men did not talk.

Shivering exhaustion finally overtook Travis as he thought that the previous night he had taken his pills and gone to sleep in his apartment in Brooklyn. He wished there were a pill that could make him wake up back there.

His sleep was tortured. He slept on his side, curled up, flipping sides constantly to stay warm.

He dreamt of New York. He imagined scenes of his childhood, and then the water would rush in and fill everything up. There was an image of New York streets filled with starving Sudanese, and he saw himself flying away before the water filled the streets and the black bodies floated up around the tips of the skyscrapers. He had the idea of the city as the capital of the world, the hub of all roads, all civilization.

He saw all the peoples of the world facing New York in their prayers, and then the water overtook the city and he didn't know if that's what the people were praying for. He heard the voice of the man with the gun, the killer. People like you have nightmares about the world burning. People like me have fantasies about it.

16

One day after the earthquake, Travis woke on a balcony overlooking the Atlantic Ocean.

The sun was still behind the ship, but the black of night had become grey, and then showed hints of blue. The air began slowly to warm. Like millions of others that day, Travis woke wondering where he was and then remembering. He made a noise as he rose and Gerry was waking too on the other lounge chair. They shared a look, sharing what they had in common.

Travis stretched and stepped to the railing.

"There's lifeboats gone," he said, looking over the side.

The lifeboats hung several decks below them. Travis pointed at empty spaces where boats had been the night before.

"Oil leak," Gerry said looking down.

Travis followed his gaze to the stern and saw the inky black cloud on the water of the rear quarter of the ship. Gas had leaked, too, and spread farther, casting rainbows off each wave.

They went inside the cabin and woke the others, Vera on the couch, Darren and Corrina in the bed. Vera gave Darren an apple from the fridge.

"Norman?" she called. "Norman?"

Corrina took her hand and walked her to the balcony.

"Come, dear, come and see this view."

It was still before 7:30 a.m. when they left the room as a group. There were a few people in the hallway, and Travis wondered if he looked as dazed as they did, wandering in the first grey light to reach the spaces of the ship.

"Is anyone in charge?" Gerry asked one man.

The man pointed down into the Atrium, which was just coming into view as they passed the obstruction along part of the interior walkway.

"People are down there."

The Atrium was a natural gathering point. Many of the ship's rooms opened up to views of it, and the bulk of the refugees considered it their base on the ship. It was where they returned.

With the skylight above they could see fully in this space, though the light was still grey.

The Atrium was already filling up the way it had the day before, only now there were more audible cries of pain as well as despair. Long shadows criss-crossed the scene, the writhing mass of injured and petrified. The light from the high crystal roof and the many mirrored surfaces created blocks in bright focus, highlighting personal traumas here and there.

As they walked down, Travis felt a quick comfort as he recognized Claude Bettman in the crowd, the man who had picked him and Darren up in the rush to get on the ship. Claude was a physical artifact of yesterday that was unchanged.

There numbered near a thousand in the Atrium, and hundreds watched from the walkways above.

Travis led them to Claude near the stairs, standing by

himself. Claude had lost his overcoat during the night, and now wore just his brown suit with the jacket undone and his open-necked white shirt.

"Claude," Travis said.

Claude looked them over, a quick assessment of how they'd made out.

"Did they come after you?" Darren said.

Claude smiled. "They did. But I'm all right. They got my coat though. Imagine that, Darren. What kind of pirates steal overcoats?"

Darren smiled.

Claude made a pirates growl at Darren.

"Arrr. Give us the overcoat! Or walk the plank, landlubber!" he said.

Claude saw the look on the face of the old woman who was with them now and stopped.

Travis was watching those immediately around them. He heard pained breathing and peered around some backs to see a man bleeding from the shoulder. He was half laying on the ground, his torso and head supported in the lap and arms of a woman who kneeled behind him. A man kneeled over him, tying a tourniquet inexpertly but solidly.

There was the little girl who had been rescued from the crashing tower on the deck, but not the man who had saved her. She was evidently with her parents now, and the man was not with them.

The captain and his team on the bridge were gone, Travis thought, but where were the other officers? Where was the hospitality manager? Time passed as they and all around felt the weight of those questions, and no one answering them. Travis saw uniformed crew here and there in the crowd, looking as lost as everyone else.

"You think you have a handle on the things that can kill you," Claude Bettman said. "You watch what you eat, you don't smoke. You worry about muggers and stay away from the dark parts of town. But you don't know. You don't know what could be falling from the sky at any moment of your life. I certainly didn't bet on the tsunami-pirate double."

"HEY!" a man's voice came above the din of the group. Travis looked around.

"HEY!" the voice called out louder.

Travis saw that a man stood on a bar, perhaps fifty feet further into the Atrium than their group. Travis knew him. It was the hero. The man who had saved the girl on deck.

"Since we're all standing around here and nobody really knows what to do," the man yelled, "maybe we should get to work. There's a lot of injured people right now, so first of all, can we have any medical workers please come down here, let's get organized. Any doctors, nurses, or paramedics, come down here. If there's any Festival officers or crew who can help us understand the condition of the ship, actually any military people, anyone else familiar with ship mechanics or electronics, please come down. I'm sure we could use some help figuring out how to efficiently assess the situation on the ship, the damage and the options, and take care of everyone's needs."

He saw the huge movement in the crowd and changed his mind.

"Wait. Let's do the medical group first, give us some time to get that organized before any of the others come down. Medical professionals first."

The man on the bar was average height, slightly overweight and broad shouldered. He had close-cropped brown hair and a square jawline. Although he looked only about forty, his skin was creased and lined, slightly pockmarked around the neck. That square jaw, thick neck and sure eyes made him appear remarkably strong. The leonine power of his face alone made it handsome.

The bar the man stood on was dark polished wood, with green-bronze marble on the countertop matching the floor. The liquor rack behind the man had been emptied before the refugees had come on board, so the servers' enclosed space behind the bar looked like a penalty box.

While most of the crowd was turning to face the man, several were already approaching him, pushing their way through, coming down from the upper levels. Travis looked back at his family, and said to Corrina, "I'd better go help. Holler if you need me."

"Go ahead," Corrina said.

He looked at Claude and nodded and waded through the crowd towards the bar.

"Are there any senior officers around? Has anyone seen where they are?" the man on the bar called.

"I saw them on the bridge," a young man in the crowd shouted. He was dressed in uniform, the uniform of a deckhand. The uniform was coated in blood all along one side. The murmur in the crowd died down greatly and this young man with a strained voice held the attention of everyone who was not tending a wounded companion.

"A lot of the senior officers were with the captain on the bridge when it got hit. Birnbaum, the Staff Captain, Harrington, the Chief Radio Officer, the Navigation Officer, the First Officer, the Quartermaster" he said. "They're all dead. But they went after the rest, too. Of the officers, I mean. I saw it."

The deckhand paused.

"I heard them, and I hid," he started again haltingly, as if any two pieces of the story together would be too much to take in. "I was on the Sky Deck, and I saw them coming. I hid in an equipment closet. I could see them come in to this lounge area, right near where the ships came together. There was a leader named Haggard. He had this yellow bandana and a big beard and this loud choppy voice, yelling at everybody. Crazy. He was telling them to bring all of us, the officers, the crew. I saw two of our First Officers come by themselves, they tried to approach him and talk to him. He shot them down.

"He'd get them coming in in groups, and they'd line them up at the railing and give them all names of their prison guards. Then they'd shoot them, and toss the bodies over so the next ones to arrive wouldn't see. I saw it all, I heard all their talk, I was right in the middle of them. They killed dozens of us. The blood poured across the deck, they made footprints in it. They'd push the officers and laugh at them slipping and falling in it. It came right into my closet and pooled around my feet."

The man stopped and tried not to cry.

"They sent most of their men room to room. Rape and pillage, he said. Each group had at least one gun, they knew there were no guns on cruise ships to fight back. He gave two hours for everyone to get back to their ship. The leader had this friend. He was quiet, but everyone was talking to him, and I heard that it was his idea, taking the ship, becoming pirates. He'd been in the Navy, they called him Commander. He knew how to run the ship. They had another guy who was a gunner. They were giving him high-fives too. For hitting the bridge. Killing everyone. They didn't even mean to collide! They were trying to come alongside and screwed it up, and they were all laughing about it.

"They kept joking about being pirates. They made our crew walk right off the deck, some of them, and if they wouldn't walk off, they shot them and threw them off anyway. They sent some of their men to find the power generator and knock it out. They wanted to destroy any communications equipment. It sounded like they'd destroyed anything on the Navy ship that could give away their own location, but the leader, he didn't seem so sure about it. I was there for an hour, two hours, who knows. They never stopped killing the whole time I was there. It got dark and I couldn't see but I could hear them scream and I was crouched down with my hands on my feet and could feel the blood coming up against my shoes.

"When it was over, and the ship pulled out, I came out. It was dark, and I slipped in the blood. I went to the staff dining room, I thought some others might go there. There were a few dozen of us there, staff and crew. There were some flashlights to see. I just sat there, I couldn't even talk. Many of them are gone now. The other staff. They took the lifeboats and left while it was dark. I didn't.

I couldn't even talk."

The man on the bar was staring at the deckhand, far across the room, waiting for more that wasn't to come.

"Okay," the man on the bar said finally. "Now the danger is gone. We have to take care of ourselves."

He looked at the couple of dozen men and women who had gathered close to the bar or were still approaching it.

"You all are the doctors and nurses? Okay."

He looked back up, taking in the whole room.

"If you have someone who needs medical attention, please put your hand up."

17

There were just five doctors, twenty-two nurses, three paramedics and one combat medic. Travis recognized one of the doctors, the middle-aged man he'd seen on the deck crying in the woman's arms just before the attack. On this doctor's face, Travis saw an anguish so ugly he forced himself to keep looking at it, as if he needed to understand.

One of the men in the group was the ship surgeon. There were two ship nurses as well. They did not know if the other nurses or doctor on staff had been killed or abandoned ship in the lifeboats.

"Do you have anyone else here you know from the ship?" the ship surgeon asked the ship nurses.

They nodded.

"Take them with you and go to the clinic. We'll need surgical tools, all the basics, okay? Every scalpel, scissor, and forceps we have. Plenty of gloves and antiseptic. We'll need spinal collars and backboards, bandages, splints, the whole shebang. Suction, oxygen, zappers, all the toys with battery packs. Let's see. Thrombolytics and morphine."

He spoke with the casual precision of expertise. The two nurses went back to the clinic, taking with them three other crew: a bartender, a DJ, a waiter.

"Go on, doctor," the man from the bar-top prodded. "How do we manage this?"

"Okay," the doctor looked around his makeshift team. "Guys, the first thing you need to know about multiple casualty triage is that the rule changes from Do the best for each patient, to Do the best for the greatest number of patients. Who are the nurses? You five will fan out. We need to triage, like this. Minimal intervention now, just opening airways or controlling external hemorrhages. Nothing else but assessment. All these guys with their hands up, get them to show a number with their fingers. Check the patients out. Salvageable and can't wait is number one — any massive trauma or loss of blood. Salvageable and can wait is number two, broken arms, non-critical wounds, 1st and 2nd degree burns. Number three is unsalvageable. Who are the paramedics?"

Travis raised his hand, along with two other men.

"Get the number threes morphine, then come help with the ones. When we deal with the ones and twos we'll see if any threes can be saved. Anyone with serious blood loss… we just don't have the blood."

"We can do a donor clinic," Travis said. "Right here. I did it in Africa. They just use the whole blood."

"We can't do blood tests," the ship surgeon said.

"Ask them," Travis said. "A lot of people that are O-negative know it."

The universally compatible blood type, O-negative.

"Okay," the ship surgeon said. "Okay. You, triage nurses, go. Get moving. Remember, one, two, three."

The ship surgeon peered into the crowd and then called out, "I need two volunteers to run back to the medical clinic. Two volunteers who know where the clinic is, can run there, and carry stuff back."

The ship surgeon sent two passengers back to work with the nurses to bring blood storage and needles, tubing, saline bags and hangers.

The man on the bar left the ship surgeon to organize the medical team.

He faced the two junior officers from the ship who had come down, as well as six military officers and dozens of soldiers and reservists. The man on the bar asked them to wait while he addressed the crowd.

"Okay, everybody, we have good news. The ship's surgeon is here, he has his staff nurses and a whole team of doctors and nurses volunteering from the crowd. We have nurses going out right now to do triage. Please do as they say, the doctors will be following them. We should have medical supplies from the clinic starting to come in around ten minutes. We have some of the ship's officers and some folks with military experience. We're going to have them come up with a plan to assess our situation as quickly as possible, and assess our food situation as well which I think everyone here is probably starting to wonder about."

Hundreds watched his face and wished for him to know what to do next.

"Firstly," he continued, "does anyone here know of any fires going on, or, well, just any information that anyone has that they think is important, I guess this is the chance to shout it out."

"Who are you?" someone shouted.

"I'm John Hesse," the man on the bar said.

Travis was watching the triage nurses approaching the first few groups where hands were still held high. The nurses took their time. Travis was aware that the crowd was yelling at John Hesse on the bar, but he continued watching the nurses. Checking vitals without instruments. Asking the questions. Then the first wave seemed to break across the room, and the nurses moved on and hands held up turned to fingers counting numbers in the air. There was a three.

Travis was familiar with this kind of work. He saw two outstretched hands go down, and Travis knew what that likely meant.

"Does anyone here know about the power systems, or about propulsions? Do we have any of the engineers or anything like that?" John Hesse yelled.

One of the junior officers huddled in front of the bar spoke up, unsure of himself. "I don't think we can get propulsion back. If they damaged the engines, we can't fix them now. I haven't seen any of the engineers. This emergency lighting we have is from a separate generator. I have no idea where it will be working or how much total power it has. But it means something's still working, at least."

"What happened to New York? Does anyone know?" someone shouted.

"We have enough to worry about here," Hesse said. "We have to consider shouting as how we communicate as a group right now, so I guess we all need to be judicious. Don't yell out information or questions unless it directly affects our activities and understanding of our situation… right now."

"I have a dead body," someone called out. "What should I do with it… right now?"

John Hesse looked down at the ship surgeon.

"We've only got two body compartments," the surgeon said, "and they won't be cooled even if there still is emergency power in the clinic. We could be here days, this could be a health hazard. Bodies rot quick. We need bodies off the ship, I'm sorry."

"I'm sorry," John Hesse said back to the crowd. "We have no facilities here for bodies, and they will become a health hazard very quickly. The dead will have to be buried at sea. Please everyone see to your own family members, enlist the help of others in moving them if needed. Everyone is really going to have to get used to helping each other. When we take care of the more urgent matters we'll have some organized body removals around the ship, but... take care of your own."

Hesse took more questions, shouted out more vague ideas about assessing the situation, and then he called off the discussion and came down to talk with his second volunteer group. It was a crowd, but he could see that officers and some civilians had sifted themselves to the front while crew and some other civilians were just behind them.

"Which of you is the highest ranking ship officer?" he said.

"I'm a second officer," a young man said. "I think that's the highest."

"Do we have any senior military officers?" Hesse asked.

"I was a colonel in the Army," an old man said, adding, "I didn't have too much experience at sea."

Hesse looked from one to the other. "You two need

to talk. We need an assessment of our power, our danger from fire and leaks, our food situation, our communications… that'll do. We also need an assessment of the best way to get some food down here this morning, you might want to get a team together for that effort. You," he pointed at the second officer, "you let the Colonel take charge, you tell him anything he needs to know about the ship. Colonel, you can take volunteers from the crowd here if you need to send teams out. I suggest you use the other men here-" indicating the officers and military men, "-as team leaders. But I'm sure you know what you're doing, Colonel."

"Before we do any of that," the Colonel said, "we need toilets. The toilets aren't flushing. Folks need toilets."

"OK," Hesse said. "You should have some crew here who can help."

The Colonel looked behind at the crowd of volunteers.

"That should do. If I need more help, I'll come back. And ask people to piss of the decks until we get the johns going."

Hesse nodded.

"One more thing," Hesse said. "Anyone you send out there, if they find any bodies, they have to be dumped."

Hesse looked at the Colonel, and his eyes wandered across the other men gathered round him. As he looked at the men, there was nothing in his eyes that asked their permission. Like that, he became the general.

18

As supplies came down, the medical team worked in high gear. The crashing of the ships had caused scores of accidents, from flesh torn open to sprained ankles to bodies and bones crushed under falling structures. There were burn victims who had hung on through the night but could never be saved this morning. They mostly spoke of fire in stern areas and someone told of the power room exploding. There were heart attacks and bullet wounds, and one man who had left New York without his insulin in a diabetic coma. Travis, bringing morphine, occasionally heard the shouts of the crowd around him and the responses from John Hesse.

There were missing family members, and Hesse designated a landing on one of the staircases as a meeting place for those split up. The staircases didn't glow green anymore. In the dull daylight, the emergency lighting was drowned out as well. All around, the fantastical lighting of the day before was gone, and now the Romanesque columns and shapes seemed an ancient, abandoned site just found in the fog.

As the morphine went out to the injured, the screaming echoing in the belly of the ship was snuffed one voice at a time.

Colonel Martin Warrant, long retired from active duty, first formed teams to construct and install porta-johns. They considered using water buckets to flush the existing toilets, but there was no way they could keep up with the demand without running water, so a whole lot of porta-johns would be needed. He put an old Air Force officer in charge of the john-crew, mainly Festival crew members, including some tradesmen and others familiar with the materials and tools available.

Only when the john-crew was organized and out did Colonel Warrant turn to his other priorities, assessing the ship and planning food delivery. He spoke to the other ship's crew and military men and women after a brief discussion with the Festival's last Second Officer.

"We will need to break up into teams. Because of the ship's size and decentralization of food and key equipment, we will split by area. We are going to do this fast, but we are going to do this thoroughly and get it right. We'll need information on damage, fires, communications equipment, power, remaining lifeboat capacity, other passengers onboard, and of course, food."

He scanned the quiet group. "First of all, who here has the faintest goddamn idea about ships' engines?"

Nobody answered.

"Alright. Who thinks they can figure it out?"

"We have scuba gear," one of the Festival's officers said. "Maybe someone could check out the propellers and get an idea how bad the hull is."

"The bridge is gone," another man said. "How could we sail even if we had power and propellers?"

"You can control the ship from the power room," the Second Officer said. "You just can't see."

"Alright," Colonel Warrant said to the officer who had mentioned the scuba gear. "Do you dive? Well, find four divers, and if you need men to lower them, take men for that too. Check the propellers, what the hell, take your time and check the whole goddamn ship. For God's sake, make sure you've got a way back onboard. Good luck. Okay, what's next? Right, who thinks they can figure out if the power room is salvageable?"

His assessment teams under way, the Colonel finally turned to food. Fortunately, there were a number of galley crew there: the Executive Chef, the saucier, the roast cook, the assistant butcher, several waiters and busboys, beverage managers, bartenders and stewards.

It wouldn't be easy, the Colonel was told: they had half their staff to prepare food, with no power, for double the crowd. So Hesse recruited more cooks, servers and dishwashers and Colonel Warrant sent another team off to work.

After his morphine round, Travis set up the blood clinic, calling for donors from the O-negatives. Occasionally, as the assessment teams left, the Colonel or some other among them would call for volunteers. One time he asked for helpers to bring food down. A few dozen lined up to give blood. It was then still before 8:30, but Travis was conscious of his own hunger as he heard that complaint repeated around the room. He looked towards his son and Corrina occasionally and was happy to see Claude Bettman had stayed near them.

After this, Travis worked with the doctors. He joined up with the sad man. His face now showed some relief in the distraction of broken bodies, his stock in trade. But he needed help. He had to amputate a foot.

The doctor's name was Joel Conrad. He was also a

New York refugee. A cardiac surgeon from King's County Hospital, he and Travis began their acquaintance by naming mutual friends from New York hospitals. After a few minutes, that talk tailed off as they each realized they might be talking of dead men and women. He was a good doctor, Travis could see that as they worked. Now he could see his face, not hidden in a women's lap, not disfigured with emotion. Conrad was a handsome man, with fine grey hair still somehow holding its part after all they'd been through. His face was tan, like some of the tourists on the Festival, which had initially sailed from Florida.

After the amputation, blood spattered on their shirt sleeves, they treated a burn victim. The patient's husband cleared his throat and kneeled down so that his face was level with Travis and Conrad's.

"Doctor. Do you think we'll survive?"

Travis looked to Conrad as if to offer whatever support he could, but Conrad answered calmly, looking up at the man after his first few words.

"Why shouldn't we?" Dr. Conrad said. "We have everything we need here. Surely we can live with some diminished electricity long enough to be rescued."

The man seemed to be looking for more than an answer to the question he'd asked. He waited a moment after Conrad spoke and then continued.

"What if no one knows about us? What if it takes…"

"Then we'll have to wait. Days or weeks," Conrad said. "Remember that whatever we have suffered here, we are still alive. We still have this freshly stocked luxury ship to support us, and each other to get us through. I can assure you that there are many, perhaps hundreds of thousands, who are worse off than us. We escaped the flood."

Travis saw Conrad grimace as he said those last words, but he let the impression go.

There was an injured girl. She had her family there, and the mother and brother were crying. The injury was less serious than it looked. Her clothes were bloodstained, but the loss of blood was not substantial, and Travis felt pride at seeing her hooked up to one of the newly donated bags of blood. He was distracted, so that only when they finished with the patient did he get a good look at Conrad's face again. The doctor stood looking away, taking a momentary breather. The ugliness contorting his face had returned, and Travis thought: it's guilt.

Sometime after noon, assessment teams began returning, conferring with John Hesse and Colonel Warrant. Then one team came, triumphantly, with food. Seven men and women came in with six-foot carts, carrying stacks of covered trays. Quickly the proud looks of those bringing the food turned. They were swarmed before they could penetrate the room.

Hesse jumped up onto the bar.

"Everybody! Please listen! There is plenty of food for everybody! But not all at once. The team getting the food will return to the galleys and prepare more cartloads, but there is not nearly enough here right at this moment for everyone — so why don't we have the kids eat first, and anyone who absolutely feels sick?"

"Why don't we just go down to the kitchen and get

food ourselves?" someone called.

"The galley can't operate with hundreds of us pouring in there. Please, give these people a chance to bring the food in."

There was a lot of screaming.

"Who are you to tell us we can't go up and get food ourselves?"

Hesse waited for quiet. In standing there above the others, his own patience was so visible it made the crowd quiet because they wanted to hear his response.

"Please!" a new voice screamed, a woman's.

Travis saw. It was the mother of the girl on deck yesterday.

"This man saved my girl," she said. "Please listen to him."

Hesse cut in quickly to the space that followed her words.

"Guys, we are in a tough situation here and we all know it. Until we get all the assessment teams back, we really won't know what kind of shape we're in at all. But I can tell you one thing — if we choose to act now through chaos it will certainly be a lot worse. We have survived two disasters right now, but if we give in to fear and panic we will create a disaster of our own that we may not survive. Please. Back away from the food carts. We'll call for kids first in a moment when they're ready. We'll have more food down here within an hour, and hopefully they'll get power to the stoves. We have right now lots of bread, cold cuts, cheeses and fruits. Our cooks will get more sophisticated as we go. We may not even have enough food here on the next round, but be assured, we will feed you. No one's ever gone hungry on a cruise ship."

One of the men who had led an assessment team came right up to Hesse and tugged at the hem of his jeans. Hesse came down to him. The tension in the crowd dissipated; the food servers were left to set up, though many stood close by watching and watching the others doing the same.

"There are others," the man said to Hesse.

"I know," Hesse said. "Some of the groups have found families hiding out or locked in their rooms. They've been telling them to come down here. If anyone needs medical attention where they are, tell the doctor."

"No, I mean a big group. Hundreds. They're in the Theater. Apparently that's the second location the captain herded the refugees in New York. There's a lot of the tourists wound up with them now as well, the ones that had rooms in the back. It seemed like they'd overwhelm us here so I told them to send some representatives to come down here and coordinate with us and share information. They should be coming any time."

Hesse nodded. As he rejoined Colonel Warrant, the crew member who had led the diving group returned.

Carts of food were continuously brought down; Travis and Conrad did not stop to eat. Bloodied, tired, and hungry, they continued. They set bones and splinted them, they stitched lacerations, they treated burns and intubated one man on a spinal board.

At some point, John Hesse returned to his perch on the bar and yelled for the crowd's attention.

"We've gotten some reports back from most of the

teams. Here's our situation. First the bad news. The generators and engines are out of commission; of course, we'll see if we can change that. We do have emergency power, as you can all see, but nobody in charge of it. That's a problem we can solve. There is a watertight compartment shut off because of the collision, we have a twenty foot vertical gash. The compartments are designed to protect the ship from a leak filling the boat, and it's working. We're not in danger from the collision anymore. There was a ship fire crew already at work battling the fires. They've closed off several corridors, but they have taken more volunteers and have things under control. We have no communications. The communications room was adjacent to the bridge and was destroyed in the attack. Any emergency signal devices would have been in the same location. We can't call for help. But this ship will be missed and will be looked for. We have to assume that authorities on land will eventually be performing sweeps of the ocean. This was done when the tsunami hit Southeast Asia, so we know we'll be found eventually, we just don't know when that will happen. Our best estimate is that there are between three and four thousand of us still on board. By my guess, that means some few hundred left by lifeboat during the night."

Immediately screams came from the crowd. One voice carried over the others.

"Why don't we use the lifeboats now?"

"There aren't enough," Hesse responded. "First of all, the lifeboats are intended for the number of passengers and crew on the ship, not for two thousand plus refugees. Second, the lifeboats are high capacity, but I don't think that those that left during the night were very efficient about it. In fact, I know they weren't because I watched my girlfriend leave in one. And I'll tell you what else. Those lifeboats will never make it back to land. It's just too far. Here, the ship can still support us until we're found. Now the good news. The ship isn't sinking. There are no major breaches of the hull, and any flooding is being contained in the watertight compartments. We also have plenty of food. That's it."

"That's all the good news?" someone shouted. "We aren't sinking and we have food?"

"What the hell do you want?" Hesse snapped. "The entire east coast of the Americas is lost, and for all we know, Europe or anywhere else could be flooded too, but we're alive, sheltered and safe. Count your blessings. All we can do now is pull together, stay organized, and survive. That's… that's our mission. Guys, we can survive here. We have food, and medical professionals, and a safe ship. We'll make it as long as we need to."

Hesse stepped down. More questions were shouted at him, but he ignored them and took Colonel Warrant by the arm. The two of them strode to a shop off the side of the Atrium. Hesse kicked the locked door open and the two went in to set up a command centre.

The first porta-johns came down and were set up along the perimeter of the great room.

The medical staff worked their way through the ones and twos. No one died out of the patients Travis and Conrad had seen to, but now they were dealing with the threes. The first one they came to was already dead. The man next to him, holding up his three fingers, had been unable to look down at his father dying. He had never seen the old man slip away. He'd spent the whole day holding that arm up, supported by his other arm, three fingers held high.

The second number three had been shot in the chest. Travis called for a nurse to bring blood. As they prepared him for IV, Conrad cleaned and studied the hole in his chest. The man convulsed.

"Cardiac arrest," Conrad said.

"Joel," Travis said. He shook his head no.

He was trying to protect the doctor from the anguish, to give him permission to move on.

"No!" Conrad said sharply, then he smiled at Travis. "Are you ready for an adventure?"

Travis smiled in answer. If Conrad was ok to keep fighting, so was he.

"We're going to do an emergency thoracotomy. I'll need a Gigli saw, large clamp or forceps, a large scalpel and scissors, and sutures. We need to intubate, and we'll need suction — the portable pump has a battery pack."

Travis ran off. He retrieved the tools and portable oxygen supply and returned in less than three minutes.

"Here we go," Conrad said. "You intubate, I'll cut."

Travis pressed tubes into the man's nose, connecting them with the portable oxygen supply. Conrad doused the chest with antiseptic, and cut shallow incisions at each side of his chest. He cut deeper, connecting the two incisions in a smile-shape across the bottom of the chest. Travis watched, amazed, as the doctor inserted two fingers into one of the side incisions as he finished his deep cut.

"I'm keeping the lungs out of the way," he said. "Now give me that Gigli saw and the forceps."

The Gigli saw was a flexible wire saw with metal handles at each end. The skin was pulled back, revealing the sternum. Conrad used the forceps to pass the saw under the sternum. With smooth, long strokes, he cut the sternum through from the inside out.

"Now I need your help," Doctor Conrad said. "Pull the skin open and hold it."

Travis did as he was told. Doctor Conrad snapped the sternum open with his hands; the crowd which had begun to gather jumped back at the noise. Blood was spattered across Travis and Conrad's arms and faces. They could see the heart now, clear and open. It was bathed in blood. Conrad used the suction, and they saw a small tear in the heart. The bullet itself had passed through the man's back.

"First thing is to suture the heart," Conrad said. "This is the only thing we've done today that I'm actually qualified to do."

His fingers moved incredibly quickly. The heart though, was not moving at all.

"Now we need to massage the heart. Very gentle, this might work quickly."

The doctor simply flicked the heart with his finger. After the briefest of pauses, it swelled and pulsed once.

"It's not going," Conrad said.

He began massaging the heart with both hands. One flat hand was applied to the front, one underneath. He milked the heart, moving his hands at a beat faster than once a second, yet so gently.

"Can you give me a free hand? Compress the aorta against the spine, this will maximize coronary perfusion."

For almost a minute the two handled the heart in silence. Sweat was pouring off Conrad's face. Then Conrad pulled away.

The heart kept beating.

"We've got it!"

Two women above them burst into tears, others cheered loudly.

Travis and Conrad leaned back for a moment.

"We just might save this man," Conrad said. "Let's close him up. We'd better anaesthetize him before he comes to."

Thirty minutes later, the two men looked around and saw no hands in the air. They stumbled over to the food carts, throwing their gloves in a trash bin, then finding cold sandwiches.

"Doctors, come here."

It was Hesse calling him from his new office. It was an art gallery, in the line of shops behind the wood columns. There was a desk near the front, where Hesse sat, calling through the open door. The door frame had been cracked around the bolt where Hesse had kicked it open. On the window, the name of the shop read, "Inspiration".

They walked towards him, filling their mouths with the sandwiches.

"Look to the left," Hesse said as they entered the room. "They brought down a few cases."

On the floor was a tub of ice and beer bottles, below two modernist, jazz-inspired beach scene paintings. Conrad reached down and took two, passing one to

Travis.

"I remember you," Hesse said to Travis. "Your boy's ok?"

"Yes," Travis said.

"When you guys get cleaned up and rested come back and we'll catch up," Hesse said.

Travis was not ready to return to his family yet. He felt, as he walked along the wall of the Atrium with Conrad, like the two of them were separated somehow from the crowd that still filled the room, just as he'd always felt separated from the refugees he worked with in Sudan. They were the desperate, he was there to help. They found a quiet sitting area under a staircase and sat down on the couch.

"Good work," Travis said.

"I can't believe we saved that man," Conrad said. "I've read about that technique, but I've never done it. I just... with all the death today, I wanted one man to live that fate wanted to take away."

"You did it," Travis said. "You saved him."

"At least for now. If he can escape infection, or internal hemorrhaging or anything else that could go wrong with a cracked sternum."

It was so sudden, the return of Conrad's face to that horrible exhibition of pain.

"Are you alright?" Travis asked. "Are you... did you leave family behind in New York?"

Conrad couldn't reply. He nodded his head and made a noise through his closed lips.

Travis waited.

"I left them all behind," Conrad said. "I couldn't find

them. I… yesterday morning, when it all happened, I called and couldn't find them. I called home and there was no answer. I called my wife's cell and there was no answer. I have two kids and I don't know what happened to them. I left them. I left them to die."

"Joel, it's not your fault. It's not your fault. Look at me, Joel. It's not your fault."

Joel Conrad looked at him as he tried to hold back sobs. "I was with another woman."

Travis could not hide his reaction. His eyes opened wide and his head jerked back under Conrad's stare.

"I was with… I was with a woman. I'd worked until three a.m. and went to her apartment and we were together when we heard the noise all around us, and we looked out the windows. The sun was just coming up and people were pouring through the streets. That's when we turned the news on. It was already too late to find my family. That's how I left my family, Travis."

"Jesus, Joel. I'm sorry. But you'll find them again, Joel. You have to believe that."

Conrad breathed deeply, and he allowed a softness to return to his face.

"Do you have a family?" he asked.

"Yes," Travis said. "They're here with me. My son and… my ex-wife and her husband."

"Why were you and your wife divorced?" Conrad asked.

"I had an affair. She found out."

They stopped looking at each other.

"I was in Africa," Travis began. "I was volunteering with the Red Cross in Sudan. I was there for two months that time, but it felt like years. She was a doctor from Italy. We worked closely together and my wife was back in New York, and her husband was in Florence. We fell in love, we were… in another world there, surrounded by death, fighting against it. There was a childish feeling of adventure. It wasn't real love, that was what I had with my wife. It was the idea of falling in love there, in a faraway land, with a faraway woman who had come there for the same reasons as me. I don't even know exactly how my wife found out. The woman had gone back to Italy before me, and when I came home my wife was gone, my son was gone. I realized the gap then between what I felt for that woman and how much I love my wife. I've been living in a kind of prison since then. Separated by just a few miles from the two people I love."

"So now you're here with her husband."

"Yes."

Conrad wiped a tear from his eye. He held up his bottle and the two men clinked them together.

"Life is horrible," Conrad said.

"It's what we made," Travis replied.

19

"First things first," Colonel Warrant said to his Chief Engineer. "Power the freezers. Next, we need some light in the galley and Atrium. Next, stoves and ovens. Then running water. I'll come for an update tonight. I'll bring sushi."

The engineer, Brenda White, stood next to him in the main engine room. The room was cavernous, three decks high. There were banks of machinery, metals of silver, brass and gold curved into pipes, cabinets, and coils. There were glass gauges, and red control dials on wall-length desks. It was all in disarray. Equipment and electronics shelving were knocked over. Bullet holes riddled the huge metal cylinders. Somewhere, something was running. Most of the equipment here was dead.

Brenda White had spent hours already looking things over here and in the emergency power room, talking with crew and refugees she'd enlisted who knew one thing or another. The bodies had been cleared before Brenda got there, but there was a lot of blood, everywhere she looked. Which explained why there were so few remaining of the engineering staff.

The Colonel left and she looked at the twenty entirely male ship's crew and volunteers waiting for her plan.

She wasn't Chief Engineer at the start of the cruise. She was a passenger. But the Chief Engineer who started the trip was dead or gone overboard, and Brenda White was an elite electrical and mechanical engineer, used to designing systems for some of the biggest factories in the Americas. But she was more used to boardrooms than factories for some years now. Now Brenda White was Chief Engineer of the Festival.

It would have taken weeks of study for Brenda to understand the Festival, but they were fortunate that a few of the specialists were still alive and on board. Most importantly, the Chief Electrician.

There were also refugees on the ship who were good at fixing things: electricians, mechanics, engineers, technology technicians of all type, plumbers, welders and general repairmen. There was no one resource that could really help Brenda unravel the ship's mysteries, but together they were able to do great things.

The biggest problem took little time to understand. The main generator room, which supplied power to the ship, was closed off in a flooded compartment. Without the generators to transfer power from the engines to the propellers, the boat would not move. The generator room lay forward of the engines and desalination area, in the section of the ship breached by the collision. The watertight doors had been sealed; there was no going in or out, not just the generator room, but all the cabins and halls directly above the generator room. The exterior walking deck at the Atrium level did not extend back past that closed section, so passing from the bow of the ship to stern required climbing to one of the top two enclosed levels, the Penthouse and Resort decks, or the open Sky Deck above that.

Below the waterline, even the areas they had access to,

the engines, desalination plant and control room, were in disastrous condition from the collision and being shot up by the pirates. Most of the systems required the generators in any case.

But the pirates evidently had not gone to the emergency generators above.

The emergency generators were running. They powered the emergency lighting on some decks, where other damage had not knocked the systems out. Ventilation and other key systems should have been running off the emergency generators as well, but there seemed to be other breakdowns somewhere.

What member of the engineering department had switched the system to emergency power, or shut the watertight doors from the control room, no one ever knew. They were dead or gone. But the ship floated still, and the generators ran because someone had done what they were supposed to.

The emergency generators put out 1,200 kW. Enough for 20,000 light bulbs, Brenda imagined, but not enough to do much interesting on a ship this size. Certainly it wouldn't move it. Still, it would last. Without the propulsion systems to power, there was an almost unlimited supply of fuel to power that generator.

There were these things to start with: power to the freezers and other galley circuits, power for some Atrium lighting, and running water to the main galley. The galley for the main restaurant was next to the ship's main food storage area, which simplified things. Brenda was certain she could get the existing emergency power to the freezers with manpower and time.

In her mind, other than the water stuff, this was a straightforward, brute force effort. They were starting almost from scratch. The existing wiring for the ship was far too complex to rebuild, given the damage from the collision, gunfire, fires and the closed-off section. Brenda gave up on the original grid quickly. The Festival's Chief Electrician was a good partner for her: smart and open-minded, he knew every inch of wiring on the ship, but was unafraid to re-imagine and re-purpose each piece for Brenda's creative ideas. He also knew the skills of the other surviving crew.

The electricians under their direction wired directly, hundreds of yards of new wire spooled out, fished between floors through existing junction boxes and transformers until finally, well after dark, the freezers jumped back to life to a great cheer among the galley crew.

Brenda White waited anxiously for word after turning the switch, and when it came back with a runner, she gave someone a high-five and went to work on the Atrium lights.

20

There was no running water because of the loss of power, but jugs were left on the tables by the galley crew. After the beer, Travis and Conrad splashed the water on their faces and arms, wiping away some of the blood.

They saw Hesse through the gallery window as they passed. Hesse leaned on the counter next to the cash register and talked with the Colonel in the small shop.

There was an explosive sound of glass smashing.

"Candy! Chocolates! Assorted Bon-Bons!" came a booming voice.

With that scream, the crowd located the source of the explosion. There stood two bearded giants. One held a rifle over his head, and gestured to an open shop door, its glass smashed out.

"Parents, cheer up your kids!" the voice cheerfully filled the hall. "Let's have some smiles back! Mind the glass there!"

Travis knew that voice. Most of the crowd knew that voice.

There was one of pro wrestling's biggest stars, holding an assault rifle, inviting the terrorized crowd for candy. And that enormous man stood in the shadow of his shaggy haired companion.

There was a fog of unreality in the ship, and this appearance of a man from TV as part of their story thickened that fog. The strands connecting life as it had been known to life on this ship were further concealed.

Passing Travis and Conrad, the Mighty Lee Golding and his companion parted the crowd.

"Hey, how ya doing?" Lee nodded as he passed through. "Who's in charge here?"

Hesse and Colonel Warrant met the two in the middle. They shook hands and made introductions. Hesse pulled them along into his office.

"I can't believe you didn't open the candy store," the wrestler said loudly, "with all our troubles!"

Travis walked on to his family. At some point, Conrad was no longer next to him.

When Hesse's office door shut behind them, the Colonel spoke first.

"How did you get the gun?" he asked Lee.

"I took it," Lee said. "From the bad guys."

"What happened to the bad guys?" the Colonel asked.

"We killed them," he looked at the gun playfully. "I guess I'm just like any tourist collecting souvenirs. But I'm happy to be the one with the gun."

They discussed numbers and logistics. Adam Melville told Hesse and Colonel Warrant that there were a few hundred in the Theater, far fewer than in the Atrium. They had far fewer injuries as well. Hesse had already sent a doctor over, which had led to Lee Golding and Adam Melville coming down here to see who this was taking charge.

"Have your people had any food?" Hesse asked.

"Yeah. There's a restaurant in the stern, just a flight up from the Theater. Italian. But there's no power for the stoves."

"There's a main galley down below the big restaurant," Hesse said, pointing to the Atrium, forward and up. "We've arranged a team to do meals until we get picked up. Right now, cold, but soon we hope to have power."

"And if we're not picked up?" Adam Melville said.

"Haven't thought about it," Hesse answered. "Not yet."

The grey-haired giant had a look of good humor on his face. It bothered Hesse.

"We're having the food from the other restaurants brought to the main galley, where we've almost got power restored to one of the freezers," Colonel Warrant said. "We'd better have your food brought over too so we can keep it from spoiling."

"Why don't you get us power instead?" Lee asked. "We don't have as much natural light. It's not a pleasant place, but if we had some light we could stay there. I like Italian."

Colonel Warrant and Hesse considered their position, in respect to their own authority to challenge Lee Golding and Adam Melville, and in respect to the gun.

"Yeah," Hesse said. "With the section closed between us, it's not easy to get stuff back to you. We'd have to carry the food up the stairs to get over the sealed sections. That's a lot of flights of stairs. We'll try and get you power right away. We'll ask our guys what they can do. We have an electrical engineer. She's a bigwig with General Electric. I think she's going to get a handle on this. But it might take time."

"How much food do you have?" Lee asked.

"A lot," Hesse said, then turning to Adam Mellville: "As long as we get picked up. I'll have them bring some tables down to the Theater."

"How much water do you have?"

"Quite a bit," Hesse said. "We have probably over a hundred thousand bottles. There's also a full 300,000 liter tank. We're trying to restore running water."

The two big men exchanged looks.

"Our engineer thinks she can do it," Hesse said.

"I hope we ain't gonna be here that long," Lee said.

Hesse shrugged. "It seemed wise to look into it."

"We've got a problem with the doors," Lee said. "We had to barricade them during the attack. We need some kind of power hacksaw to get them open."

"Well, how did you get out?" Colonel Warrant asked.

"Obviously there are some open doors. But we would prefer more open doors. So, if you please, send a saw."

The representatives from the Theater returned to their refugee center with smiles. Adam enjoyed his time with Lee Golding. He liked being surprised, and Lee Golding was always surprising. Adam was rarely with someone who drew attention away from himself.

Travis quickened his pace in the Atrium crowd, and his son burst forward and jumped into his arms. Travis needed the boy; he hugged him for a long time before he spoke.

"Hey, champ. Long day, huh?"

"Yeah."

"How'd it go?" Corrina asked.

"Exhausting. We won some, we lost some. That guy running the show… I hope he knows what he's doing."

Gerry stood a few paces off with Claude Bettman. Vera stood by herself, and Travis imagined that the old lady had been standing all day.

Soon Hesse called for attention, standing on the bar-top. Travis saw that the two big men had stopped on their way to the staircase to watch.

"I know a lot of you are wondering about the lifeboats right now," Hesse said. "Here's what I think, after talking with some of the ship staff. There are not nearly enough lifeboats for everyone. The lifeboats have bare food provisions and their range is small. We don't even know how far land is or what the conditions are. We believe we're over 200 miles from shore. From the old shore, that is. No lifeboat will make it. The ship has a lot of food, it's a luxury cruise line. It's equipped with over three weeks of food. I think we're a lot more likely to be found in this ship, than any lifeboat would be. So. I don't see any percentage in taking a lifeboat."

Hesse went on, about water, powering the freezers and lights, and volunteer rotations.

"He's got it all figured out," Claude said to Travis. "But see, he's counting on the idea that no one will steal food from the kitchens to bring a little something extra on the lifeboat. Look around. People are thinking, he doesn't think the lifeboats are a bad idea for the ones who take them — but that they'll screw everyone left behind. These folks are thinking, what does that have to do with me?"

Travis said nothing. He had a flash recollection of a refugee camp in Sudan, and the sea of anguished black faces. Emaciated bodies wearing rags. Red Cross workers carrying on, keeping their concentration on tasks, as if on a raft in that sea. He felt again that complete vulnerability, his tiny island of white safety amid that sea of black desperation.

John Hesse finished talking, and Travis watched the two big men walk away to the staircase out.

A boy ran up to Mighty Lee Golding, and the star wrestler signed something for him.

"I need a walk," Travis said. "Why don't we go get some fresh air on deck?"

Corrina agreed, and they offered to walk Vera back to her room. Gerry and Claude stayed in the Atrium.

"Pavel, you look tired," Vera said to Darren. "Beautiful boy."

Darren looked up at his mother but kept silent. The foursome walked up four flights of stairs and along the hallway to Vera's cabin. Travis carried Darren after the first flight. Vera's room was at the far end of the hall, among the penthouses.

At the end of the hallway in the dim light something caught all their eyes at once. Legs protruded from a corner. With one step further they saw the whole body. It was the gunman from Vera's room.

He had a knife in his back, and dark staining spread across the orange.

Some history from the prison perhaps had followed him, or some disagreement in conducting the raping and pillaging.

Vera was on him at once, screaming, without enough breath for it. She landed on the corpse and pulled the knife from his back, plunging it into him again and again, trying to scream. She stabbed twice more before Travis grabbed her arm as she drew it back. He held it gently until she dropped the knife.

She pulled her arm from Travis and stood up, an old lady, wild and blood-spattered. Corrina held Darren to her waist. Vera looked in all their faces.

"What happened?" she said. "What happened?"

Travis held her as she went limp. He walked her to her bedroom where she lay down.

Vera regained her composure and looked up at Travis.

"You can stay here tonight," Vera said. "You will be more comfortable here than downstairs with the mob."

Travis left Corrina and Darren in the living room, and went back to the dead pirate. He turned the body. There was the gun, in a pocket. Travis took it. He hadn't fired a gun in years; he'd never fired a pistol. But he wanted that gun now, and at the same time, didn't want anyone else to have it. Didn't want anyone to know about it.

Travis walked the gun to Vera's galley, under his shirt past Corrina and Darren, looking for a place to hide it, thinking through what was likely in each drawer or closet: food, cutlery, towels, pots, baking dishes.

Finally he went into the bedroom. Vera was already asleep. He opened a closet, stood on his tiptoes and pushed it to the back of the top, empty shelf, out of sight.

They left Vera to sleep and found their way, away from the gunman's body, to the small walking deck, shaded by the deck above. Chairs and tables were overturned and left on their sides, helter skelter. The sea was calm, and there was something fearful in its unbroken spread as far as they could see. The ship made no wake now, it sat as solid as an island, the small waves breaking against her hull. The oil spill had spread and now encircled the ship. The black curtain delineated their drama. Beyond that frame, within that frame.

They stood at the railing.

"I love you," Travis said quietly. He knew he shouldn't be saying this. He felt ashamed for himself saying it but he couldn't stop. "Corrina, I love you and Darren. That's all I could think about when I ran from my place, and in the crowd at the dock, and when I thought we were going to get shot. Maybe when we get off the ship-"

"Oh Travis," Corrina said, shaking her head. "Please don't"

Darren looked up at the two of them, mindless of their words, and smiled.

Hesse and Colonel Warrant were in different places for much of the day, but before the dinner crowd arrived, they caught up in the office.

"We need to do some serious risk analysis," the Colonel said.

"The guy with the gun is a risk," Hesse said.

"Yes, he is," the Colonel said.

"But what can we do?"

"Don't give away too much, the less he knows about Brenda and the power and everything, the better. And the less he's around the better. That's not a guy who gets told what to do. The more he's around, the more he's gonna argue with you, and sooner or later the guy with the gun wins the argument."

"Let's just keep him happy and fed and far from us," Hesse said.

"That's all we can do. Maybe the Mighty Lee Golding's a sweetheart. I heard Killer Kowalski was a vegetarian."

In the Theater, Lee sat in a front row seat with his wife and Rick's wife while Rick sat facing them on the edge of the stage.

"I wish I would have been there," Rick said, "Man, I wish I could have seen their faces."

"I bring joy," Lee said. "It's what I do."

"They must have pissed themselves when they saw two giants and a machine gun."

"Well," Lee said. "I wasn't there to frighten them. Just to make sure we're planned for, whatever they're doing."

"They seem like they know what they're doing," Rick said. "They got a freezer going there, I'm sure they'll get ours hooked up. I mean, I trust them and all but I'm glad they saw you and Adam and the gun."

"Why do you trust them?" Jessica said. "Are you that good a judge of character? You can judge a guy on the other side of the ship that you haven't even seen?"

"Well," Rick said, "they sent the doctor."

Back home, Jessica's mother lived in the mansion with her and Lee.

Jessica had been a shy child, afraid of the world, but in her mother's poor house she had been a princess. She dated and married famous Lee Golding, and her character had grown louder and more confident. With Lee's support, she'd gone back to school, and then quickly ascended the corporate ladder, becoming with each step more extroverted and sure. She worked at a major insurance company as a vice president. In The Mighty Lee Golding's palace in suburban Atlanta, her mother still called her Princess.

"God," Jessica said. "If we don't get off this ship soon I'll use that gun to shoot myself."

21

They walked forward along the dark-stained wood planking around the bow end of the Penthouse Deck. The sun was descending so that it caught them straight on from the side. Corrina and Darren were holding hands. They saw others on the deck, some at the brass railing alone, some in canvas deck chairs with spouses or children. No one said hello, no one nodded as they passed. They were all together, but each group was alone on the deck.

"I don't see anybody out there," Darren said.

There was nothing but the green and lace waves stretching out into the haze.

They continued onto the larger foredeck. Rows of deckchairs were tumbled over each other. No one seemed to care to clean any of the mess now. Two small semicircular bars rung around a large hot tub, sitting half empty and dead. They walked to the railing and looked out.

The ship was moving, Travis thought. The sun was at a different angle tonight.

I hope this sunset doesn't bring more surprises, he thought.

"There's a lounge there," Corrina said. "Let's check it out."

They walked through the glass doors into a gleaming white piano bar. The room seemed more orderly than the exterior deck. The heavy furniture had been less upset. The salon had most of its ceiling as glass, open to the sky. The blue of the bar and tables, the black of the grand piano, gleamed immaculately in the light filling the room through the glass ceiling and walls.

"Play something," Darren said.

Travis sat at the piano. He knew only how to play rockabilly style, simplified Jerry Lee Lewis. He couldn't play something so happy, so his fingers just sat on the keys for a moment.

"I don't feel like playing, Darren," he said. "I'm too tired."

He saw the disappointment further sap the energy and hope from the boy.

"Travis!" the father barked in a mock rendition of Corrina's rough voice, "Don't bang the piano! Take a lesson before you play that thing!"

Darren brightened. Travis's impersonation was unmistakable; the voice, accent and cadence sounding just like his ex-wife's, but more so.

"Travis! Why do you hate my ears? Stop that banging!" Travis said, leaning his forehead in to Darren's. "That's what Mommy said."

Long, long ago, he'd used jokes and impersonations to make friends, to make people laugh. To make his father laugh. It got him through high school and college. He'd become so serious at some point in his adult life, and so sad when his marriage had ended, but he always kept that part of himself for Darren. He shared laughs with his boy, almost as a secret, like his father, a living room clown, had shared with him.

"Maybe we should stay here tonight," Corrina said, "The seats are like couches."

"We could look at the stars," Darren said.

Gerry and Claude sat on the wall of an indoor garden in the Atrium.

"Do you wonder what kind of world we'll be going back to?" Gerry asked Claude.

"I try not to," Claude said in his smooth growl. "I'd like to delay returning as much as possible, myself. Until I get to thinking what a real delay would start to look like on the Festival. I do believe we may be nostalgic for this quiet moment soon. I do believe all our possible futures will be… unpleasant."

"I think I'll take my unpleasantness on dry land, if I have the choice," Gerry said.

"Dry land is a lot further away than it used to be," Claude said, looking out at the darkened mass of refugees in the Atrium.

22

Brenda and her team worked through the night. Once the freezers had been powered, wiring other circuits in the galley was more straightforward, so she'd turned her attention to the Atrium. Then, the Chief Electrician had seemed better equipped with his knowledge of the ship to lead that effort, so she'd turned to running water.

She thought of the thousands above dependent on this water, and how, out of those thousands, there would not have been more than a handful like herself who could, from scratch, deduce the principles and working of this complex and badly damaged system and bring it back to life.

She worked solidly for close to twenty hours, along with a core crew. Colonel Warrant proved to be as helpful as he was demanding, sending good food regularly and, when they finally took break from what they considered a very successful first shift, they finished with fine cigars and Scotch.

Brenda went back to her family and slept in the loud Atrium for ten hours before returning, getting caught up by Colonel Warrant, and getting back to work, still trying to repair the water system, still trying to expand the reach of their emergency power.

As each day went by without rescue, the work took on the feel of a full-time job. The longer they were on the ship, the more they had to think ahead. As it became a full-time job, the cigars and Scotch became an end of shift ritual. The supply on board was immense, and Colonel Warrant had commandeered it, treating his invaluable engineering team to the best of the best.

While Hesse and Warrant daily added to the list of necessities for the ship, Brenda began a side project, her own idea of redundancy. There was a full tank of fresh water still to be tapped, and a seemingly endless supply of bottles packed for the three-week cruise. Still. There was a double-load of humanity aboard, and no end-date on their occupancy. She never communicated her idea to John Hesse or Colonel Warrant. It had been threatening rain all day. Brenda remembered the weather report calling for heavy storms along the coast. So she set a crew up on a water collection project. They built dozens of large catch basins topside, and used a series of hoses to collect the water in a giant reservoir down near the desalination room.

Within three days of her starting work, Hesse asked her about the vast tubs of metal, plastic and nylon scattered on the top deck.

He didn't give his blessing to the work. But Hesse didn't want to push his ownership of Brenda's efforts too far. He was sensitive to the idea that the only basis for his leadership was the goodwill of everyone involved.

Then she began to tinker with the communications system. Here, the Chief Electrician aboard had little help to offer. He'd never himself worked in the radio room. The Chief Radio Officer and his staff were missing. Brenda began surveying the equipment. Doodling diagrams. Thinking about it, while working on her 'proper' tasks.

Brenda freelanced like this because, as they finished those first urgent tasks, and she talked with Hesse and Colonel Warrant of what work to continue with next, she was never completely in agreement with the game plan.

The ship would never move under its own power. So the only way out was through outside help. To her, it was straightforward.

"Who cares about light? What have you all got to see?" Brenda White said on the third day.

"We have thousands of people scared to death on this ship, and we don't know how long we're going to be stuck here. If we want to avoid panic, we need light," Colonel Warrant said.

"Well, I'll need access to the Theater to find the main line in."

"Look," Colonel Warrant said, "they've got that guy with the gun. If he knows about your work, who knows what he's going to want to do. We need to keep him in the dark."

"Except you want me to turn on his lights," Brenda said.

"We have to take care of everybody," Hesse spoke up. "Just find a way to get power to the Theater, and the Italian galley, and try to avoid the guy with the gun."

"Sure, standard work," Brenda said. "Look. Let's think about this. This amount of wiring is days of work. Maybe weeks. If we want to get the communications going, that's a huge project too. We need to devote time to it."

"We need to take care of the people on this ship," Colonel Warrant said.

"But what we could find out with radio contact could change everything."

"How?" Warrant said. "Whether a rescue is coming today or next week, we should be preparing for the worst, and that means making this ship habitable. I've seen that satellite equipment, it is broken beyond repair and we'll be wasting time trying. You told me yourself you know next to nothing about satellite receivers and we have no crew left with experience."

"I can figure it out," Brenda White said, frustrated. "I need time to do it."

"When we have stable water. Stable power to the galleys. Emergency lighting to get safely around this damn ship. Ventilation and toilets so we don't all get sick. Then communications," the Colonel said.

It was a massive ship, and there was not enough spare wire to simply rig new lines as they had with the first freezers. They had to find the breakdowns, or scavenge and join together unneeded wiring systems.

She wondered if the communication gear would do any good anyway. If there were anyone there to listen, anyone there to help, wouldn't they have as likely been found by now by search efforts? This was a big ship, you could see it a mile off. If they'd done air sweeps, like after the tsunami, the ship would have been spotted by now. It was a day and a half later. What was taking so long? Just how bad were things back home?

So she plodded along with her work, and the systems kept breaking down or overloading.

Everything Hesse and Colonel Warrant needed was always urgent. She did as she was told. She was happy to be occupied, though it was hard on the family, her being away this much with the work. They just sat around in the Atrium.

The girls were going a bit crazy, Brenda thought, and her husband as well, but she had to do this work. Somebody had to. She worked on the communications stuff every chance she got, but it was far beyond her experience and there was a lot of damage to overcome. Brenda had had no experience with this kind of equipment since college, and what training she had was far out of date.

She rigged a powerful spotlight to the deck, pointing up at the clouds.

That Colonel Warrant, he was micromanaging the amperes. With such limited and inconsistent power, Warrant wanted to know how every bit of that resource was used.

Brenda knew it would be a long time before the satellite communications would work, and she also knew they weren't getting off this thing without help, so the spotlight was her other secret, after the water basins.

The spotlight, and its 10 kW and 45 amps, was a secret in plain sight.

The spotlight was obvious at night, beautiful in fact from the deck. But no one ever asked her about it.

23

In the next days, Travis, Gerry, Corrina, and Darren had less contact with the crowd of refugees who stayed mostly in the Atrium. To the refugees in the Atrium, their little spots on the floor, on the couches, or on spread-out blankets, were their homes. Travis and the group, including Claude Bettman, stayed in the piano lounge. Vera had invited them to stay in her room; Corrina had answered that they would stay in the lounge but come to visit her. Gerry and Travis disposed of the bodies of her husband and the gunman.

They were not alone. The tourists that knew of the lounge, who had been using it before the flood, would stop in in small numbers simply seeking a comfortable place away from their rooms, especially when it was cold on deck. Then a few other refugees discovered the room and moved in. Each individual or group kept to their own section. Some of them became acquainted with their new neighbors. Most of the forty strong population kept to themselves, and at night it was whispers in the dark.

The second night in the lounge was especially clear-skied, and Darren stared up at the great spill of stars above him, his father nestled behind him, pointing up, drawing silly made-up constellations in Darren's imagination, telling silly stories about the characters in the stars. Darren trying not to laugh out loud, burying his face in his father's shoulder and chest.

Darren took a liking to Claude Bettman. Claude could see that the kid was withdrawn; maybe that was the way he always was, maybe it was this situation. Claude was a widower. His daughter and grandkids were in Indianapolis, so he had only to worry for himself living to see them again. He was a professor of ancient history at New York University. He kept Darren entertained with his tales of ancient cultures and legends.

Darren listened, and Professor Claude drew him out, testing him with questions on the meaning of the stories he told. Somehow, in the midst of this Great Flood swallowing up the Earth, the kid still found magic in tales of dragons. It seemed to Travis, listening, as though the ship itself were slipping through the mists out of the everyday world and into myth and magic, of No Time and No Place.

Travis went every day to John Hesse's shop; nothing was changing, except that people were getting anxious each day that nothing changed. Out of the several thousand gathered in the Atrium, there were always a few crying at any given time. Travis picked a Crier of the Day. The competition was tight; crying alone wasn't usually enough. Anyone could cry, release a bit of the stress. To win Crier of the Day usually required out-loud sobbing of one's thoughts, a public display that one had lost control.

Hesse had located the keys to most of the shops; those with any food had been raided, their shelves empty like the stores Travis had run past just a few days prior in Brooklyn. A few, like the jewelry, wine and cigar stores, had been smashed and raided by the pirates while others, like the fashion boutiques and gift shops, had their security and integrity respected still.

The officers and crew that remained had not quite lost their identity as a group. Some slipped off their uniforms and joined the waiting lives of the refugees, but most enlisted in Hesse's efforts, and were put to useful service by Hesse, or Colonel Warrant or Brenda White, each of whom oversaw specific projects. There were musicians aboard, and some gave impromptu concerts. One magician dressed up twice for kids shows, in a corner of the Atrium.

Brenda's team had yet to succeed in bringing power to the Atrium other than the original emergency lighting system. The skylights helped, bringing triangles and rectangles of light to most of the public parts of the ship, but in the evenings it was very dark, with just those emergency lighting tracks along the walls near floor level.

The wounded were brought down to the medical clinic. Travis and the medical squad tended the bedridden and changed dressings. The ship's surgeon came by each day to check on the in-patients, and he kept office hours for any others to come see him with new problems.

Perhaps the most valuable were the chefs, many of whom remained from the original crew and were reunited, efficiently running a galley with no power and no running water initially. Everyone on board was well fed. Power availability increased, and portion sizes were shrunk compared to cruise norms, but the meal quality made everyone feel a little less besieged and desperate. They had lobster and prime rib with a garlic crust that was the talk of the ship.

Food service was an enormous effort. There were two

shifts of galley workers, including the chefs, servers, dishwashers and others, and they rotated each of the three meals, with two buffet servings per meal.

They had, over days, accumulated the food stocks from the French bistro, the American burger joint, the Mexican taqueria, the Thai-Fusion dining room, and every other food shop on board — save the Italian restaurant. At last, running water reached the galley, which made cleaning much easier.

They kept the same servers at the buffet table for each of the two meal servings, to help discourage repeat customers. Still, they let clients take away multiple servings for their families or friends in other parts of the ship. Hesse had reasoned it best to encourage satellite groups, to keep things more efficient in the food service. He also, as time went by, followed up on the supposed groups that consistently came for extra meals to take away. They told where they were staying, and here and there, Hesse went to check them out or sent others to.

Some were hoarding. Two of the culprits were a young couple, tourists staying in their own cabin. John Hesse walked right in on them. He found a fresh garbage bag and loaded the food into it while they watched.

"Half of this would be rotted in a day, you idiots," Hesse said.

The young man shoved him. Hesse swatted his arms away and grabbed the hoarder by the throat. His face became bloated and purple.

"If you mess with me, I'll drag you in front of that crowd and we'll see what they think. Don't get out of line again."

Hesse still held the garbage bag with one hand, but he easily slammed the other man into the wall before dropping him to the floor. He stepped in front of the woman, shoved his face at her and growled, then left. The food could be repurposed in the galley.

John Hesse had always been the leader. It was never something he questioned, it was all he knew. His friends thought he lived a charmed life. He was always on top. That kind of proof in his instincts made him easy to trust, easy to follow. But Hesse knew better, he knew the difference between himself and others and why they thought that of him. He never complained.

He saw the world as people who complained and people who would rise to the challenge. When he'd once seen how complaining made him look weak, he'd given it up altogether. Hesse was a bit of a solipsist. His strength of character, indeed his ethics, came from the thought of what kind of person he'd want to be if this were all a game he were playing.

Much of the ship had taken on a putrid smell. In the first day of the power outage, nearly every toilet on board had overflown due to their electrical mechanisms. Human waste had soaked through floors and into carpets all over the ship, and Hesse had organized the excruciating task of cleaning and bleaching the affected areas, with no steam cleaners and before the running water was restored.

Travis took to walking on his own. There were enough hours in the day for it. On the fifth morning on the Festival, Travis made a discovery. The spa. It had its own complex on the Resort Deck, the first mostly enclosed deck, below the open Sky Deck.

In the spa were fitness rooms supplied with stations of various apparatus and machines, and racks of free weights and dumbbells. There were aerobic rooms of stationary bikes, treadmills, stairmasters and rowing machines. There was a hair salon, an acupuncture clinic, a honeycomb of massage rooms. There were men's and women's lockers.

At the centre was a beautiful, long indoor swimming pool in a modernized Roman style. It was orbited by four smaller hot tubs. The tubs, and to a lesser extent the pool, had just begun to show signs of algae growing, from lack of cleaning and circulation. At the head of the pool was a large white marble Poseidon, trident raised, looking more majestic than threatening.

Under the statue, a plaque:

I begin to sing about Poseidon, the great God, mover of the earth and fruitless sea, God of the deep who is also lord of Helicon and wide Aegae. A two-fold office the Gods allotted you, O Shaker of the Earth, to be a tamer of horses and a savior of ships!

Hail, Poseidon, Holder of the Earth, dark-haired lord! O blessed one, be kindly in heart and help those who voyage in ships!

"So you're the old earth shaker what did all this," Travis said to the God.

Travis stripped naked and dropped his clothes over Poseidon's arm.

"Well, keep an eye out."

He plunged into the deep end. It was a shallow deep end — a pictogram specifically banned diving on the side of the pool — so he dove shallow and long. No rules, he thought. The water was cool and beautiful. Afterwards, he found a towel in a closet he tore open. He wrapped it around his waist and lay down in a tan and red-trimmed linen lounge chair looking out long windows at the sea. Travis had a stocky frame, big arms, big chest. His belly too was big, a little bigger each year. He was losing weight now, he considered. On a cruise ship.

24

Travis was beginning to recognize many of the faces. Some days, he noticed a few missing, and sure enough, a corresponding lifeboat gone. He knew that meant fewer crew left on the Festival, as the lifeboats were difficult to deploy without familiarity. It also meant that someone who wasn't going with them was helping them, because someone had to be left behind working the davits to lower the boats.

He wondered why anyone would do that. Were they 'sacrificing' themselves by staying behind? Or did they just think it was safer on the Festival but were happy to help? What was the context, or relationship there?

Travis saw the great grey-haired man a few times on the deck, always alone, watching the sea.

He tried to keep Darren away from the crowd, but couldn't entirely. They'd go down for meals. The whole ship came together then, and they could see just how many they were sharing the ship with. Then many would disappear back to their cabins or whatever corner of the ship they had made their own.

Vera didn't like to leave her room; they would bring her meals to her, generally. Once in a while, she'd forget things, usually her medication which Travis supervised. She never forgot that Norman was gone, though she several times mentioned Pavel.

Near the end of the first week, Travis sat with Darren

on the Sky Deck. They listened to a man playing banjo on a chair nearby.

"Do you think he was a musician for the ship, or do you think he was rescued like us, and brought his banjo instead of a suitcase?" Travis said.

"Ummm, I think he's like us," Darren said. "He brought his banjo because he's all alone and he wanted to play music if he got lonely."

A basketball shoot-around started at the court in front of them. Travis watched them pass the ball around, shoot and put in lay-ups.

The Mighty Lee Golding was one of the players. He didn't have the gun. He had the ball.

"Can you take one more?" Travis asked.

"Sure," the big man said. "I'm Lee Golding."

Travis introduced himself.

"I recognized you. I saw you at Madison Square Garden against the Samoans, maybe twenty years ago. It was great. You tossed Trog through the announcers table."

"You're with us," the Mighty Lee Golding said, and they began a game of three-on-three.

The third man on their side was a pylon, but Travis and Lee could play. Lee mixed fearsome intensity with a suddenly relaxed, amiable laughing humor. He could not be stopped inside. He couldn't dunk, but he could almost drop the ball in off the backboard. Travis was shorter than all three of their opponents, but he had a fadeaway jumper that was hot, and he milked it. He used the pylon on their side for pick and rolls, and almost laughed at his teammate each time he was knocked to the deck.

Travis was happy. All the bad went away for a moment, and his only connection outside the game was awareness of his son watching him, and looking pleased.

"Go, Daddy, go!" Darren yelled.

Afterwards, he high-fived Lee, and the big man grabbed his hand, and pulled him into his sweaty bulk. Travis was helpless in Lee's arms as he shook him. The bigger man laughed and with a butt-slap sent Travis to high-five the pylon and their opponents. His son had the biggest high-fives for him.

"Yay Daddy!"

Travis had deferred thought on the sweat problem while he played, but afterwards he could not ignore it. Nor was there anything he could do. He'd have to let the sweat dry and keep on wearing the stinking clothes. And he'd probably keep doing it as long as there was a game on.

The day after the basketball game made it a week on board. Sunday to Sunday. No one had come. There was an awful presence in the Atrium. No one on board had expected to be here more than a few days, even after the attack. For them to still be uncontacted after a week was inexplicable. It brought a very real change to the psyches of all: there was no longer the expectation to be saved soon. They had to live on this ship indefinitely. It was felt acutely as a third disaster. Flood, Attack, and Abandondment. Each of the three a different flavor, they came so fast on each other that it seemed the laws of nature had turned upside down.

Hesse had felt that, and suddenly the vast stores of food on the ship seemed clearly limited. Fishing was organized. Hesse and Warrant decided not to use the lifeboats with their very limited fuel and the chance for more desertions. They fished from the lowest decks above the Festival's waterline. Nets were sunk down below the oil slick, and dozens of weighted, hooked lines lowered.

Brenda White felt the weight of a week's work, heavy thinking, heated arguments, full-body pain from the physicality of wiring. The ship was running. It was time for a break. This time she shared a quick beer with some of her co-workers, and returned to her family. Her husband was exhausted, having stayed up to care for their five-year-old through a short-lived stomach bug, so she let him rest while she took the kids off to the playroom.

Brenda had checked out the playroom when the family had first come aboard for the cruise in Florida. The kids had pleaded to stay and play, but she wanted to relax by the pool, so she'd promised they'd come back. Now they had their chance.

The room was lit only from the grey light through the windows. None of the video games worked, nor did the various electronic gimmicks around the room, but the kids didn't notice. They ran from Brenda at the sight of the room, 1,500 square feet of colorful oversize toys, slides, and ball pits, all theirs. In the center was a kid-sized cruise ship, orbited by different international scenes: an ice island with fake ice blocks to play with, and huge seal and penguin stuffed toys. There was a strangely isolated Paris, with an Eiffel tower and play bakery, and an ancient Egypt with 8-foot pyramids, containing rising tunnels exiting by a slide.

The old noise of her kids being kids came to her, and she relaxed into a beanbag chair and smiled.

When Brenda thought it might be time to wrap it up, another kid arrived.

Corrina Adamson introduced herself and her little boy, Darren. It was their first visit to the playroom. Brenda introduced her kids to Darren, and they were off into a tunnel.

Corrina heard Darren's laughter coming from the tunnel, and she laughed, but her eyes teared up.

"I know," Brenda said. "I know, darling."

Corrina sat in the beanbag chair next to Brenda.

"I can't believe we never came here before," Corrina said.

The kids came flying out of a tube, down a slide, running over to the next play structure.

"We could get rescued right now and the kids would cry for more time," Brenda said.

They both laughed, and the kids' laughter came from the play ship.

Brenda stayed another hour, and Corrina and Darren played themselves for another hour, until they rolled together, red-faced laughing on the polar ice floe.

That night in Vera's room, they ate small deli sandwiches. Corrina and Claude played chess on his travel board in the zip-up leather pouch.

"Can you tell me an African story?" Darren asked.

Professor Claude gave Darren a quick look and a smile.

"There is a story the Ashante peoples told, of two princes and two magic spiders."

His attention was back on the chess game, the story seeming to flow from him without his influence on it.

"The father of the princes was a wise king, much loved by the gods. When it was shown to him by the sky god that his time was coming to an end, he decided to share his kingdom between his two sons. And so he granted each prince a tribe over which to be chief. But the King was worried that his sons might grow jealous and slay each other. And so, on his death, the king gave up his place with his ancestors for a wish. His wish was for Nyame, the sky god, to come to each of his sons and promise them a paradise in the afterworld, should they remain each at peace with his brother, and his brother's tribe. But Nyame was wise and knew that men live for today and forget what is to come. So the god came to the princes while they slept, and gave to each a magic spider, which could find its way to, and kill the other of the princes. So that each prince knew, if he were to overreach, and take that which belonged to his brother, that his brother had the spider with which to destroy him. The tribes were happy and prospered under their princes, but the princes were afraid. Each prince knew that his brother could release his spider to kill him at any time. The fear grew and grew in them, until the night of the feast of the ancestors. With ghosts in the air and the veil between life and death so thin, each prince sent their spider, and each was in turn killed."

They all waited for the next words. Corrina looked up from the game. The Professor didn't notice. He moved his castle, taking Corrina's queen bishop. The story was done.

"For God's sake, Claude," Gerry said. "Darren has enough death already."

"Oh," Claude said, looking up from his meditation on the chessboard. "I'm sorry. I am so used to these stories I suppose I don't think of them as happy or sad or scary."

Claude returned his attention to the game. Corrina had his queen.

"Sorry, Claude," she said. "You were distracted."

"Don't be sorry," he said with a smile.

Travis was trapped in Claude's story about the princes and the magic spiders.

"What will happen?" Darren said. "I mean, if no one finds us."

"Someone will find us," Gerry said. "Remember, Darren, if things get really bad, there's always the lifeboats. Just remember that, if you ever really, really hate it here, we can always leave."

They were quiet. When Darren went to pee off the balcony, Claude said to Gerry: "The lifeboats are suicide. But you're right, it's the only way off."

25

With the coming of that second Sunday on the ship, nothing felt the same. A comet had fallen from the sky once. Then, comets had rained from the sky, and now each looked up for falling comets.

Lee had taken a backstage dressing room behind the Theater, where they slept with Jessica on the couch and Lee on the floor. They had a flashlight, but slept in total darkness.

"The whole Theater is rattled," Jessica Golding's voice came in the black space. "You're the only rock for everyone. But you're nervous because the Atrium controls the power and you can't see what they're doing. Imagine how they feel knowing you have the gun and they don't know what you're doing."

"They got us the power," Lee said. "They got the message I'm watching."

"Do you think they did that out of pure kindness?" Jessica said. "Or does it suit them to keep us separate? They gave us light so they could keep us in the dark, Lee."

He rolled onto his side and looked up at the space where she was.

Twelve years old, Lee Golding was in jail in Mobile, Alabama. He was a freakishly big kid, but only had a kid's strength. The police treated him roughly. His cellmates treated him roughly. He'd only stolen a Coke, and only because Therese Blackburn had asked for it.

The police knew his father, and that was no help to him. He didn't get scared overnight in jail. He got angry. He imagined someday he'd be in control, and they'd be scared of him. They could do their worst to him; he could take it. But he was just a kid. It wasn't right to push around a kid. He wished they'd held him and charged him, so a judge would see, but they were scared, he knew that was why they'd let him go after two days. They shouldn't have done that to a kid.

He got bigger and soon had a man's strength, even at 14, starring in basketball and football as a freshman. He loved playing. He was in control. He imagined crowds that weren't there, announcers beside themselves at this most poised and powerful force in sports. He won basketball championships and Super Bowls with his sisters and friends in his front yard.

He believed in his fantasies, and they soon came true. Still the kid, excited, unafraid, he bound down the alleys of countless stadiums and arenas. His theme song blaring; his gown trailing him. He reveled in the glorious physicality of wrestling. His body, his skills, his persona, at the heart of the game. Then there were the movies, three years in Hollywood, two hits, and best of all, the sensation of watching himself, thirty feet high on a screen. It was never strange to him to become a star. He'd imagined himself one for so long.

Being on the floor in the dark dressing room didn't bother him. Comfort and ease had never been part of the dream.

On Tuesday, he played three-on-three basketball again

and ran again into little Travis Cooke. This time they were on opposing teams. Again, Travis's fadeaway was on. Even with Lee leaping at him, stretching his incredible arms, Travis could fall backwards and float the ball above his hands.

Twice Travis pulled that move on Lee. Lee could always get his baskets backing his way to the net and reaching up for the pass. But Travis kept coming back and evening the score. He was tiring Lee out.

A third time, Travis took Lee one-on-one, slashed at him, then stopped on a dime, pushed off his front foot and drifted backwards, the ball coming up to shoot as Lee leapt forward after him. Lee's hands came down through the air on each side of Travis's arms. The big hands pummeled Travis's face, the ball flew far off target and bounced away against the fence. Travis fell down on his back, his head slamming the court.

"Sorry. Let me get you up," Lee said.

On one of the counters in the galley of the Italian restaurant was a line-up of cell phones. Built into the stovetop was one of the few outlets on the ship to carry power. Without Colonel Warrant there to ration their amperes, Rick and Jessica and a few others had been keeping their cell phones charged. They were useless for communicating, but a few of them still found comfort in keeping their phones charged. Just in case.

On Wednesday of the second week, the Italian restaurant ran low on supplies: the endless bounty of gourmet food had been reduced to a final array of unmatchable products. The Theater, or the Italian restaurant, were feeding not just those refugees who had originally been sent to the Theater, but those whose suites had been destroyed, like Lee, Rick and Adam, or whose suites were aft of the closed compartment, which made travel between fore and aft so difficult.

At first, more of them slept outside the Royal Theater, but as days went on many returned, preferring the emergency lights of the Theater to the absolute darkness of the suites and so much of the ship.

"I've been in the main kitchen. It's huge," Rick said to Lee and Adam. "But you think our food is going fast? Man, they're feeding five times as many as we are."

"They were," Lee said. "There's a lot less of them now than there used to be. Hesse over there hasn't been so convincing in keeping people from the lifeboats. A third of that group has jumped ship."

"Why do you suppose our group has stuck together more?" Adam asked.

"The gun," Lee chuckled. "It has a certain charisma of its own."

"My wife thinks so," Rick said. "She keeps telling me how much better she feels that it's our guy who has a gun. You know, who knows what people would do if there wasn't a gun to answer to."

"Just watch the Atrium and find out," Lee said.

Rick and Lee went to see Hesse about new food arrangements to include the Theater group.

Adam Melville stayed behind. A chill had grown in his relationship with Lee Golding. From the beginning, when Lee had asserted his leadership in the Theater, he had gravitated to Adam as a partner. Adam had a certain aura about him. His eyes glowed.

He had worked with Lee on the logistics of their group, they had spent hours in discussion on the best courses of action to maintain the longest survival on the ship, and the two had acted together as ambassadors to Hesse and the bigger group. Then, Rick Dumas had somehow made them a triad. Adam disliked Rick. He didn't trust him, and he could see in the Mighty Lee Golding certain character traits that Rick Dumas helped to bring out- it wasn't something he could quite put his finger on.

Adam was not a religious man anymore. As a child he had grown up with Sunday school and Christian camps. He had won Bible contests; his mind retained incredible amounts of information and he had spent hours learning whole chapters by heart. In the early Seventies he had become a Christian hippie. He gave his mental efforts to his own interpretation of the text, and soon became disillusioned with the everyday flatness of organized religion. He became just a hippie, and said he was spiritual, not religious, but he always read the Gospels, even while searching for answers in the Upanishads of Hindu and Buddhist Mahayana Sutras.

He trained himself in electronics, and in the nascent field of computer science. Without formal education, he became a tinkerer and soon one of the earliest tech entrepreneurs, a living symbol in certain communities, of the link between hippie and silicon San Francisco.

He'd done well, and had started and sold off several companies during the booming Nineties. He was a groundbreaker, and he had inspired a mystical loyalty in the staff of each company he began. With his unique appearance he'd become a Silicon Valley legend. Now sixty-five, Adam had lost none of the energy and strength of youth. His great arms were still as powerful as they appeared, and the mind worked as intensely as the eyes showed.

Adam had divorced and sold off his latest company in the last six months. He'd booked this cruise to imagine what was next, and it struck him how those converging turning points in his life had freed him up for this trip to witness this turning point for the world. He was obsessed with information and digital technology and often saw things in terms of information manipulation, computer programs and logic flows. He imagined Lee and Rick going to the Atrium as an arrow in a logic diagram, and he wondered what would be in the next box.

26

Rick enjoyed the looks he always got walking into the Atrium with Lee, like a celebrity. It was a place of sadness and Rick liked smiling in the middle of it, knowing eyes were on him and his friend. This time, there was a different atmosphere. There was fear. At first Rick thought the refugees were scared of him and Lee. He was excited by it. Then he understood that it was not directed at them in particular. It was just everywhere. There was fear in the Atrium, and by the time they got to Hesse's office, Rick had it himself.

Hesse was with the Colonel; Rick could not remember his name.

Lee shook the Colonel and Hesse's hands as they entered the art shop.

"How are you for food?" Lee said, while Hesse's hand was still hidden in Lee's own paw.

"We're managing," Hesse said. "Are you ready to join our food plan?"

"I don't know," Lee said. "Maybe we should think about joining you guys down there. The Theater's nice, it's a comfy space, but the dining area's getting pretty messy."

"We can't handle you here," Colonel Warrant said. "It's just too difficult to handle these crowds for food alone, let alone the sanitation and sleeping space. Do you have any idea how much work it took to wire the

Theater? We'll bring the food to you. You guys keep taking care of everything else yourself. It's working."

"What do you have left in Little Italy?" Hesse asked.

"Meats gone," Lee said. "Veggies gone, eggs gone. Have a bit of cheese and pasta still. There's crackers and nuts and lots of cooking oil. What have you got? How long can we last all on your kitchen?"

"We'll have to lower the rations," Hesse said. "Not by much. We have enough to last a couple more weeks, but we can lower it again in a week, and again the week after that, well… we can last over a month if we have to. That's including the Theater, of course."

"Food will last longer if your people keep deserting," Rick said.

"Yeah," Hesse said. "I've done what I can. I don't really have any right to stop anyone from taking the lifeboats. That's what they're for, right? It doesn't hurt us and I can't stop it anyway, so frankly, I have more important things to worry about. I'm staying on the ship, and my concern is everyone else who stays on. Anyone who wants to leave takes their own chances."

Lee pulled the gun off his shoulder with one hand and slapped it down in his other palm.

"We could stop them," he said, smiling. "You just have to ask."

"We're not asking," the Colonel said. "You'll hurt yourself with that thing."

"Or somebody," Hesse said.

"Yeah," Lee agreed. "Or somebody. What about the fishing? I seen you got lines set up all along the starboard."

"The fish are coming up covered in oil. We can't eat from this ocean, at least until this oil spill breaks up and we drift on. Maybe this storm will help."

"Or we get hungry enough," Lee laughed.

"We still need our doors opened," Rick said. "You were supposed to send up a power saw."

"It's in a flooded compartment," Colonel Warrant said. "We can't get it. You'll have to keep using the doors you've got."

Their first meal from Hesse's crew was arranged for that evening. It would be a long trip for the carts.

"We have a group working on the service elevators," Hesse said.

Rick and Lee Golding left. Colonel Warrant and Hesse watched them through the glass storefront.

"Is the power saw in a flooded compartment?" Hesse asked.

"No," Colonel Warrant said. "That boy's a risk. I take risk management seriously."

"Maybe we should have had Brenda work on the satellite gear," Hesse said.

"John, that's a smart girl, but sometimes you have to reckon for yourself what someone is capable of. That gear is broke. And Brenda White told me herself she knows next to nothing about satellite receivers. We did the right thing. She'll be working on it soon, if we're still here, and if she can get it going, well, that'll be when we need it. For now, we've got things running here and we can take care of ourselves. We did right."

They drifted off into their own thoughts, looking out the storefront at the mob.

"You have any family?" Hesse said.

"Not really. Wife left me a long time ago. My son was killed in Afghanistan. You reminded me of him the first time I saw you up on that bar, you know that?"

He paused, almost happy imagining his son, getting a feeling of connection with him through Hesse.

"How bout you?" he added.

"My family's from Chicago, they'll all be fine. My girlfriend left in a lifeboat the first night."

When the food came at last to the Theater, the rain had picked up and it could be heard on the thick glass of the skylight stories above. The food came, trolley after trolley. The food was in bulk and uncooked, meant to give the Italian galley three meals to work with, so that only one cross-ship delivery was needed each day.

It took more than an hour to feed everyone. Then, the rain came so heavy that it became the evening's distraction. Four hundred or more leaned back and stared at the darkness above them from whence the noise came, never stopping, never letting up.

Rick was restless. He took his wife for a walk.

At forty-seven, Rick Dumas' life had been successful and satisfying. He was a top seller for his company in the Dallas-Fort Worth region. He had lots of friends, and a beautiful wife. He'd always had lots of friends, and always had beautiful girlfriends. He was friendly, a good listener, but he had a secret to successfully navigating social situations, and all situations were social to him. He found the most powerful person in the context and he made them like him.

Rick and his wife made the long trip to the Atrium; he

couldn't think of anywhere else to go. He wanted his wife to see him talking with John Hesse. Families and small groups squeezed past him in the hallways. There was an open door out to the lower level promenade, the wind keeping the door open despite its return spring. Rick and his wife were deafened by the sounds of the storm in the moment they passed it by.

The Atrium felt different again. There were loud voices and much movement in the dark. Rick could hear agitated families and groups passing information: the lowered rations; the Theater was out of food.

It was not like his previous visits, a crowd muted by fear and tragedy. It was a powder keg.

The power went out and it became very dark. Around the room came children bawling and men and women screaming in frustration and fear. Lightning illuminated the room in diffracted rays of crisscrossing light.

The thunder clapped and the glass pyramid above shook.

27

Travis was in the galley with Hesse, cleaning in the dim light granted by Brenda White and Colonel Warrant in their amperage rationing. There were thousands on board, but Hesse was somehow always at work. He usually took the worst jobs. Travis, like Gerry, Claude and Corrina, took shifts occasionally. They spoke little as Travis scrubbed the food prep surfaces and Hesse studied the supplies. Travis watched him.

"You're from New York, right?" Travis asked finally.

"Yes," Hesse said.

"Did you ever play rugby?" Travis asked.

"Yes," Hesse said.

Travis nodded. "I thought so."

"Yeah," Hesse said. "I was with the Village Scottish. My God, I thought you looked familiar, all this time I thought I knew you from somewhere. Where'd you play?"

"Brooklyn, the Rebels, back, oh, ten years."

"Oh!" Hesse smiled, slipping back to happy times. "I've been retired for a while, but we used to play you guys a lot. We always won."

"Yes you did," Travis admitted. "You had an amazing scrumhalf. Guy was near pro level."

"Not quite, but thanks. It was me."

"Yeah," Travis said. "I know."

"The Rebels," Hesse said. "We used to beat you boys

pretty good, but you had this flanker who nailed me one time, broke my arm."

"That was me," Travis said.

"Oh my God," Hesse laughed. "You were dirty, man!"

"You were killing us! I had to stop you. I took you out, man. I put you down good."

They laughed.

There was a sound of thunder, and the power went out.

Travis and Hesse said nothing. The sounds of their breathing showed that each was all right in the dark as Hesse looked around for his flashlight. When he had it turned on he spoke.

"No sense stopping," Hesse said. "We'll be getting food ready in the morning with or without power."

He hung his flashlight from a rack above the counters and joined Travis in cleaning.

Their hands worked in the light as their heads were in the dark.

"On my first Red Cross mission, we were in Haiti," Travis said. "And we had this power outage. I was in my tent, just a battery lamp on the table, and I was reading. And drinking. Drinking and reading. In comes this monkey."

"Is this a joke?" Hesse asked.

"No, no," Travis said. "This is true. The monkey comes in, and he's staggering. I point my flashlight, and I notice three things. He's got a liquor bottle in one hand, he's dead drunk, and he's bleeding profusely. So he's drunk, and I'm drunk, and I stumble over and pick him up. He's all playful. He's so drunk he doesn't even feel anything. But he's been shot."

"You're picking up a bloody monkey in Haiti?" Hesse said. "You're not worried about AIDS?"

"Myth. Haitian monkeys never had AIDS. Anyway. I'd been in Haiti a few weeks. And it was bad. And this poor drunk little monkey, he's all limp in my hands, and making faces at me. I decided I had to save him.

"I got a friend, a nurse, and we turned on the lights in the operating theater, they were on the back-up generator. And of course, I'm a paramedic. I've never done surgery. But you know, I'd seen it all. And I'd taken courses. How hard could it be? We figured he was drunk, so we wouldn't need to anaesthetize him. Actually, the bullet had passed right through him, didn't hit anything. All we had to do was sew him up. And I'm wondering, how did this monkey get the booze? And is that why he was shot? Did he steal it and get caught? Or did someone just shoot a drunk monkey for fun?

"The monkey slept it off in my tent. Next thing you know, he's my buddy. He hung around all the time. We quit drinking together, actually. We used to do tricks, for the kids. Stupid drunk monkey. I wonder whatever happened to old Lord Disco."

Hesse laughed.

"Yeah, he was a good dancer," Travis continued. "So that's what I think of when the power goes out. Haiti and Lord Disco and my first experience as a surgeon."

Hesse slapped Travis's back.

"I like that," he said.

"I have a ghost story too, if you like ghost stories," Travis continued.

"Of course."

Travis waited, letting Hesse's laughter and smile dissipate, letting the silence back in. Then, in a quite different, darker voice he began.

"It was on a night just like this. Dark and stormy. The wind was fierce and the rain lashed the house."

Their heads perked up as they heard the noise, a percussive sound. Like jungle drums, getting louder. Just as Travis realized what the noise was, the galley doors were flung open and a stampede of humans rushed in. They had flashlights, and lifejackets with blinking lights, and cameras flashing. Travis and Hesse were blinded by the lights in their faces and then swarmed. Travis was punched from the blackness around him, then again. Arms grasped around him and he was pulled down.

He heard a struggle around Hesse, and Hesse's voice and others blowing out in exertion. He stopped struggling, hoping they would leave him, then he was punched again in the face and he fell to the ground and couldn't move. They were taking the food. There were dozens of them. The feet pounded by him unendingly until his eyes shut and he went to sleep.

When he opened his eyes, they were all gone. Hesse was gone too. He got up in the dark and made for the door, feeling along the countertop, around the pantry, along the wall of cupboards. In his desperate hurry to get to his family, he fell several times in the dark, as the longest hallway returning to the piano lounge had no windows and no light at all. Once, he hit his head on a cracked open door and bled from the cut.

The rumors of a run on the lifeboats reached the

piano bar just as Travis did. Groups were already huddling in conversation or hurrying towards the exits. The rain was hitting the glass walls so violently it felt like the room was shaking, like a stadium of fans thundering.

"What happened?" Darren said.

Travis was wet and disheveled. He had a bloody split lip from the brawl as well as the cut on his head. He looked exhausted. His chest heaved with his breath.

"I was with Hesse in the galley," Travis began, speaking to Corrina, and to Claude who came upright in the lounge chair. "Some group rushed us and took food, now everyone's rushing on the lifeboats."

"What do we do?" Gerry said. "Do we go to the lifeboats?"

"Look at that storm," Travis said.

They turned to the open glass walls. In the moonlight they saw shimmering sheets of rain, exploding in tiny millisecond white flashes on the windows. There was a decision to be made that their lives depended on, and the immediacy of it increased with each other group that ran out from the lounge into the hall towards the lower deck. The more that panicked, the more need to panic.

"You want to be in a lifeboat in that?" Corrina said.

"These are big boats," Gerry said. "They're meant for emergencies."

"We could be hundreds of miles from shore," Corrina said, "Do they have food?"

"They have everything," Gerry said quickly. "Food, water, they've got an engine, we could get somewhere."

"Which way would we even go?" Corrina said. "We've been drifting for weeks. What's the range of those lifeboats? Have they got enough food and fuel to get us in?"

"They've got no range," Travis said.

"How much longer will our food last on the ship?" Claude asked.

"We don't know," Travis said.

"How can you not know?" Gerry asked. "I thought Hesse had this down to a science."

"I don't know because people are stealing the damn food!" he said.

"God," Corrina said. "Travis, we have to do it. Let's go."

Travis looked back out at the storm.

"You have a child here," Corrina said. "Damn it Travis, we listened to you to get on this boat, but now it's time to get off it."

"Claude, what are you doing?" Gerry asked.

"Staying."

"You think the food'll last longer?" Gerry said.

"No," he said. "But there's more places here to hide."

They were aware again of the action around them, some groups leaving, others huddling together, just watching. The groups made their decisions nakedly in front of each other.

Travis insisted on getting Vera. He sprinted to her stateroom, down the hall of the same deck. Within minutes he came back alone.

"She won't go," Travis said. "She just wants her comfort."

"Amen," Claude said, stretching out on the couch.

"Okay," Travis said. "Goodbye."

Professor Claude stood and gave them each a hug. There was a stiffness, they each thought the other was making a suicidal choice.

"Try not to catch a cold," Claude said, smiling at Darren.

Down four interior flights of stairs to the lifeboat level, they rushed out into the rain, Travis carrying his boy.

It was difficult to see in the dark as the rain and wind stung their eyes. They stayed in a pack as they moved along the slippery deck to the nearest set of boats. Corrina fell and Gerry grabbed her and pulled her back to her feet before she hit ground. They soon saw the mad press of people trying to get into the lifeboats. The lifeboats were kept at deck level, so only the gates and doors had to be opened, still someone needed to lower the boats and Travis again wondered who were those people.

Travis had seen the posted pictograms for lowering the lifeboat and they were complicated. He hoped there would be a crewmember in his group.

The boats had capacity for 150, but there were hundreds at the doors of the first one, and who knew how many already inside. It was the pier all over again, but this time no police, no crowd control. Just the animal crowd. In the dark, in the rain, individuality was lost. All that could be seen was a live mass, a giant organism struggling for its survival. Gerry led them around the back of the crowd, past one, two, three lifeboats.

Then there was a scene. Neither the tourists nor the refugees had had any chance for an evacuation drill, but there were still enough crew on board to lead the proceedings. As Travis and his group came around the back of the third lifeboat mob, towards the railing where there was a gap in the crowd, they could see well over the side of the ship. Some kind of soft chute led from the deck down several flights to four inflated rafts below.

The chutes were spinning and swaying with activity, and they could hear screams from the rafts as evacuees landed on each other, or missed the rafts entirely.

They couldn't hear the splashes over the wind and rain, but they saw the men and women waving up out of the water, swimming out in the dark at the life rafts, or waving back up at the ship for help.

Again, they avoided the mob at the raft-chutes. By the fourth of the huge lifeboats the crowds seemed smaller, by the fifth they thought they had a chance to get in.

You were all in, or you were out. Travis held Darren tight to his chest, Corrina and Gerry pressed their bodies against his back, and they became a part of the living mass. Pushing, and soon being pushed from behind. There was no movement it seemed at first; Travis could just make out the door through the rain, above the heads. Not the door, but the part of the living mass where it met and flowed into the fiberglass walls of the covered lifeboat.

Travis's throat began to tighten, he felt a sudden swelling feeling, and then his chest tightened and tightened. It was an asthma attack; his breath came short and sharp.

There was a familiar surge. Travis thought he could see the mass pushing a little bit more of itself into the vessel, just as he was able to move forward about three feet. He willed himself to keep watching and moving as he struggled to breathe. There was little choice, there was no room to bend or spread his arms in the crowd.

He turned his head, and saw the next set of davits letting out cable and the boat dropping, one side swinging low then the other violently dropping, past the hundreds who still pounded with their fists on the closed shell. Then Travis saw the davit operator jump the three flights down. So that's how they got on the lifeboats, he thought.

Another surge, Travis moved one step closer. The ship was rocking now with the waves and the crowd was so tight that they held each other up as they slid across the deck. Travis was dizzy now, and his vision seemed strange. He looked up and saw the spotlight, solid and blurry at the same time in its passage through a million moving drops of rain.

28

The power went out in the Theater. Lee sent a few of his men to check the ship, to find out if there was power elsewhere, but Rick returned before they did.

"They're going for the lifeboats," Rick said. "I could hear them all in the Atrium. They were raiding food and everyone's panicking and trying to follow them before it's too late. It's chaos, and it's black everywhere."

Lee ran out of the Royal Theater with the rifle and a flashlight.

They couldn't do this, he thought, bounding up the stairs. But there was no law to stop them. Hesse had said as much. Hesse and the Colonel's control was a joke, but he had the gun. So he'd be the enforcer. Golding's Law.

The lifeboats and life rafts were at the Atrium level. From the Italian restaurant, Lee had to climb four flights of stairs, run down the dark Penthouse Deck corridor, and down four more flights. The adrenaline surge was in him, and he hardly slowed. At the Atrium level, he forced open a door and went into the rain, walking solidly in the wind. He was familiar with weapons, and he worried that the gun would jam in the rain. This had automatic and semi-automatic options, which was good. He didn't quite know what he'd do. If they were leaving, they damn sure couldn't have the food. On the other hand, the more that left without extra food, the more food would be left for those remaining. How could that work?

Still, he had the gun, which was good. There were so many of them, and it was so hard to see in the dark, through the rain. He'd have to make liberal use of bullets to frighten them away from the boats, but how would he get the food? Their screaming came to him over the echoing rain from down the walkway.

He reached the first lifeboat with his heart beating in his throat. His only animal thought was that they were taking his food. He began firing above their heads in single shots, trying to get their attention. The crowd around the first boat turned.

"Give me the food!" the Mighty Lee Golding shouted holding his gun above his head so they could all see.

Only the first few at the edge of the crowd could hear him, the rest just stared, waiting.

This was the mob. The same that screamed and lost themselves in their screams at the arena. They were one monster with a thousand heads. He fired above their heads again and waded into the crowd, as some fought to get away and others fought to get into the boat. The sea of bodies parted around as he marched quickly towards the boat, firing a few more shots in the air. He got to the door, throwing a smaller man off the steps. The lifeboat was already beyond capacity.

"Give me all the food," he screamed in the closed hull. He fired through the roof.

Nobody moved. Something made the lifeboat buck, and Lee fell hard against the wall. A man jumped at him. Lee caught his jaw with his big elbow, then smashed the stunned man's face with the butt of the rifle. Screw it, he thought. There was a console- he shot it. He stepped back out of the lifeboat and shot up the davit control boxes and soft spots. There were the loud pings of ricochets, and Lee knew he couldn't let fear of that stop him.

When he got to the next boat, more of them just scattered, which made it easier. But he couldn't see any other way — he couldn't stop them from taking the food unless he stopped them from going. He should have organized first, he shouldn't have gone alone. He shot out mechanisms and controls for the next boat, and repeated that, so that hundreds had scattered before him. There were too many boats. Some of them had to be in the water by now. He switched the rifle to fully automatic. It made everything faster. The sounds of the ricochets came over the gunfire, but Lee didn't see anyone get hit. The rain picked up suddenly and he was drenched as if in a waterfall. He looked up at the heavens and saw the spotlight, the only light on the ship. He felt a kind of ascendance, as if he were rising above this crowd he fought.

The living mass around Travis's group propelled them in jerks. The sound of gunfire pierced the storm, and the living mass held its breath and stopped convulsing. The sound was unmistakable, through the rain and wind. It came again, single shots. Then a burst, coming closer, and they heard screams, and reverberations of the fire against the ship.

"Daddy?" Darren said. "Are they back?"

Lee Golding, Travis thought.

"No," he said.

Was he trying to get on a lifeboat? Or was he trying to

stop them, as he and Hesse had tried to stop them in the galley? With that he realized he was now with the same group he had been fighting less than half an hour earlier; he recognized several faces that had appeared in the flashing of lights around the galley. The madness of it. He was struggling, competing and cooperating with the ones he'd thought monsters minutes ago, while another man with a gun threatened them all.

There was a loud sound like a machine breaking down as the mass again surged forward, and they all waited for the next sign of the gun. Why hadn't he brought his gun? Travis thought. He'd been to Vera's room and never thought of it. He would kill Lee Golding if he came near his family. But he had no gun. There was thunder that blocked everything out, and then the noises of gunfire and metal percussions were all around them, like the gunfire was part of the swirling tempest itself.

The gunfire was not heard in the piano lounge far above. The lounge had returned to its calm equilibrium. Those who were staying were staying. Only the sounds of the storm now.

Professor Claude Bettman stood and walked to the piano. It was dark, no one noticed. He began to play a nocturne of Chopin. It was not loud; the rattling of the glass all around them was loud. Only those in a few of the spots closest to the piano could hear.

A woman yelled for Claude to be quiet. A man, holding a child, shouted back to play.

It was not a technically difficult piece, but one that, with the right touch, rang out with subtle flavors. Professor Claude played fluidly, just louder, just softer. It was a sad piece, but, here and there, hope, in bright chords. Then gone, as if it had not been there at all.

It was a good piano, a Bosendorfer concert grand. He'd wanted to play it for days. Why not? He lost himself then in the music. It seemed to him the most beautifully he'd played in his life. God, he'd always wanted to play a Bosendorfer, why had he let this one sit here untouched?

Chopin on a Bosendorfer in the storm, as though each note were itself a drop of liquid gold.

When he finished, he could hear the applause from all the spots that could hear. He had a wet hand on his back and turned to see Travis, and just about in the darkness, Gerry, Corrina, and the child. Travis was breathing loud and slow.

29

He couldn't keep this up, Lee thought. He'd have no bullets left. He'd be left behind on this ship, and he'd have no bullets. He shot out another boat's engine and davit mechanisms and moved on.

He fired again, single shots here and there, at the boats or davit mechanisms. Up the deck he walked, past each lifeboat, scattering the mobs but not waiting for them, trying to disable the boats as quickly as possible, hitting the engines, the hulls, the davit mechanisms, but bodies tumbled from the shots. There was the other side still. They'd still be evacuating. There were so many more boats, running off with the food. But he was too worried for bullets to keep trying to stop them. He'd stopped many but he couldn't stop them all. He had to get out.

He knew he could never blend in with the crowd. He was too big, even in the dark, to mistake. He stormed through a gangway into an inner hall, his gun ready. He knew that just a short side hall separated him from the Grand Atrium and a whole bunch of people who would now want him dead more than each other.

He found a stairway and hurried towards the Theater. Up four levels, across the dark Penthouse Deck, and then back down a stairway astern of the closed compartment. He felt safe, insulated from the madness and violence left behind. His legs finally began to twist under him. He rested against the wall and caught his breath. Now the gun had been used, and violence was in play. He had only stopped a fraction of the lifeboats, a fraction of the stolen food. He thanked God he had the only gun.

The Theater was still dark when he arrived. He wondered how many here had left. He'd have to wait till morning to find out.

He broke the taboo against speaking in the overnights and shouted out.

"It's over. Every lifeboat that didn't get away already has been shot up. And so have a lot of them that tried to take food. Get some sleep, we don't know what we'll be facing tomorrow, but there's going to be some angry, bleeding thieves out there."

There was noise in the dark in reaction, quickly ebbing.

He found Jessica. They often slept in the dressing room, but they also had a place by the stage they'd made relatively private, and they stayed there sometimes when they were nervous of being cut off from anything. He lay down with her, and as the Theater returned to sleep, he couldn't. He peered into the darkness, imagining shapes, black against black, and the only sound was the rain. The spectral shapes moved and he replayed the vision of thieves filling the lifeboats and saw himself shooting at them. He saw a woman hit by a bullet, falling in to one of the boats. Had he seen that? Or had he just imagined it?

When sleep finally came, its arrival seemed to slide right into its departure. He opened his eyes, and light was in the room through the small skylight, not a real sunlight, but a grey light, a shadow light, through the cloud and lighter rain.

It seemed most of his Theater group was still here; Jessica had disappeared.

He found his wife backstage in the dressing room.

"I shot them," he said. "I don't know how many."

She was muted by the event. In the dark she stood and grabbed Lee and kissed him.

"Calm down," she said. "Calm down. Lee, they asked for it."

"I know," he said. "I know. I might have saved all of us, who knows how many could have gotten away. But all them I stopped, how will we find their food? How will we ever get it back?"

"That's not your problem," Jessica said. "You stopped them. Get Hesse to clean up the mess."

"How many of ours went?" Lee asked.

"I don't know," Jessica said, "not many."

"There were hundreds of them out there, maybe thousands," Lee said.

"All from the Atrium," Jessica said.

"Maybe it's not too late for us," Lee said. "I shot up the boats, but maybe we could find one that works. We could get some food and just get out of here."

"Lee, think," Jessica said. "Those lifeboats will never reach land. We'll be floating with two armfuls of food. Which boat do you think will be found first? Here we have a huge kitchen and the gun. You did the right thing, Lee."

Lee said, "I need to see Hesse. I'll get Rick."

Lee thought about bringing Adam, but while he could be sure of Rick's support, he didn't feel that way about Adam Melville anymore. Walking the long distance between the Theater and the Atrium, Rick and Lee could see what the night had done. They still passed individuals or small groups here and there, but they were not like people now. They were furtive and quick, like animals. They either knew what had happened, or what was worse, they knew only that something bad had happened but not what.

In the Atrium, some power had been already restored. Lee was struck by the quickness of the repair with all that went on that night. The emergency track lighting glowed in the dim dawn let in from the glass ceiling above. There were much fewer here than before. Fear and hatred appeared on faces here and there that recognized Lee, or his gun.

They found John Hesse. He was in his office, with two women. Hesse saw them through the window, his face grave. He waved Lee and Rick sharply to wait.

It was not long before the women wound up their business and left. Lee and Rick entered.

Hesse looked at them strangely. He was standing, they sat.

"They found a girl. Raped. Sixteen years old," Hesse said.

Each let out an expression and then waited.

"In a bathroom," Hesse said.

Lee and Rick sat motionless. Hesse stayed standing, by the counter.

"Well, what are you going to do?" Lee said.

"I don't know," Hesse said. "Last night, a lot of things went down. We have dead bodies, dead bodies, bleeding kids."

Hesse stopped there to see Lee's reaction. They stared at each other in silence. Finally, Lee spoke.

"I did what I had to do. And I have an M16 and you don't."

"Fine," Hesse said. "You have an M16, and I don't. So you can watch your own back. But with all this mess, here we are this morning, and everyone still has one ship to live on. So all I care about is how we survive from here. Now there's this rape. Anybody who has a woman on board that they care about needs to worry about this."

"Yeah," Lee said. "So how are you going to deal with it? You couldn't stop your own people from stealing food."

"We need to find this guy," Hesse said. "We'll figure everything else out, but we can't let this go. Those women, it's one of their daughters. They've been staying here in the Atrium. She says the girl had never seen the guy before, so he's probably from the Theater or in a stateroom. But she could describe him- and if he's a refugee he'll be in the same clothes."

"So, the first step would be to check for someone like that in the Theater you're thinking," Lee said. "And you're just offering a truce with me to get that."

"I'm not at war with you," Hesse said. "We don't need more blood. We want to feed everyone, and get everyone off this boat. Those folks that stole food stole it from us too. We can still get back to normal, Golding. But everything falls apart if rapists are unpunished and everyone knows it."

"Are you blind or stupid, Hesse? It's already fallen apart. You've got people who tried to steal our food, and you'll go right back to keeping them alive, but you're mad at me for trying to stop them? Do you seriously want to sit here and waste time worrying about one girl? Wake up. We have thousands of lives hanging by a thread now. I let you have your little podium up there and let you get on with organizing and running things. Now look. The food's gone."

"Not all of it," Hesse said. "There's quite a bit left, maybe a week's worth, maybe more with the Italian leftovers. We don't really know how many of us are left yet, or how much we can get back from what was stolen, so it's hard to say exactly how long the food will last, but we've got a while yet."

"And how is it you have power back and we don't?" Lee said.

Hesse rolled his eyes.

"Our engineer and her men were up all night getting the generators running again. And guess what? They'd blown because of the circuit powering the Theater. So they had to disconnect it to get power back here."

"Who are you to decide who gets power? It's pitch black in there at night."

"Look, we have thousands of people getting their food or living here."

"You had thousands, looks like a lot fewer now. Guess you didn't really inspire a lot of faith did you?" Rick said.

The Mighty Lee Golding stood.

"I trusted you," Lee continued. "All our lives in your hands. I said, when I first came down here, he's got things under control, he's already got things going on. So I let it stand. This is the result. From now on, I call the shots."

He leaned over the counter, his gun hanging behind him. Hesse could have gone for him then, and grappled with Lee before he could get his gun in hand. Lee hoped he'd try.

"No," Hesse said. "No one here'd put up with that, not the Colonel, not the staff, not the people out there."

"They'd put up with it if I killed you."

Lee pulled back and grasped the gun by his side, holding it underarm, not lifting it to aim at Hesse but threatening with it.

"If you kill me," Hesse said, "they'll kill you."

"Who?" Rick said.

"Anyone," Hesse said. "We all know what you did last night. No one will make anything of it because last night a lot of things happened that we can't do anything about now. But if you kill me you won't have a moment's rest on this ship. The moment you kill me, you'll be marked. Someone will get you. We'll get power back to the Theater. It's still a safe place to use as a hub. Trust me. No one wants to see you here in the Atrium again."

Lee laughed.

"Are you for real?" Lee said. "You threatening me to stay away? You stay away from the Theater. If I see you, I'll kill you, and I guarantee no one there will be bent on vengeance. Get our power back, or I'll be back. Send the food, or I'll be back. And I'll know if you're shorting us, I'll have eyes in here checking your rations. You got anything to say to me, send someone else to say it or bring me down. I'm telling you, stay away from the Theater. I don't like you."

30

In the morning, as they had every morning, the groups from the piano lounge went down to the Atrium for breakfast, joining a steady stream of tourists and squatters from the staterooms.

The crowd was significantly smaller than it had been. There was coffee. The food was late.

Hesse came up onto the counter top.

"I think you all know something about last night. There was a lot of food taken. There were people hurt. All the lifeboats are either gone or shot up. I'll get into that in a second but first I know you are all wondering about the food."

The longer he spoke, the more he regained his strength.

"We're going to be fine," he continued. "We need to stick together. We're going to have to cut down the rations again, but we can still last well more than a week, eating decently. We'll have two meals a day now, skipping lunch. The portions, like I say, will be a little smaller. If we have to change again in a few days, we will, but I think everyone should still be getting enough now. The food's just going to be a little late today."

"What about the guy with the gun?" someone said.

"He's from the Theater," Hesse said. "He went to save our food. He's just like everybody else. He just wants to survive. Last night some of us went a little crazy. It isn't going to do any good now to try and figure out who did what last night. We all know it didn't go well for anyone. If everyone just trusts each other, and no one tries to steal our food, there won't be any more violence."

Hesse looked slowly over the crowd.

"The professional wrestler with the gun just wants to survive," Claude said. "Like that's not a scary motivation, right?"

He fixed a look at Travis. "What would YOU have done if you'd had a gun last night?"

Travis was stunned. Did Claude know? It was impossible. But why hadn't he taken his gun last night, after all? What would he have done with it? Would they be on a lifeboat right now? What would he have done with the stolen food?

"That guy's bad news," Gerry said. "Have you spoken with Hesse about him?"

"No," Travis said.

Would he use his gun? Travis wondered. Would he trust it to another's judgment or was it his choice alone to make?

His whole life he'd wondered how to live right. He tried, but it was like chasing a phantom. Working hard meant being less of a dad. His emergency work abroad meant being less of a husband. He never really felt like he knew how to live right, but he tried.

He'd wonder if he really was good, or just acting at it.

Now, again, he wanted to do right. He wanted to help. He didn't know how.

"I know some of you tried to get away last night," Hesse said. "I know some of you tried to steal food, and I know some of you were there in the galley when I was attacked. But there is no way we can survive if we don't turn the page on last night. There are no more working lifeboats, so our only option is to work together to live here until we're rescued."

"How are we going to get off this ship?" someone yelled at Hesse.

"We just have to be patient- there's no doubt that, eventually, there will be rescue efforts. After the flooding in Indonesia, there were sweeps of the ocean within days. It's obviously been a major catastrophe, but eventually, people are going to come looking for the thousands and thousands who will be lost at sea."

"Man is smoking crack," Professor Claude said. "Indonesia, it was the rich countries helping. Who helps when the rich countries get it?"

"The other thing," Hesse continued, "is we think we can get the communications system working. We have some good people who know what they're doing and we think that'll be ready sooner rather than later."

"What's taking so long?" someone said.

"For one thing," Hesse said, "the satellite dish was structurally damaged. It's taking some time to get that in working condition. The rest of it is electronics, and I can't tell you what's involved. It'll take what it takes. They've only been working on it a few days. The first priority has always been getting more power and redirecting it where we needed it to survive. We couldn't do both things at once."

The food came at last, but it was slower in coming than in days before. It was another hour before Travis's group ate. A half-cup of scrambled eggs, a thumb of sausage, a small slice of melon. It wasn't so bad, Travis thought. Some of the chefs must have stayed.

Rumors of what had occurred in the night filtered in to the Theater as well. Men and women went in and out of the Theater freely, and the events of the night had spread across the ship.

When Lee came back from the Atrium, he was something beyond a leader and protector of the group. He was a force.

There were no announcements here. There were no arguments.

Adam watched Lee sitting up on the edge of the stage, talking with his wife and Rick Dumas. He felt sick and went for fresh air.

He liked being outside on the ship and took a circuitous path around the Sky Deck before returning to the Theater. A strong wind blew through his long hair. It was cold and dark though it was the middle of the day; the ocean was steel grey, kicked up into large swells. The storm was preparing to return. We haven't things bad enough, he thought. He looked up at the great spotlight and followed it as high to the heavens as he could make it out.

As Adam came back in from the fresh air he was struck by the smell of the ship. The consequences from the toilet overflows over a week ago, thousands of unwashed live bodies and dead bodies left to sit too long, the poorly managed porta-johns, and a dead HVAC system. The air was heavy. It made him queasy.

As he opened the great door at the bottom of the

Theater and looked into the hundreds in their lounge chairs above, the smell overwhelmed him. It rushed down over him, flowing out the open door. He thought he would vomit. He turned from the scene quickly, rushing back through the hallways, not seeing the faces of those he passed by, although, striking as he was, all eyes always turned to him. He felt better as he got out of that Theater air, but he kept moving.

Adam Melville's life had been a quest, and the clues always had come to him. He was one of those men who felt fate in their life, and he'd never run from it. But here, there was the greatest mystery and no clues. So many people were in so much pain, and he knew it was much more than the silly practical issues Lee tried so hard to resolve. If it were Adam's fate to help here, he could not see how.

He found an empty stairwell. He shut the door and fell to his knees and prayed in the dark. There he had a religious experience.

Dear Lord, he said quietly, his hands covering his face, rescue us from our fear. Let us understand your plan. There must be a meaning to it! If this is punishment, show us a way out. I know I've been lost to you for many years but I've tried to do right things in my life. Please.

Adam knew, in the end, this was all there was to prayer. Please. It was obvious what they needed. Please. However many sinners there were on board, or anywhere the flood had hit, there were innocents too. Please. In the Bible, God showed himself so that the people could look on his miracles and know He had touched the world. Please.

He asked God to let them live, or, if they were to die, that God would show them how. So that, if it were God's plan, they could die without suffering, and in such a way that they would have a better life to come. He prayed for all those aboard the ship, he prayed for those off the ship. He prayed with such intensity that his flesh grew red behind his grey beard, and sweat came from his cheeks and his fists bruised his forehead. Show us the way to live, or the way to die.

He stopped praying and stood. He understood, not everything, but the outlines of something. He knew he was where he was for a reason. Something needed to be done that only he could do. He returned to the Theater.

Adam's hair was wet with rain; his clothes wetly hugged his enormous frame. The man entered at the bottom of the stairs by the Royal Theater's left aisle. He walked along the front row, making eye contact through the crowd as he walked. There were people on the stage, it had been home to a couple of dozen. Adam walked onto the stage, and even in the dark, his presence was tremendous. He found an empty spot, fell to his knees and entered into prayer.

A wave of quiet propagated from the front rows out. Soon, all eyes were on the giant on stage, on his knees, his head held up, eyes screwed up tight, his big hairy fists up in his beard. For minutes it went on, and many wondered how long they would watch this man pray.

A man and his wife on the stage came over to Adam. They knelt next to him. An old lady went up, then a man.

Several more joined Adam on the stage, others fell into prayer where they were. Rick felt himself laughing nervously in the buzz of several dozen quiet prayers.

No one stood until Adam did. The spell broke. He looked around; the sounds finally came to him. He smiled, turning to those who had knelt next to him. They shook hands smiling. More came to him and shook his hand, thanking him for bringing God onto the ship.

31

The ending of the first week on board had brought a spiritual and emotional sickness to the Festival. The ending now of the second week brought a physical epidemic. People were getting sick. There was a bad flu bug; one in four were sick with cramps and muscle pain, diarrhea and vomiting, or respiratory infections. It was the mold and bacteria from the toilet spills, Travis knew. The ventilation system had been repaired, but the ship was too filthy to air out that easily. Darren was sick, and Travis, Corrina and Gerry took turns comforting him as he vomited or lay shivering on the couch in the piano lounge.

They continued to split their time between the piano lounge, Vera's stateroom, and the Atrium. Although Claude would leave them for periods of time, Travis found himself attached to Claude, as his son was. He was fascinated by Claude's optimistic pessimism. Professor Claude seemed always to expect the worst, but never seemed dismayed. Sometimes Travis was attracted by the attitude, sometimes repulsed. It was as though Travis held it as an article of faith that the worst had occurred, and the Professor felt as strongly that the worst was still coming.

One night, Corrina said offhandedly, "This limbo is hell."

"What's that?" Claude asked.

"The not knowing," she said. "We have no idea what our world and lives are going to be when we get off. I think it's the worst stress right now."

"No," Claude said. "God, no. This boat is home now, and everybody's starting to realize it. Pretty soon people will be asking what it means if this is all we have. Think about this. Human beings don't change. Our DNA is no different from- pick your favorite historic savage. Nazis slaughtering Jews, Romans slaughtering Carthaginians, Portuguese slaughtering Africans, whoever you want. There's nothing in us programmed any different. Just what we grew up with. And this isn't where we grew up."

"You're a real ray of sunshine, you know that?" Travis said.

"Travis," the Professor said, "you've seen people in so much worse conditions in your Sudan work, in Haiti. Why do you keep thinking we've hit bottom?"

Yes, Travis had seen worse. He'd seen humans so far from humanity. What had to happen to take them there, he wondered.

Travis continued to explore the ship. He felt like, if he gave Gerry time alone with his wife, Gerry would likewise give Travis time with his kid, which happily sometimes meant Corrina as well.

He sometimes fantasized that they would survive, but somehow Gerry wouldn't, and then he'd feel guilty for imagining it and he'd punish himself with the thought that Corrina would never return to him, whatever happened to Gerry.

The electric card locks of the cabins had remained operational through it all. Each had its own battery to power it, which meant that many abandoned cabins were locked. Travis had watched now, day by day and week by week, as more and more of the bolts were smashed open, the doors splintered around them. There were no secure spots, but the ship still seemed to contain vast secret places, dead and dark areas.

The huge casino, built in an old west style, was a haunted ghost town. Then, there would be life where it wasn't expected, a hidden pocket, like the library, where they found a number of refugees would pass much of their time quietly in the Alexandrian-inspired space, amid white columns and upright desks, leather chairs and mosaic floors. They read histories and sciences, trash and art. It passed the time.

An afternoon several days since the run on the lifeboats, came a miracle.

Travis wandered alone. He passed through the Champagne Room, which had become one of his favorite spots. Many of the crew and ship staff had camped out here after the collision and the loss of so many crew berths. Occasionally, the musicians on board gave concerts there. Travis had seen a Flamenco guitar duo on one visit.

The Champagne Bar had the best lounging booths on the ship, the softest carpet, snooker tables, and an ice bar which Travis had watched melt over the first days on the ship until a wet stain had spread over the carpet, evaporating and drying slowly in the cold wet atmosphere. Now there was a moldy smell in the room, but it still charmed Travis because the room had so little natural light, but all day through showed the pleasant glow of the battery-powered electric candles on the tables, which lit up the room like lightning bugs at night.

Travis had just entered the room when he heard a woman screaming in the dark.

"It's alright, Cassie," another woman's voice said, followed by more voices and encouragement.

Travis ran over. Several flashlights illuminated the scene. A woman was in labor, lying on the floor. Her pants were off. A friend supported her from behind. Dr. Joel Conrad kneeled between her legs.

"Travis!" the doctor shouted. "Get to the clinic! No one here knows where anything is. You know what I need? We've got water already, need everything else."

"On my way."

Travis flew.

When he returned with soap, gloves, forceps, scissors, sterile pads, sutures and needles the delivery had progressed. The woman was crying, and only one of her friends continued to encourage her, as others backed away fearing tragedy. The father knelt behind her, silent.

"Push!" Conrad said.

She cried and grunted.

"I've got the head," Conrad shouted.

The umbilical cord was tangled. Travis and Conrad worked together to get it clear.

"Almost there," Travis said. "Come on!"

The woman screamed, her friends again encouraged her, hope returning, and then the baby's cries pierced it all.

"A healthy girl!" Conrad shouted.

There was a cathartic cry from around them, and

around the room, a joyful sob.

From the shadows came a long swirling and bubbly run of notes from a clarinet, and then the musician's comrades joined in, a small jazz combo with a joyous Dixieland tune. Travis held the baby and cleaned it, while Conrad tied and cut the umbilical cord. Travis's eye stayed on the tiny toes, and he thought of Darren's birth, that beautiful boy. He'd felt so much hope on that day, and on this day, he couldn't help but feel it again.

The father took the baby, both of them crying. He collapsed to his knees and passed the girl to the mother who sobbed uncontrollably.

The sound of the clarinet, trumpet, trombone, banjo and tuba soaked them in a heavenly joy, and they all laughed and cried.

"Trying to work here!" Conrad complained with happiness in his voice as he cleaned and sutured the mother's skin tears.

Travis too found himself on his knees laughing and crying, and the band played on. Suddenly Travis was pulled up and dancing with strangers in the dark, and soon they all danced in a circle around the mother and father and baby and doctor. They had all hungered for something to let them feel good. He thought of his baby boy, the first time he held him, and the smile stretched so far his cheeks began to hurt.

When it was over, and he'd thrown out his gloves and washed his arms, Travis felt high. He put his arm around the doctor.

"How have you been?" Travis said.

"Good now, my friend. Come, let's celebrate. Come

with me."

The cardiac surgeon put his arm around the shoulder of the paramedic and led him down a large hallway, then down flights of stairs to a small side-hallway, where they could hear rock-and-roll music.

32

"Welcome to the Viking Sports Hall," Conrad said, "or as I like to call it, the Bowels of the Festival."

It was a Viking themed sports bar. There were rough wood long-tables, bulky beams overhead, and creatures of Norse mythology in sports jerseys. Eight-foot Thor, holding his hammer in the air, wore a Michael Jordan pinny. The All-Father Odin, on a throne, wore Fran Tarkenton's purple Minnesota Vikings jersey and cradled a signed football in his lap. Big screen TVs dotted the walls between the portholes. They were here just above the water level, and it occasionally washed the window with green spray and champagne foam, so that they felt as though traveling in a Viking longboat.

Dividing the booths, extending from the outer wall were replica ship masts with carved maiden figureheads, each with famous sports jerseys painted to their torsos. There was Edmonton's 99, Cleveland's 32, San Francisco's 24, and Brazil's 10.

There were a few dozen refugees and tourists in the bar, and the sound of loud chatter. A stereo system played Bruce Springsteen, and a young man and woman, dressed in informal server's outfits in the ship's colors, served drinks with smiles on their faces to customers with smiles on their faces. They'd get tips occasionally.

There were young and old, two very pretty girls danced, people sat in booths and at tables, in groups freshly made or with their own. They drank pitchers and cocktails. A young couple in the corner booth smoked a joint. Travis saw the woman Conrad had been with on the deck. It seemed like a lifetime ago.

"The bartenders opened it up," Conrad said, leading Travis over to the bar. "The captain had them lock up all the booze, but the captain — he dead. What'll you have? It's on me. Everything's warm, by the way, but we got a guy working on siphoning some juice for the fridges down here. And the beer taps work. They got the stereo on batteries, can you believe it?"

"Guinness," Travis said.

"One Guinness, one scotch and soda. Big one this time, Sue-Anne, what are we saving it for? A better class of customer?"

Sue-Anne laughed and got them their drinks.

"Yeah. The bartenders are good people," Conrad said as they carried the drinks to their table. "They work a few hours, then let some of the others work behind the bar, and they drink, or go out, wherever the hell they go. They've been raiding the cabin mini-bars. They sleep here. In the back room. They just make sure the bar's well stocked so no one bothers them. I assume they're engaging in what we call sex, but who knows?"

Conrad's mistress sat at a table with a tourist couple. Conrad sat next to her, and the couple made space for Travis. Conrad introduced him around. The couple were honeymooners, Travis figured. Conrad's mistress he introduced as Marianna. She was very beautiful, and smiling. Conrad told the others how he'd worked with Travis after the pirates.

"What have you been doing?" Travis asked.

"I'm retired from medicine. I keep getting dragged back in, I admit. Yesterday I killed a guy. Well, I didn't kill him. But I didn't save him. Man, bullet wounds are getting old. We've been staying in a stateroom on the fifth deck- abandoned. Left some nice clothes though, don't you like this shirt?"

"It's silk," Marianna said.

"Are you by yourself?" the man next to Travis said.

"I'm with my family, kind of," Travis said.

"We just met," the woman said, her arm entwined with the man's. "I was actually on the cruise with someone else. But it's funny, you can fake loving someone your whole life until you think you're about to die, and then you don't want to anymore."

"I'm sick of talking about that stuff," Conrad said.

"The way I see it," Marianna said to Travis in a New York Puerto Rican accent, "we're gonna die or we're gonna live if we get rescued or not. Either way, we can't do anything about it. My gramma always taught me not to worry about things one cannot affect. So… let's party!"

She screamed a party scream, YEAAAAAH, and raised her beer, and the couple screamed and raised their drinks, and Conrad raised his. Around, a few others screamed and raised their drinks.

Travis raised his to the other four.

It was strange at first for Travis, a room full of smiling people. He hadn't seen that since it had begun. He was disconcerted. But he felt great seeing smiling people again, it was intoxicating. He enjoyed Claude for the same reason, he seemed unaffected by what went wrong, and in his humor Travis felt an outlet for the stress inside himself. Here in the Viking Sports Hall it was an unexpected vacation from the seriousness of everything. He realized he was smiling, too, at their audacity, their exuberance in the face of everything. Their defiant exuberance.

He stayed for two more beers. In his hungry, tired state he felt drunk. In the end, he pulled his wallet out and tipped the bartenders twenty dollars. He had sixty-five left. He wondered at the idiocy of holding onto this money and thought of throwing it all on the bar. But wouldn't he feel like an ass if a little money somehow came in handy later?

When he walked out, Conrad called, "Next time bring the ex!"

Gerry Adamson sat alone on the Penthouse Deck promenade. He had a piece of paper and a pen. He looked out over the ocean and tried to see in it monsters of the deep, mermaids and sirens, and Odysseus searching for his way home. All he saw was the ocean. He wrote.

The end of the world came
And we no longer asked, who to die by fire and who
by sword
We all died by water.

Six days after the lifeboats left, the rations were cut again. They were eating stews now to stretch the meat. Still, it was enough to live, and still, somehow, everything was delicious. They occasionally included pastries; strange and fanciful deserts that seemed so out of place with everything else. The Festival's Executive Chef began to struggle with the ingredients they had. Flour and eggs were used in more substantive recipes, but what could be done with marzipan, mascarpone, baking chocolates, berry compote, and icing sugar?

33

Corrina took Darren to the playroom every afternoon. It was supposed to be a daily play date with Brenda's kids, but Brenda would often postpone or not show up at all as her work dictated. Occasionally, other kids were there, and Darren played with them. Corrina didn't care; she went with Darren everyday and they played together. Some days she'd have a heavy heart crawling through lime green plastic tunnels.

She knew some would consider this, her indulgence of her boy, frivolous or disrespectful. She didn't care. There would be heartache enough for everyone. She didn't need to make it worse than it had to be. If Darren could come out of all this not really understanding until he learned about it in school some day, that would be fine. Things weren't that fine though. Here, Darren was struggling. This was her best medicine.

As she slid down, Darren in her lap, she heard familiar screams as Darren's friends came running to take him away from boring old momma. Corrina got to her feet and walked over to Brenda. They hugged.

Holding hands, they fell back into the beanbag chairs.

"Close your eyes," Corrina said. "I'll watch the girls."

Brenda closed her eyes and fell into solid sleep to the sounds of the kids' screams.

After an hour, Brenda opened her eyes and the kids were still screaming.

"I took this cruise to relax," she said. "I never worked so hard in my life. It's like a Twilight Zone episode. I think my husband is behind it. All these years he begs me to slow down my work, to take a break, even a sabbatical from power and electronics and all that beautiful stuff. So I do it. A lo-o-o-ong cruise. And now I'm in this Seventh Hell of wiring and power management. And it's constant. I close my eyes and dream about voltages and capacitors."

Corrina had been surprised when Brenda's work had carried on after the first week, when power and water were stabilized. But as she questioned and understood the endless succession of issues, emergencies, and new demands, she knew Brenda would be working like this until whatever end was coming.

"What are you working on now?" Corrina asked.

"The communications, always," Brenda said. "But we're trying to get power to the toilets. They're wired to the emergency power system, and like everything else, we'll have to get them back bit by bit. Like everything. With all the sickness, this is getting to be a serious priority. But we were really getting somewhere with the satellite, too. I wish we didn't waste so much time, I wish we didn't always have a million things to take care of… we could be talking to someone!"

"Oh, hello," Corrina said into an imaginary phone. She slipped into an exaggerated Long Island accent — with South Carolina under it. "Yeah, this is Corrinna. Uh huh. Yeah. Yes, I'll hold."

She held up her invisible phone and whispered to Brenda, "I'm on hold."

Corrina put the imaginary phone back to her ear. "Yes,

could I get a cab? We're on the Festival.... Yeah, that's right. OK, you'll honk when you pull up? Oh, what am I wearing? Yeah, it's the same underwear I put on like, three weeks ago. Uh huh. Yeah, it's nasty. Oh, you like that?"

Brenda was laughing, wiping tears from her red eyes.

"There's a party tonight," Brenda said. "Did you hear about it? Leon and I are going. We even got a sitter. Some of the bands are having a dance party in the night club."

"Really?" Corrina said. She looked out at Darren and smiled. "Yeah, I love to dance. And we have the luxury of a live-in babysitter right now."

"Travis?" Brenda said.

"Yeah, well, he never was much of a dancer anyway," Corrina said.

"Do you still work together well as parents?" Brenda asked.

"I suppose we're all outside our comfort zone right now," Corrina said. "We've probably spoken more these couple weeks than the last couple years."

Corrina paused. Spending this time with Travis had been emotional for her. She couldn't talk to Gerry about it, so she'd been blocking it from her mind. She wished she could forget things, as Vera did.

"I couldn't take him back, you know?" Corrina said quietly.

Since that first time they'd met, Corrina had always seemed cheerful and strong to Brenda. Now, she sounded sad.

"I wanted to punish him. But I never wanted to ruin his life. He is a good man. I wish he could be happy again in his life, without me."

"You can't fix everything," Brenda said. "Or everyone."

Brenda took her kids back to her cruise suite, the same she had moved into that morning in Florida.

As the sun went down, they met up in the disco: Corrina and Gerry, Brenda and her husband Leon, and dozens of others. Brenda flicked a switch and the strobe lights and spotlights came to life, circling the room. The crowd cheered and clapped, and Brenda took a little bow as the first band, a small salsa combo with acoustic guitar, bass, trumpet and shakers came up on the stage and led off with "Besame Mucho", driven by a powerful syncopated bass line and trumpet blasts.

The crowd kept the cheer right up and rushed to the dance floor. Corrina pulled Gerry out, and Brenda and Leon followed them. The band played with fire. It was for them a greater release than for the dancers. They'd been doing cruise gigs a long time, sticking together as a group. They came from the same village, and they left it together and stayed together. They veered between Mexican boleros, Cuban mambo, Brazillian samba and Latinized versions of American hits.

Gerry and Corrina were very good dancers. It was what they did nights at home in their apartment when Darren slept. Looking around at the dozens, if not hundreds, crowding the dance floor, Corrina was pleased to again see faces she'd seen once or twice but then lost to their private routines. It felt like a reunion.

The Mexican quartet blew themselves out and bowed their way off the stage, glowing with sweat in Brenda's glorious strobe lights. They were replaced by a Jerry Lee Lewis style piano player, who unveiled the grand piano, hidden by a black tarp in the shadows, with a deft yank. They all danced, and smiled at each other in acknowledgment of this special moment they were sharing, the spirit they still felt as humans. When the rocking piano player played himself out, he was replaced by the Dixieland band.

It was the show of their lives.

There was no alcohol, but they felt drunk. Brenda and Corrina stumbled out to the promenade to cool off.

"You did all this?" Corrina said.

"Well. I talked to some people," Brenda said.

"You're amazing," Corrina said.

"So are you," Brenda said. "You'll make it."

Brenda pointed at her spotlight, snake-like in the mist.

"What do you see when you look at that?" Brenda said.

"I see a shout out to the world," Corrina said. "We're still here. We ain't going away."

They looked back out over the water. The music still reached them. They listened to the song and Corrina tapped her feet.

"*Heaven,*" she sang along, "*I'm in heaven/ And my heart beats so, that I can hardly speak.*"

34

In the morning, Vera sat with them in the piano lounge. She too had been sick, and Travis was struck by how she'd wasted away. The winds were gone outside, and the air pressure seemed to change. Vera spoke.

"When I was a girl, I was in the Siege of Leningrad. For two years, we were alone, trapped by the Nazis and their bombs. My house was destroyed. My parents killed, my brother. I was spared. I wondered why. I tried leaving; there was a caravan crossing the ice of Lake Lagoda. The Germans bombed the lake. I fell in the water. It was a miracle. I survived again. I was a beautiful young woman-then I was an animal, living in rubble, scavenging."

At first Vera had seemed focused, speaking slowly, as if considering how best to reach her point. But she began to seem tired and disconnected, rambling.

"Two years like this. The bodies littered the streets, dead from starvation, from the cold, from the bombing. You don't imagine what you can think when you are so hungry, when death seems so certain, not just for you- for everyone.

She paused and considered what she had said.

"There were cannibals then. I wondered sometimes how we did not all kill each other. But we had the Nazis to hate. But why would any God have saved me from Nazis and winter and hunger to bring me here?"

While she spoke, Corrina had pulled Darren towards

her, but he struggled away from her breast to face the old lady, listening seriously. When she finished, Claude looked at the boy.

"And your dad thinks I'm the party-pooper, huh Darren?" he said.

35

Days after Travis's visit to the Bowels, Hesse found him at dinner and pulled him into the office.

"I need your help with something," Hesse said.

Travis nodded.

"We've had suicides," he paused to catch Travis's eyes, then continued. "There's a fair number that we know of, maybe a dozen. I'm sure we'll find more. People come and tell us when they've found the source of the smell down the hall. There's no way we can keep it from spreading. The rumors, I mean. That will make things worse. But we can keep people from seeing it, and seeing how many there are."

"What are you asking me to do?"

"I need you to take a few guys who can keep their mouths shut and get rid of the bodies. Do it after the daytime crowd disperses and everyone's in their hiding places."

Hesse gave him a list with directions and a flashlight.

"What's happening with the communications?" Travis asked.

"Soon," Hesse said. "Soon."

The same confident I've-got-a-plan tone he had for everything, Travis thought. But Hesse did have a plan. He'd expected this, too.

Travis took Claude and Gerry to visit the staterooms on his list.

There weren't any lights in the rooms. The emergency lighting only lit the hallways, and only enough to walk by. Gerry circled the first room with the flashlight.

"On the couch," Travis said.

The man sat upright on the couch, his head at an awkward angle. They could see the blood, dried and browning. He had slit his own throat. The knife rested on the couch, just out of his grip.

"I suspect an inside job," Claude said.

"No way," Gerry said. "The butler, in the library, with a razor-sharp wit."

Travis looked at the wound. He'd gotten the air pipe but not the arteries. This had been slow and painful, and he would not have been able to scream.

Travis wondered why Hesse had asked him to do this. What was there in Travis that he would be chosen out of everyone as the perfect guy to clean up suicides? The question bothered him.

Travis and Gerry took the arms and legs. This was a less expensive stateroom than Vera's. There was no balcony to throw him off of, as there had been for Vera's husband and the man who had killed him. The windows were sealed. Claude led the way with a flashlight, out of the cabin, down the hallway. There was no promenade or foredeck at all on this level, so up a flight of stairs they carried the dead man. It was heavy work, and they paused several times to rest and adjust their grips, but they met no other passengers on their route. Out on the deck, the soft rain and breeze cooled them satisfyingly. They hurried across the deck, and without pause, lifted the man over the rail and dropped. There was no sound after that except their own heavy breathing.

The next was a couple. They rotated so that they took turns with the body and the flashlight.

"There's something romantic about a double suicide," Claude said.

"I'm not that into commitment," Gerry sputtered.

At the railing, Professor Claude said, "Why couldn't they just throw themselves overboard anyways?"

"There's something of the exhibitionist in a suicide," Gerry said.

"Yeah," Claude said. "They're making an argument. We get it. Life sucks."

As they walked back to the next spot, Travis shined the flashlight on Claude's face.

"So who do you like in the World Series this year?" Travis said.

"I think we can pretty much eliminate the Yankees and Red Sox," Claude said.

"And the Braves and the Orioles and the Marlins," Gerry said. "Could be the Rockies' year. Remember how the Saints played a season away from home after Hurricane Katrina?"

"Yeah," Claude said. "Ain't life unfair?"

Next came the teenagers. They did not joke in that room. Two dead, and a lot of blood. They looked beautiful.

One had evidently killed the other, then done himself by the wrists. The knife was on the floor. It looked like his had been painful and slow. There was a balcony here, and the work was done quickly.

Travis wondered at the trauma he'd seen in the last

few years of his work, the nightmare of Sudan and nightmares of it since, the loss of his love and family, guilt, and now this, and still he fought. His life had been unhappy for three years since he'd lost Corrina, but somehow he still fought for it. Would Corrina? They both had Darren to fight for. Kids didn't kill themselves. Not often. He'd never seen one as a paramedic. Darren, the indestructible, saving all their lives.

The last one was at the opposite end of the ship. They were forced to take a circuitous route around the sealed compartment, outside again, inside again. The night was becoming late, the moon and a slice of star-filled night were just visible in a chasm in the cloud cover; the moonlight lit up the chasm walls so that they could see the full depth of the clouds above.

"They uncovered some archaeological ruins in northern Peru," Professor Claude said. "The remains of a human and animal sacrifice. Fifty children and as many llamas. This village literally sacrificed its future. For something. What do you imagine was bad enough that they'd sacrifice their kids for god's mercy?"

He laughed a haunted laugh. "Same DNA, same DNA."

When they entered the final room the stench was horrible. This one had been sitting for days. They found him in the bed, killed with medication, an empty bottle on the nightstand.

"Oh," Travis said, as the flashlight passed over the man's face, "crap."

The other two did not bother to ask, they waited.

"The ship surgeon," Travis said.

"Huh," Claude said. "Physician, heal thyself."

On the walk back they realized they were passing by the Theater. They were outside the back doors and Claude held the flashlight on the sign for a moment.

"The next bodies we'll be tossing will have bullet holes," Professor Claude said.

"Just stop!" Travis said. "I hear this from you over and over, I'm sick of it. I feel your voice pecking at the back of my brain."

"That's the truth!" the Professor said. "And I imagine if I put money down right now that things were going to get worse before they get better, neither of you gentleman would pick up that bet."

"Well, your money's no good here, Darkness," Gerry said.

Travis laughed, the spell broken.

"You're a pretty funny guy, Gerry," Claude said. "But you're still only a rebound husband."

That night, Travis lay on the carpet in the piano lounge, his son sleeping above him on the plush curving bench of the booth. He had nightmares again.

In the morning, Travis felt haunted from the night's chores. At the Atrium, he saw Doctor Joel Conrad waiting for food. He looked awful, his skin was a bad color and his eyes were bloodshot.

Before Travis could approach him, there was a scream.

"FISH!" a man shouted.

They all turned to see a group of men on the stairs, smiling all.

"FISH!" the man screamed again. He held a basket teaming with headless fish.

"We've got nets full of clean fish," the man yelled. "We'll eat well tonight! We'll need a few more volunteers so any of you good with knives, please come by the kitchen after breakfast… if you're not too busy."

There was a cheer from the crowd, and Travis saw Hesse cheering too. It had a sharp effect. Travis felt it in himself and knew everyone around him felt it. He guessed that they couldn't possibly catch enough fish to feed everyone, but the ticking clock in their galley would slow down, at least.

It was good news, so rare, it thrilled them.

"Have you been back to see the baby?" Joel Conrad said, coming next to Travis.

"No," Travis said.

"Pneumonia," the doctor said. "She could hardly breathe last night. I put her on antibiotics. I've been to see her this morning and she already seems a bit stronger. She was able to feed again, at least."

Travis felt sick himself at this news. Did God have to do this too?

The ghastly doctor grabbed Travis's arm. His grip was still strong.

"We delivered that girl," the doctor said. "Death will have to tear her from my hands."

Travis smiled. It was good to see fight left in the good guys.

36

Lee and Rick spent days sounding out the crowd in the Theater. People were upset. There was anger at the Atrium for being in control when things went wrong. They were convinced that the other group was giving them the short end of the stick. It was a suspicion that had grown and fed on itself each day and each incident, seeded here and there by Rick and his wife, who loved to talk.

Soon, it became impossible to imagine that they weren't treated as an unwanted burden on the main group, bound to get secondary service in all cases; in food, in use of the electrical power, fresh water, in any kind of warning or communications on anything going on- like the lifeboat panic. If they weren't being sacrificed yet, they would be soon, they were sure of that.

Since the run on the lifeboats, Rick and Lee's talks had pushed more and more of their group to that attitude. There was a growing desperation that whatever chance they'd had before the run on the lifeboats was greatly diminished. For days, Rick and Lee listened. They judged their peers, what types of ideas they had.

When they began organizing, first Lee and Rick confirmed those they guessed would follow them easily. Then they picked from that pool the ones to draft. Lee avoided Adam in his recruitment. Adam had led a few more prayer sessions, at random intervals. It bothered

Lee that he didn't at least go somewhere that everyone didn't have to watch. Lee didn't trust Adam anymore. He was angry too, like Adam had ruined what could have been a great friendship.

Lee and Rick took thirteen men and seven women to raid the central galley. No one else was told.

There was great excitement about the enterprise.

At last, they were doing something. They had taken upon themselves the action to save their group.

They went at night, when the dinner cleanup in the galley would be over, and there would be only the two guards.

It was very dark. They crossed over the sealed section on the open Sky Deck, in pairs, to avoid alarm if anyone were out for a stroll. They reunited in an unlit service stairwell as soon as they were beyond the sealed section. They went slowly and quietly, along corridors less traveled. The ship's main Aquarium Restaurant was spread over two decks, with the lower floor opening to the Grand Atrium. The galley and food storage was below the restaurant, one deck below the Atrium.

Outside the galley, they went terribly slowly. Lee and another man were in front. Lee walked out of the darkness, and could see into the open door of the galley. He walked in. There were two guards, in a set of rooms barely lit by emergency lamps, with many shadows.

"Get on the floor," Lee said. He didn't even hold up the gun hanging from his shoulder, but the guards saw it.

They lay on the ground. The man behind Lee signaled for the others to come in. Some had rope, and they went to tying up the guards.

"What are you doing?" one guard said.

"We're saving ourselves," Rick said.

"Are you going to make us starve?"

"Get them in the closet," Lee said.

The two men were stuffed in a storage room, their mouths taped to keep them quiet.

None of the raiders were familiar with the galley, so the work was slow. The facility was massive, and not all visible at once. There was a lot to take in. They found that one side of the galley had been emptied out, and everything that was left was consolidated on the other side.

They worked in pairs, looking for food cupboards and storage areas, and through each refrigerator and freezer. Rick darted between each group as they made a basic accounting of what they had found.

He grabbed Lee.

"There's not much," Rick said.

"Everything we can carry," Lee said.

They began arranging trolley carts, throwing on enormous hunks of meat in freeze-dried plastic packaging. There were cheeses and sacks of potatoes and vegetables. They took flour, pasta, eggs, milk, buns, and sauces. There were a lot of condiments. They found metal trays full of the fish catch, filleted and frozen.

Eleven carts went back, slowly through the halls in the dark, much more so being carried up seven flights of stairs before running astern on the Sky Deck, and carrying them back down to the Italian galley. The first flights of stairs took them under two minutes each. The last few, five minutes or more, with carts dropped and picked back up, food falling and being found and restacked by the light of cellphones.

They left two of their team behind, to pack the frozen foods in the Italian restaurant's freezer.

On their return, the galley raiders sent a scout first to ensure that nobody had noticed their activity. So it went, as they brought three trips of food down to the little galley near the Theater. What was left then in the main galley was not much, but they still argued over going back a fourth time. They were exhausted, wearing through even the adrenaline of the night. Still, Rick, soaked through with sweat, wanted everything.

"If we leave them something," Lee said, "they won't attack, not right away. It'll give us time to prepare defenses. This took way longer that I expected. If the next shift of guards gets up there and finds their friends tied up, in the galley, they'll set a trap. Just be satisfied with what we got. We should've kidnapped one of those cooks though."

They went downstairs, into the backstage entrance they normally used.

Lee stepped up to the Theater stage in the last dark before dawn. He called loudly for attention and began speaking. Only the track lighting along the aisle stairs was on at night, so that Lee could be just barely seen on stage.

"Everybody wake up and listen."

He only had to say it once, in his full stage voice, and wait a moment to know he had their attention.

"There's not enough food on this ship for everyone. Some people are going to get food and live long enough to get rescued, some people are not and are going to get sick and die. That's the fact. I sure didn't like it that other groups were in charge of that decision. I don't know what's gone on over there, why it is, but they're half-wild. It was those guys that ran off, those guys that stole the food, those guys that left us to die here. They're animals. They've been dealing with rapes and suicides. Animals. We weren't going to leave those people in charge of our fate anymore. We've brought the food back to our kitchen here."

There was a lot of noise and many shouted all at once.

"Are we still going to share it?" someone asked.

There was angry discussion going on across the Theater, trying to make sense of this newest development.

"You're not listening," Rick said, walking up on the stage. "There isn't enough food. We have the choice to live or die. Don't you understand that we've been caught in the biggest disaster that's ever hit America, or the world maybe? Do you think anyone is going to blame us that we took the food instead of waiting for them to cut us off? The only thing that matters is living and dying."

"And anyone who disagrees," Lee added, "can leave now, because you aren't welcome, and you aren't getting any food, and you can tell them down there that they're not getting any food. This is war now. If you want to live, you fight for it."

"I won't," Adam said.

He stood alone, near the top of the main seating, but all those who sat in the balcony or could not see him knew who it was.

"We are still men," Adam said.

"Then you'll die," Rick said quickly.

"We will all die," Adam said. "But you will die wrong. I won't."

Adam began walking down the aisle.

"Friend," Lee said, "I'm saving the lives of everyone here."

"No," Adam said, "you're destroying them. And I never was your friend."

He turned. Now he could see the entire Theater, even if only the outlines of people in the dark. He did not need to stand on the stage; he was a stage.

"Look at you all," Adam said to the rest. "You blind mob. You pack animals. You cast off your self into the mob, and think right and wrong can be cast off as well. This is your choice. If you think it's worth killing hundreds of innocent people so you'll have a better shot to live a few days longer, stay here with him. If you believe in God, if you believe in decency, and that there's anything in the human heart more important than how many beats it has left, then come with me."

Every little couple, family, or group seemed in intense deliberation.

"This is the time to decide," Adam said, "What do you stand for?"

He slowly began walking down the aisle to the open door at the bottom. Others stood in their seats as if to follow, and then, here and there some did: individuals, couples, and families.

Of those that stayed, some watched the ones leaving, others turned away, or hid their families from watching.

A man yelled for his wife. She was in tears, walking

awkwardly down the aisle, as others scrunched themselves up to let her pass. The man called for her, exasperated.

"You're wrong!" she shouted back. "You were always wrong!"

In the hall in front of the Theater, Adam gathered over forty people. They spoke very little, each consumed with the events moving their lives.

"I know a place we'll be far from here," Adam said.

They followed him up the dark stairs, up, up, so many flights of stairs, to the Sky Deck, then along that open space to the structure at the very edge of the ship, the solarium tower adjoined to the blasted bridge. Up one more flight there, they found the glass-enclosed hall dark under the cloudy sky.

"We'll stay here," Adam said.

"But what will we eat?" someone said.

"We'll talk with the group in the Atrium. They'll get the food back. There are still much more of them in the Atrium."

"But he's got a gun!"

"There aren't so many of them now, most of them left in the lifeboats!"

"I thought we left them so we wouldn't be fighting over food. What did we leave for?"

"Go back then!" Adam snapped. "Do you think things will be easier with those scorpions? Golding was right- at least one of the groups will die. But who has any reason to guess which it will be? Or whether, in the end, they won't all die? Who wants to stake their soul on it? Look out there!"

He pointed out the glass walls at the black sea and sky.

"This is what God has given us. Uncharted waters. We thought we understood the earth. Our own arrogance. We do not understand our own bodies, even. We think that, because such-and-such has never occurred before that it won't occur. But the world can die in a day. Every day of existence is uncharted territory. Every civilization on earth has a flood story. None of them saw it coming- there is no special warning that you live in momentous times."

He was so strong and full of energy, it seemed the fight with Lee Golding and the long walk up had only woken his full power. Then his voice dropped- the energy he projected was still there, but it was suddenly controlled very tightly.

"Let's capture this moment. Let's all remember how it feels to be this scared, this desperate, this far from human society."

They slept there. In the morning, when the sky became a lighter grey, but still before the sun could be seen, Adam took two others and went down to the Atrium.

37

The next morning Corrina walked down to the Atrium for breakfast with Darren, Travis and Gerry.

It was early; many in the lounge were yet asleep. Corrina knew before she made it down the stairs that something was new and bad. Though more isolated than on previous occasions, there were again the sounds of wailing and crying on the floor, the unhappy sounds carrying over the general tumult of angry voices from the still sparse early morning crowd.

There were no breakfast tables.

She stood off by herself with just Darren, holding his hand. No one in the crowd knew anything. There was no point speaking with anyone. She waited, a few children and mothers cried, voices argued. Then there was a different noise level from one end of the Atrium, and the crowd parted, and Hesse came through the crowd and stood up on his dais. Behind him, standing on the floor but still standing out, was the giant of a man Corrina had seen before, the one who had accompanied the gunman from the Theater.

The big bearded man alone seemed the same after those weeks.

"I've been waiting for enough people to get here before announcing it," Hesse began. "The galley was raided last night. The group from the Theater beat and tied up our guards and took most of the meats and breads...most everything. Lee Golding led them. The big guy with the gun. The same one that shot at some of you when you were trying to get out in the lifeboats. Now we still have some food! I'm sure that's the first thing that's on everyone's minds. We won't starve. We have food still, and we're catching fish. But it's going to be tough.

"The other thing," he continued quickly. "We now have an antagonistic force on board with us. We're going to have to deal with that."

In the sliver of a pause between Hesse's sentences, someone yelled out, "Who's that guy? He was with Golding before."

"This is Adam Melville. He wouldn't go along with the raid. He and some others left the Theater. They thought they'd better not come down here, all of them, in the middle of the night, so they're settled in another section, the solarium upstairs."

"Who's going to feed them?"

"We are," Hesse said.

The noise of the crowd was silenced by the sharpness of Hesse's continuation.

"But we're going to find a way to get that food back. We outnumber them probably three to one. I'll be talking with the Colonel about this. We will be getting control of the food back. I also want everyone to know that we've had progress with the electrical work that's being done. The back-up power is stabilized now where we need it most. They think there's a chance we'll get satellite communications going."

Several people yelled at once. "What's taking them so long?" was heard.

"The radio room was destroyed. You know that. They had to scavenge equipment and build from scratch down in the power room. Look, our engineering people are not even experts with this kind of gear, and they're trying to figure it out as they go. They've already gotten us the power needed to live. They'll get us in touch with the world. We have a group in the galley now going through what we have left of the food. The team up there will have something down shortly. I'll pass on more info as we get a better grasp of the situation."

Corrina was surprised there had been no more questions. She couldn't think of any herself. It was just another twist of fate that had been brought on them, and against which they were powerless.

She remembered the bus ride from Charleston when she was seventeen. She had run away from home and school with Sasha, holding hands on the bus bench, looking out the window as the country rolled by along the I-95. She was terrified. Everything was open to her, and there was neither shelter nor guardian for whatever waited in the whole wide world. She remembered Sasha crying as they left the state, but Corrina never stopped smiling until they stepped off the bus in Chinatown in Manhattan. She never was so excited again. However scary life was, it was hers to create.

Now, she was one of the helpless. She looked over the strange and familiar faces amid the gold pillars of the Grand Atrium.

38

Travis Cooke sat in Hesse's office with Colonel Warrant, the engineer Brenda White, and the refugee from the Royal Theater, Adam Melville. Adam Melville had two others with him, a man and a woman from his group, who waited outside.

Travis was not really sure why John Hesse always seemed to involve him in things. Perhaps it was his experience in emergency work. Maybe there was a trust built from fighting the first galley raid together, or of familiarity from that long ago meeting on the rugby pitch. Hesse just seemed to lean on him. Travis was both proud that Hesse had picked him out of the hundreds there as a kind of confidante and glad to have the opportunity to be involved, to actually have a say in how things were handled, and the chance to do things himself and to know they were being done right. He was also happy to have had the chance to speak now and then with Warrant and Brenda White, and Hesse of course, to gain the confidence that he had that these deputies did things right too. No matter how bad things were, Travis felt, you're always better off with competent people.

"We can cut their power," Colonel Warrant said. "We can kill the galley, cut their lights."

"We have to go right past the Theater to cut their power," Brenda said. "They'll be watching. There's that gun."

Everywhere they argued, there was that gun. Yes, and there's mine, Travis thought. Something kept him from telling of his gun. It was a key fact, and it was his alone right now. He wasn't ready to tell it yet.

"Why did we ever set up their power?" Brenda Wright said. "If we'd just said no, there would be no Theater group now. We could have gotten the satellite going, we could have told them there's a lunatic with a goddam machine gun!"

"It's not a machine gun," Colonel Warrant said. "It's an automatic rifle. You've been working on the satellite for almost two weeks now and we haven't gotten anywhere."

"I told you it needs time," Brenda said. "Sometimes you need to trust people who actually know what they're talking about!"

"Sister, calm down," Colonel Warrant said. "You've done good work, don't take things so personally."

"Calm down!" Brenda shouted. She stood. "Calm down! They have all our food. The tank is almost empty. The basins are almost empty. We don't know what we'll be drinking tomorrow. Jesus, what did we need a colonel in charge for? Were we hoping for a war?"

Brenda fell back down in her chair and heaved a great sigh.

Adam Melville offered to tell them what he knew of the vicinity around the Theater, and the layout between there and the Theater's galley.

"Forget that," Colonel Warrant said, "we know every inch of this damn ship by now. The question I have is, are you and your folks going to help us if we have to overpower them."

"No," Adam said.

"So you left those with the most food for the least people, to come live off us, who have the least food for the most people, and now you won't contribute to our cause?" Colonel Warrant said.

"Colonel," Adam answered, "We left them because we weren't going to kill others to save ourselves. Why would we leave those that already had the advantage to come to you, only to now do the same thing? We wouldn't fight you before. We won't fight them now. Golding is a bad one. But there's a lot of others in the Theater who are just trying to stay alive, and however your plan works out, there's going to be people hurt. And it all may not make any difference. I don't know whether we're going to live or die, but I know there's higher stakes. And remember something else: what you have left in that kitchen is not your food to give. It's all our food. And if you don't see it that way, you are Golding."

There was quiet, and Travis could see, among this small group, that some could respect that answer and some couldn't.

"Would you be a messenger?" Hesse asked. "A go between to see if they'll share the food, like we did with them?"

"What good will that do?" the Colonel said. "We can't trust them, and we can't leave ourselves at their mercy."

"We can learn," Hesse said. "We can find out how they're guarded, maybe how their galley is guarded. We can even figure out a way to know where the gun is- if the gun is busy in the Theater, maybe we can overpower whoever is in the galley. For God's sake Colonel, I don't want to walk into gunfire. Maybe we can get some scraps of food, enough for breathing room, while we figure out how to take them on."

"I'll do it," Travis said.

Adam never indicated whether he wanted the job, whether he would have taken the job. He simply nodded in acknowledgment that the job was Travis's.

Brenda spoke then about the electrical systems.

"The power is stable, but I don't know that I can get any of my men back to work with that gunman on the loose. The power room and the communication equipment are beyond the Theater, and with the compartments sealed off, there's just not that much choice in how to get down there. Even if we could get to the power room, the wiring to the Theater is shared with ours until right below the Theater. If we wanted to cut them off, that seems a dangerous place to be mucking about with a flashlight and wire cutters. Plus, we'd wind up thawing the food in their galley."

"Goddamnit, why did they put everything we need in the stern?" Colonel Warrant said.

Brenda looked right at Hesse and continued.

"On the other hand, if I did get in there, I could start a fire right under them."

"We were lucky to get the fires under control once," Hesse said. "We'd be suicidal to start one on purpose. Even if we wanted to kill them all."

He paused and they all were stopped on that thought, that it had come to that thought.

"Most of their doors are permanently shut since the

pirate attack," the Colonel said. "We need to know which doors are in use, and how they're guarded. If we could shut them in-"

"Then what?" Hesse said. "We starve them? Sooner or later they'll make a way out."

"Let me talk to them first," Travis said. "Let's give them a day to cool off. I'll go up in the morning and find out what I can find out and we'll see where we are."

Brenda went on about the water.

"For now, we still have water pressure from the tank, but we'll have to cut rations again."

"What about the catch basins?" Hesse said.

"We just can't rely on the catch basins," Brenda said. "If we go without rain for a couple days, we'll be real thirsty. However! There is another possibility. They all told me we couldn't run the desalination plant to make fresh water from sea water without the engines running, but I've figured a way. It'll take a lot of fuel. Which means we'd run out of power, sooner. It'll also take a lot of time, and frankly, I need to be working on the satellite link. But look, if it gets bad and we need to make fresh water, I think we could do it."

She looked from face to face trying to read their confidence or fear.

After the meeting, Travis wondered why he held back about the gun as he walked away.

He was uncomfortable and not ready to return to the Piano Lounge. He visited the Champagne Bar to see if the baby had recovered. He was disturbed by the news. The baby had responded to the antibiotics at first but then had gotten worse, not just the coughing but diarrhea, and vomiting any food she managed to take in. The mother looked half dead with exhaustion and fear.

Travis hurried to find Joel Conrad.

The Vikings Sports Hall had changed. Instead of music and laughter hitting him first, there was a cloud of marijuana smoke in the still air of the hall. The mood inside had changed. It was a zombie version of his first visit. As many were there as before, but the air was filled with smoke. The men and women looked wild, their faces and eyes intense and sickly. It was quieter. Some leaned back smoking. Others just leaned back, while a few lay motionless on the table or in their booths. The ship-wide epidemic of wet coughing was terrible in here, and a dozen or more chests rattled with their breath.

There was still rock-and-roll music playing, but there was no one behind the bar. There was a brick of hash, a plastic bag overflowing with marijuana. Scattered on the bar were assorted drugs and paraphernalia.

He found Dr. Joel Conrad sleeping in a booth, by a statue of Jimmy Connors. Travis shook him awake.

"Travis!" he said at last. "Oh, Travis. I'm happy to see you."

He stank.

"Joel, the baby is dying."

"I know," Joel Conrad said sadly. "It's the flu. Norovirus. The pneumonia came from the flu. We fought the pneumonia, but the flu never went away."

Travis protested with stammers and stutters, trying to force the doctor to see a solution, something they could try.

"It's this ship!" Conrad exclaimed. "The ship poisoned

her, it's poisoning all of us. The air is making the whole damn ship sick with fecal bacteria. In natural earth, our waste feeds life. Here, in this construct, our waste is destroying us. We make ourselves sick here."

"You can't quit on us," Travis said. "That baby will die."

"YES!" Joel Conrad stood. "Now you see! That baby will die, and soon! And then we all will die. Let me die in comfort and with some fun, is that so wrong? You all are going to get worse up there, and you'll tear each other apart. I don't need to watch that. I've done what I could, but there's no more to be done. We've got an abundance of fun here, hash and coke from the staff, weed from the refugees, and of course, there's the clinic. Leave me go out with a smile."

"Yeah," Travis looked around the zombie bar. "Have a blast."

He felt dizzy going back upstairs. He passed through the Atrium and tried to regain his focus on his mission for tomorrow. The faces in the crowd struck him: so lost, hopeless and stupid. Travis was no hero, but he wasn't weak, and he felt sorry for those who were — not weak necessarily, but weak compared to their circumstances. Looking at the faces in the Atrium, he felt sad for them. You could see it on their faces: there was nothing they could do for themselves. He wanted to do something for them.

He went out on the walking deck to escape the wretched air. The cool wind refreshed him, but the low, heavy clouds seemed to be weighing right down on them, as if the pressure of the clouds themselves were raising the tensions on the ship. On this side of the ship, all the lifeboats were gone and there were a score of empty davits hanging over the side.

39

They believed in Adam Melville because he had the strength to do what they needed to do, but could not. He had been on this runaway train into violence and conflict and he had jumped from the door, and shown them there was a place to land. He had gone against Lee Golding. They'd been intimidated by the giant that was the Mighty Lee Golding, but Adam wouldn't be. He had a big back they could all shelter behind.

The rain was back. It was loud on the glass roof of the solarium and it was dark inside. Adam was lying on his back, looking up. It was still early and others milled about or sat or stood in their small groups. They kept a distance from him, most of them. He could block them out as he looked up. In the darkness of the sky, an underside of a cloud was illuminated by the ship's spotlight. The heavens themselves were made seen by that light from the ship below, a cylinder connecting two spots in an endless darkness. That's what Adam saw.

He was becoming more comfortable with what had happened.

He'd always believed in God, sometimes perhaps with more definitive ideas of what that meant. But he always knew there was something, and if there were something, it would be participating in this. If there was one thing he understood that others didn't, it was that this was an Earth shattering event. Biblical. God would be involved.

Adam had always known he was special. He'd always been where he was supposed to be. Here was a flood, and he was on a boat, and the very fact of their lack of rescue after all this time testified that the world was gone, or crippled at the least. So God was showing himself through Biblical methods- whether this was self-referential of God, or merely a manner of showing Himself in a way he and others would get, Adam didn't know. Either way, God was communicating through that Bible, re-inventing the story of Noah and the flood, when the animals and people were kept safe on the ark as the corrupt Earth was cleansed.

And here he was, a giant of a man, with flowing hair and beard, and a loud, deep, clear voice. All he needed to complete the part of prophet was a robe, and he could get one in any stateroom. He chuckled. He was giddy, and embarrassed at himself for it. It was exciting, though. Adam forced the lightness from his mind and refocused on the seriousness of his position. There were many people to save.

In the night, he walked the ship. He liked the darkness.

Yea, though I walk through the valley of death. He entered an abandoned stateroom he knew of — between those like him who had lost their rooms in the attack, and the refugees, many of the abandoned rooms had found sub-letters. There were many fewer on board than there had been, but Adam knew of a few that were still empty. He also knew that there were floaters around, those that stayed in different rooms each night. In this particular room, he went to the bedside nightstand and found a Gideon's Bible.

He took it to the spa, part of which lay directly under the solarium. He had found cupboards full of electric candles, and he lit them, creating a pagan atmosphere by the pool. Soft light danced on the water. He stripped and dove in.

Afterwards, he sat in a lounge chair and read the Bible by candlelight. It all flooded back to him, each story, the turns of phrase, the mysteries and the certainties. He felt a kinship with the men and women of the book, the doubts and strength needed to face a rock-solid world that suddenly revealed God. He was up there till the dawn, then rejoined his people.

There were a few in prayer. There were always a few in prayer. It had only been a day and a half since they'd left the Theater, but it had been a long day and a half, and through it, there were always a few in prayer. There hadn't been much else to do. Those that had come felt less inclined now to travel the ship, to mix with the other passengers. So most remained in that one great room on the peak of the ship.

Adam kneeled and prayed himself, and when he did, many others began praying too. This time, Adam noticed. Prayers, he reflected, may be other than just pleas. They can be promises, praise or thanks. Yesterday, Adam had pleaded. Today he thanked — for life, and for the life he'd been given. For the world and for being separated from it in this moment. For the chance to know God.

As he prayed, a few of his men came up with the day's bread. They had volunteered as the food-carriers the day before. Adam paid no heed as they arrived. The food-carriers expected the onslaught from the starving group, but with Adam solid in his place, no one else went, and the food-carriers quietly looked for a place to set their trays.

Adam had now been a day without food. Seeing the tiny rations his group had received yesterday morning, he had resolved to suffer double the privations of the others.

When Adam finished his prayers he saw the food and went for his small portion. It was an awful bread, and some kind of potato stew. The stew wasn't too bad. There wasn't much. He wasn't sure if any actual meat was in it. Not in his cup. It wasn't too bad though, for a hungry man.

There were some dried herbs in it. Parsley. Thyme. That bread was awful though. He soaked it in the bottom of his half cup o' stew. When he was finished, just seconds really, the rest ate.

"I want to say," Adam spoke up, and the room listened. "I've been thinking a lot about what has happened to us. You are here because you know something. I don't care what religion you are, they all believe the same thing: that there is something eternal, and that being good matters. And we all know that siding with Golding was bad for whatever it is that we carry that is eternal.

"Once the Hebrews were slaves in Egypt. But what was their relationship to God then? No one had heard from Him in hundreds of years, since the days of Joseph. Then, bam. Miracles. Plagues. Exodus. Doubt. Redemption. I can tell you, I believe that a flood that destroys the world and leaves a small group alive on a ship, I believe God is there. We say everyday, how come

God doesn't show himself? How come nothing happens anymore like what happened to Noah? Well. Hello.

"I haven't spoken to a lot of you. Maybe you're not religious. But if you believe in God, how could you not believe he's here, one way or another? Maybe some of you don't believe this. Maybe some of you just came along because you couldn't go along with what Golding and them were doing. That's fine. I'm glad you came. But here is what I think. For us to be sitting here this long with no rescue, we all know what that means: the world as we know it has been destroyed. I think that we are lucky enough to have been given this chance, to be placed on this ship and saved from the flood, and given a chance to do right while God is watching. That may mean dying, but if God isn't saving us, I think we're beyond man saving us at this point. So the rest on this boat will die too. But we'll die in control.

"Where were you when the Flood hit? Whoever you were, whatever you were doing, the flood crossed your life and your life changed. You don't need to be the person you were. You've survived three disasters. Flood, attack, and abandonment by the world. Now, here, we are blessed. Our lives are short and our options are limited. We isolate ourselves. We live deliberately. We know our end."

None of them knew what Good looked like anymore, they were desperate to know it. Now it appeared as a giant man with a beard, and they were all prepared to follow it.

40

"Travis," Rick said.

Rick was holding the M16. He had spotted Travis approaching the restaurant.

Travis had given a special hug to Darren before leaving that morning, knowing he would be facing that M16. Travis had made his way around the Theater, from a distance. He'd spotted sentries at some open doors and ducked away before they'd seen him.

He wanted to learn what he could of the layout around the restaurant and galley before he presented himself to Lee Golding to talk. But Rick Dumas had seen him first.

"No soup for you," Rick said laughing. He had his hand on the pistol grip of Lee's rifle.

He showed no sign that he would fire it, and Travis inwardly ticked off a sigh of relief at surviving the first checkpoint.

"I want to talk to Golding," Travis said.

Travis could see into the darkened galley. Although it was daytime, there was very little natural light seeping through. There was some kind of light around a corner that provided a glow over the parts that were in Travis's field of vision.

Although he couldn't see any food, he could smell it. Something had been cooked recently, it smelled good, and he realized he was very hungry.

Rick saw the nostrils flare as Travis first felt that

aroma.

"You know, I had this one shore excursion booked," Rick said. "A culinary excursion in Helsinki. A wine and dine in a Finnish farmhouse. Reindeer steaks. Roast moose sausages, and pastries and berries. Bet that sounds pretty good to you right about now."

"You talk a lot, don't you?"

Rick paused. He chuckled.

"Let's go see Golding," Rick said. "Frisk him,"

A man came out of the shadows and roughly patted down Travis from his ankles to his armpits.

"Cruise security has been tight since 9/11," Rick said. "You know how it is."

Rick picked up his cell phone from the counter.

"What does your GPS say?" Travis said as he shook himself loose from the pat down.

"Wish I knew," Rick said. "Phone's only good for taking pictures now. Someday I'll invite you over for the slideshow. Let's go."

The Theater was beneath them. Rick and the gun and two other men walked with Travis down the stairs. They went into the Theater through the back entrance, to the dressing rooms behind the stage. There was more security: other refugees Travis had seen around the ship. They exchanged pleasantries with Rick and the other men. One of the two guards stared hard at Travis, the other looked around him and through him as if he didn't exist. They walked down a hall and around a corner.

The Mighty Lee Golding was asleep sitting back on a bench. His feet were on the floor, his legs straight and crossed at the calves. His arms were raised and his hands clasped behind his head against the wall, his enormous belly vibrating in snores with each in and out breath. They stopped in front of him.

God, you slept well when your side had the gun, Travis thought. He wondered what Lee Golding dreamt of; what was his perfect outcome now? Rescue? A safe and sane world to come home to, where he would be charged with murder? Did he dream that there was another gun?

Travis looked at Rick and the other two who still made no move. Travis kicked Lee Golding's feet, knocking one off the other and uncrossing the legs. His security detail tensed around him ready to take him down, but did nothing. Lee was quick to his feet. Not long to come from sleep to fight, this one.

The fight in Lee Golding died down as quickly and he said calmly, "What?"

"I'm making a quiche," Travis said, "Could I borrow a cup of milk?"

Lee Golding laughed, Rick laughed, the other two men laughed. Finally Travis chuckled.

"Hey, you never wanna lose your sense of humor, am I right?" Rick said. "I knew I liked you. Seriously, Lee, we oughta adopt this guy, he's good people."

"Seriously," Travis said, "we'll starve."

"Seriously," Lee said, "I don't give a shit, and I'm not adopting you. But I appreciate the levity. These are hard times."

"It's gonna get a lot harder," Travis said, "when all those people in the Atrium and the cabins get hungry enough, and you're stuck here in one little room on a boat, with one gun."

"It's an M16 buddy," Lee Golding said. "So you just pick which few dozen volunteers want to get shot first, and then bring it on. By the time you cowards are hungry enough to fight, you'll be too hungry to fight. This is a defensible situation we got."

"Yeah?" Travis said, "We've got a goddamn Army colonel, and an electrical engineer who has the whole ship figured out."

Lee went into the Mighty mode, with his full stage voice and face: "It ain't helped you so far!"

"Yeah," Travis roared back in a spot on impersonation, his eyes just as big and angry as Lee's, his voice as bombastic and self-important, emphasizing and slowing odd syllables. "And think how safe you'll feel with a thousand enemies outside your walls with no options but killing! And you're here touching up your goatee!"

"Is this how you ask for milk?" Lee said. "What the hell? You risked getting shot just to come here and tell me I'm not well liked?"

He turned to Rick and grabbed the gun from his hand, Rick letting it go like it was hot. Lee lifted the rifle, switched the safety, cocked it and checked the chamber for a round. He held it to Travis's face, nonchalantly with one hand. Travis stared up the barrel, down the arm to Lee. He studied the wrestler's face and saw in it some kind of question. Lee didn't know what to do. Travis turned to Rick and saw that the small man seemed drugged, coked up. His face was flush; Travis could see his neck throbbing with his pulse. On Rick's face was written: DO IT!

"How many rounds you got left?" Travis asked.

Lee lowered the gun, and then handed it back to Rick who had the unmistakable look of disappointment, of adrenaline unused.

The Alabama Assassin's hands came up more quickly than Travis could have imagined, crossing each other to grab the sides of Travis's head just as Lee's body spun and dropped, and Travis's head came down fast and hard over the big man's shoulder. Travis's limp body bounced up and back to the ground.

Travis lay absolutely still on the floor, his arms and legs flayed in snow angel form.

"Oh yeah" Lee Golding shouted. He made a V and wagged his tongue at Travis through it. "Golding gonna getcha!"

Rick stood over Travis's head and focused his cell phone camera.

"Cheeeeese."

41

A snake coiled across his dreamscape and looked at him.

"Smile," the snake said.

The snake opened its mouth and swallowed him.

Travis woke on the jogging track up at the Resort Deck. They'd carried him a long way, he thought. It was still daylight, barely. His head pounded, his jaw felt like it was broken in pieces. He lay still staring at the grey sky, a cold drizzle in his face, returning to the reality of where he was. He rose and in doing so saw a measuring cup on the deck next to him. It was filled with milk. He lifted it and smelled it.

It smelled a bit off, but it was white and swirled in the cup like milk. He drank. It wasn't too sour. It spilled down the jaw line, off his chin, and then he felt something lumpy and slimy go down his throat. He dropped the cup and ran to the railing and vomited. The milk was gone quickly and then he shook and convulsed as his stomach tried to force up stuff that wasn't there.

Lights came on and off in twinkles orbiting his face.

42

Jessica Golding had her own dressing room, the only individual dressing room. The star's room. Well, they had been booked first class after all. Lee didn't stay there too often. He didn't like being cut off, not knowing what went on beyond the walls. Lee was her eyes and ears, he told her everything.

Her husband had always been a strong man, but she had never seen him so intense, so self-assured. He had the gun. He'd killed the pirate. Most importantly, he'd been the one to decide that it was lunacy for everyone to die. He had turned this Theater into a haven.

He was her eyes and ears, and her hand in action. He was doing everything to protect her, damn any other casualty. She looked at herself in the mirror. If you die here, you deserve to die here, she thought.

She had never been beautiful, but there was something very alive in her that had made her attractive. She had long blonde hair that was frazzled and dead looking. On this ship, she had long since run out of, and anyway lost interest in, hair spray. The lines around her eyes and her mouth, the open skin pores of her cheeks, were no longer masked under makeup. They now defined her face. Her lips were still full and red, her eyes still intense.

She'd once cultivated flirting relationships with other men as a way of controlling Lee, but that had been lost to her since the flood. She had control of Lee now; that was undoubted.

Years gone by now, she had learned of an affair of Lee's with a fitness instructor at one of his gyms in Atlanta. It had been bold and offensive, carried out in front of mutual acquaintances in addition to Lee's business partners. The insult was so great her sister had implored her to end their marriage. She had not.

Lee's actions had been so blatant, like a child flaunting authority, that ending their relationship seemed no victory to her. Using the incident to increase her own control over her husband was fitting and just. Her husband was a strong man, and that made the victory all the greater. She loved him more since she'd flipped their power structure.

He came in to the dressing room with the gun. She knew he had a guard at the door, one at the end of their hall, and another at the back entrance, which led to the backstage area. They owned the Theater and the restaurant. But the halls and stairs in between were no-man's land. It was a nerve-wracking thing having only one gun with so many places to be, but what mattered most, in the end, was themselves. So Lee erred on the side of holding the gun if he was unsure.

He collapsed on the small couch. Since the war started, he'd been throwing himself down in exhaustion. She could see new lines in his face and knew his nerves were getting to him. That gun weighed heavy in his hand, and she knew, as she put her hands on him, that he was her hand but she was the blood that coursed through it. He was her muscle, but she was his strength.

She curled up with him. He took the couch all up himself, and she nearly had to sit on him. The gun was standing upright in the cushion behind his right shoulder. He put his huge hands around her thin neck and began to rub her shoulders.

"You look stressed," she said.

"Nah," he said.

This was his sanctuary. She was his sanctuary. But still she held herself stiff in his hands. The big hands were not at all gentle, working harder to soften her out. They hurt, but still she showed no sign, and he rubbed deeper. He was distracted.

"What happened?"

"They sent an ambassador," Lee said. "They're begging."

"They couldn't be that stupid to think after all this we'd just share."

"I'm telling you," Lee said. "The guy went up to the kitchen to beg for scraps."

"What did you do?"

"I knocked him out. With the Mighty Head Mash, baby!" Lee laughed.

"They're trying to find the gun," Jessica said. "They're probing you."

"Nah," Lee said.

He sat upright and moved her legs off his lap.

"You think?" he said. "What do you think they'll try?"

"Do you want to wait to find out?" she said.

"What can I do?" he said, "I already took all their food. I've got the gun. I've set up guards, rotations, alarms."

"And now you'll just sit back and wait?"

"Time is on our side, baby. They have no food, and

they're getting weaker by the day."

He got up and stood, shifting from one foot to the other, rubbing his hands together.

"They know that too," she said. "Do you think they're just going to roll over and die for us? They're backed into a corner."

"What more can I do?" he said, "What do you want me to do? I haven't got enough bullets to kill them all, you know."

"Do you need to kill them all to stop them?" she said.

He stopped moving, one hand caught in the other.

"No. No, there's just… that Hesse. The Colonel. And this Travis Cooke. Maybe the engineer. But what am I supposed to do? Just kill them for no reason?"

"You shot at them in the lifeboats," she said. "You took their food to kill them all slowly. But you won't kill them fast? What are you scared of?"

"I need to know what they're up to," he said. "I need spies."

He left.

43

Travis was in the stern when he awoke with his milk. He stayed outside just a few strides before picking a stairway that was exceptionally dark. It was never hard to find dark spaces on the ship with the electricity so drastically rationed. Mostly though, they all sought the light, and all that was active was in the light. Travis wanted the dark. It was relaxing, and there was something hypnotic of descending into it, imagining a place lit up on the other side.

He went down several flights without seeing anyone, then looked and listened for over a minute before venturing into the halls of one of the cabin decks. He was still in Golding's domain.

He found the abandoned cabin in the dark. His gun was where he'd left it, between the mattress and box spring of the untidy bed. He had guessed that he would be frisked. If he had brought the gun, he'd be dead now. He couldn't explain why he'd hidden it here, closer to danger than safety, except that he wanted it close at hand. What circumstances could have led to his being able to retrieve it if he had been in pressing enough danger to need it, he couldn't imagine, but he'd wanted it close at hand just the same. He knew there was a time for guns. He had felt they weren't there yet, yesterday.

Today, as he replaced the gun in Vera's bedroom closet, he thought he'd be using it soon.

He met up with his group at breakfast in the Atrium.

"What'd you find out?" Claude said.

"I don't know, not much. They seem like they don't have any plan either."

"What did you expect? Them to be working on a space ship?"

"I don't know. I guess I just hoped that someone had a plan for getting us out of here other than just fighting over who starves last."

"Well," Claude said, "I hope you like fish."

Breakfast was sugar, a thin slice of frosted cake and a quarter of a mushy fruit. Corrina kept quiet, smiling as she handed down Darren's napkin with the food. Darren did not smile back, and he too kept quiet. He was not well, Corrina thought. He'd borne it all so well when it happened, even the shooting of Norman, and she'd expected that first shock to be the worst of it. Bit by bit, the stabbing of the dead man by Vera, the shootings during the lifeboat crush, the continuance of everything, had turned him into something else. Darren was far away. He was a dirty, smelly automaton, more and more withdrawn, except perhaps in the playroom or while sitting with Claude. This day, his head still ringing from the Mighty Lee Golding, Travis tried harder. He began by forcing his own smile.

"Guess who has a birthday coming up?" he prodded the boy.

"I forgot," Corrina gasped.

"Do you want a birthday party?" Travis continued to Darren.

"How do you even know the date?" Corrina said.

Darren didn't answer for a moment, he withdrew into himself and his imagination, but then he looked up at his daddy.

He remembered his birthday party. His daddy and mommy and Gerry were all there, his cousins and the kids from his class, and the girl down the hall, and everyone was happy, and his mommy made a dragon cake. They had a treasure hunt. When he blew out the candles on the dragon cake he wished for more birthday parties with his daddy and mommy and Gerry all being happy.

"How?" he said almost inaudibly.

"We'll go the games room," Travis said. "They've got board games, and foosball. They even have Hungry Hippo. We'll invite your friends. And your dad and mom and Gerry will play with you as long as you want. We can do a treasure hunt. And your dad might just know where to find a band looking to do a show."

Darren smiled. His imagination took him to that place. Travis felt a hand on his shoulder, and peeked sideways to see Corrina smiling at him.

After breakfast, Travis stayed to talk with Hesse. The others walked back towards the lounge. Gerry spoke with Claude quietly. They told Travis they were going to take a look at the remaining lifeboats, and see if any could be repaired.

Corrina offered to go with them but Gerry had shook his head no, and spoke low so Darren couldn't hear.

"I'm worried about that psycho with the gun getting the same idea. Take Darren back to the lounge."

The way back, up the stairs, down the corridor, up more stairs.

"How come we're able to live with Daddy here?" Darren asked.

"Things are different now," Corrina said. "We want to be all together."

"Can we still be together after?" Darren asked.

"I don't know, honey," she said. "Don't ask about that now."

She knew how much it hurt Darren to be apart from Travis, however much he now loved Gerry. She knew also how much it hurt her to be apart from Travis, however much she loved Gerry. All that pain was still because of Travis. She wondered, was she strong for denying her love for him? Or just scared?

Corrina held Darren's hand. The corridor on the Penthouse Deck was walled in, not opened up to the Atrium, and was completely dark except for the thin track of lighting along the floor.

Corrina was grabbed with an arm across her throat so fiercely it knocked the breath from her and choked the air off before she could scream. The man shook her viciously, pulling her back on her heels and through a door he pulled opened with his other hand.

She heard Darren crying for her and running in after them into the room. It was brighter in here, the curtains were drawn across the windows, but there were some little slivers of light slicing the room. She heard Darren running and crying and the man pushed her down against a counter and turned. In a sliver of light Corrina saw the man's fist come across Darren's face so that the boy was thrown back into the darkness she could not quite see into.

"Run," she screamed.

She had a moment's freedom in the man's grip, and she turned to punch at him, connecting with his face, but the man didn't seem to notice it and pinned her wrists and pulled her into the living room, down onto the floor, tearing at her sweater, shirt and bra.

She screamed again for Darren to run, and was distracted by the thought of Darren seeing this. She went out of her body, and could see herself there, thrashing and trying to find air while the man held her throat and pulled at her pants. All she thought of then was the prayer that her son not be there to see.

He became more violent and it became more painful, and she began to cry. She blinked her tears away and saw the attacker's face for the first time as she adjusted to the darkness. He was just a boy, she thought. He could have been one of Gerry's tenth grade students. The boy didn't seem to see her, though he was looking right at her. Her eyes became full of tears again so that she could not see him anymore.

"I've been watching you," the boy said, panting. "You're so beautiful. I've been waiting. I've been waiting for this so long."

When it was done, the boy pulled up his pants and was gone. Corrina cried as she rolled over on her side, holding one hand around her bruised neck and one hand squeezed between her bare thighs. It hurt to cry. Everything hurt.

When she opened her eyes she saw at the same time as she seemed to first hear, Darren on the floor crying in the corner of the living room. She crawled towards him, pulling her pants up but undone. Coming closer she saw the blood on his lip; she remembered the fist hitting Darren's temple, and it occurred to her that he'd possibly continued trying to fight, until perhaps giving up, and she might not even have noticed.

When she reached him she embraced him, pulling him to his knees, she on her knees, and they joined together in crying to a synchronous beat.

When their crying stopped, a great silence came up around them. She pulled Darren to his feet. Her baby. She was overwhelmed with the idea that his life was broken and irreparable. They walked back to the lounge. They found their spot around a lounge-chair table unoccupied, and uncrowded by any groups at nearby tables, and they sat there quietly.

In a way it didn't happen. No one around her knew anything. No one was there to see that it had happened. There were no police to report it to. The only mark, its only history and existence, was the pain.

All her life she had spent overcoming her beauty. As if she had the power to do that. It was all just a joke. Any man could take from her whatever he wanted at any time. She'd felt so strong, as if she'd learned the secrets how to deal with the world on her terms. No, she thought, she never had learned to protect herself. She'd fooled herself into believing the world's protections were her own invention.

44

Travis found the Colonel alone in Hesse's office, and they waited together for Hesse to return. Hesse and Brenda White were doing their own recon work, checking for safe routes to the emergency power room, hoping Travis would have give them a bit of a distraction. Travis waited with Warrant.

"Brenda's stayed behind," Hesse said when he returned. "She doesn't want to have to keep crossing that gun."

"Anything touched?" Colonel Warrant said.

"Not really, no," Hesse said. "I don't think they've found it."

"If they haven't found it, they haven't looked," Colonel Warrant said.

"It's a big ship," Travis said. "That room's a needle in a haystack."

"Not at all," Warrant said. "They're not looking. So what are they doing?"

"Waiting," Travis said. "They've no plans, honestly it doesn't seem like the concept of a plan to get themselves off the ship has even occurred to them. Like they've convinced themselves that only some of us can get rescued, so if they can outlast us, they WILL get rescued."

"Anything else?" Warrant asked.

"They've got a lot of bullets left," Travis said. "I saw some magazines on Golding. But it's still only one gun.

Golding's sharing it, at least with that little guy, his name's Dumas, maybe with some others. The gun was in the galley with Dumas when I went there, and then they took me down to Golding at the Theater."

"How close did you get before they found you?"

"Well, there's just no way to approach the Theater or the galley without being seen. The galley's wide open, with glass walls and they have sentries around the Theater. Except, I was noticing the Theater doors are really heavy doors, without windows. So I wonder if there's any way to isolate the outside sentries, take them out without getting any attention, or just shut them off from the Theater somehow."

"How does Golding seem?" Colonel Warrant asked. "And the other guy he gives the gun to, Dumas?"

"They're nervous," Travis said. "I think they feel that since they have the food, we're coming after them."

"Well, they're right," Hesse said. "But they must know we're fishing, so they don't know how long we can wait."

"I don't think they have anything specific planned against us," Travis said. "Anything more, I mean."

"They will," Colonel Warrant said. "Stupid can't last forever. We've got to act soon."

"Even if we took the galley when the gun wasn't there," Hesse said, "even if we got all the food back here, what's to stop them from taking it again? They've got the gun."

"We need to take out the gun," Travis said. "It's the only way."

"He's right," Colonel Warrant said, "we can kill Golding, or we can kill all of them, or we can let them kill us. I think you'll agree, the most palatable option is the fat man."

"So how do we kill Golding?" Hesse said.

"I have a gun," Travis said.

If Travis had said he had a nuclear weapon or an escape rocket he would not have gained a more powerful response. Both men froze, their eyes and mouths open wide.

"Colt 1911," Travis said. "From a dead pirate. Seven bullets."

"HOOOOOORAH!" the old Colonel cried out.

Hesse fell back in his chair with his arms spread wide, laughing.

The Colonel clapped his hand and stomped his foot, and a painting fell off the wall, the glass smashing and they all laughed. They were intoxicated with hope.

They made him confirm several times the existence of the gun. When they began to calm, Travis told them he'd found it and had kept it hidden since.

"So how do we do it?" Hesse said.

"I'll do it," Travis said. "I'll kill him. I hate the guy."

He did too, he thought. He had an actual enemy he wanted dead. That was a first.

"Do you know how to fire a gun?" Colonel Warrant said. "Never mind. You'll have to trust me. I'm very good with a pistol. I'll show you my trophies when we get home. I'll kill the fat man."

"If we're gonna do this, let's figure it out now," Hesse said. "Time is not our friend."

"The restaurant is one deck above the Theater, and aft," Colonel Warrant said. "There are three staircases that are clustered around there. Now, there's one hall on the restaurant level where all these staircases arrive. There's an open view of it from the bathroom. If I can get in that bathroom-"

Travis shook his head. "They'd see you from the restaurant. They can see that whole hall if they're looking that way."

Hesse thought a moment. "You said they brought you down to the Theater, did anyone stay in the galley?"

"Yeah," Travis said. "There was another guy there."

"What about Theater side?" Hesse said to Warrant. "Travis managed to see the sentries without being seen, maybe you could."

"Very risky," Travis said. "I think to keep a real watch for Golding coming out, you'd be spotted eventually. Besides, I think he uses the rear entrance, from the backstage area. There's a sentry there too, but there are definitely hiding places around the corner from the sentry. If you just waited, you could ambush him there eventually, you'd hear him coming."

Colonel Warrant tapped his fingers quickly on the table. He was sitting, Travis was sitting, Hesse was standing, moving around, looking out at the Atrium mob and the faces that occasionally looked back at him hoping for something.

"Alright," Warrant said, "give me the gun."

"I haven't got it with me," Travis said. He'd been waiting for the request so he answered without pause.

"Well, where is it?" Warrant asked.

"Hidden upstairs."

"OK," Warrant said. "I'll do this tonight, in the dark.

I'll get in position and wait there till morning."

"Do you think going alone is best, or would you want a point man?"

Warrant thought.

"No," the old soldier said at last. "Two people is just twice the chance of being heard or seen. I'm better alone."

Then he smiled and showed all his yellow teeth and silver caps.

"I'm going to kill that fat man," Colonel Warrant said.

Travis left. He would return with the gun for Warrant tonight.

Golding, he thought, gonna getcha!

Up at the lounge, he saw Darren and Corrina sitting alone. As he got closer, he knew something was wrong. Without knowing why, he ran to them. Corrina burst out crying, and he put his arms around her. There were red marks all around her beautiful long neck. Darren just sat quietly and looked away.

"Just a boy. He was just a boy," Corrina whispered into Travis's ear.

45

He pressed her to his chest, knowing only the urge to protect her. She sobbed once more, then inhaled and held it, looked up and seemed to be waking, realizing where she was. She pushed Travis away, crying louder. He began to loosen his grip, trying to understand. She hit him in the chest. Someone grabbed his shoulders and threw him hard backwards and he saw it was Gerry, putting himself between Travis and Corrina. Travis instinctively reached to throw Gerry away when he saw the look of terror in his son's eyes, watching.

Travis backed away. What had happened? His family had been hurt, he knew. Now he had to stand back and let Gerry deal with Corrina. He raged at Gerry in the instant, then saw again his son and calmed. Overflowing with worry for him he grabbed Darren and held him tight. A dumb, sad expression on Travis's face, he smothered the boy, his right hand going up to the back of Darren's head, rubbing it and rocking it. He turned Darren so that Travis could look down into his face, and he felt himself breaking seeing the sadness of his son.

The six-year-old face was blank, but Travis seemed to see cracks deep down in the wet, red eyes. Travis felt as if someone had taken away his most precious thing, and that which he felt he owned most securely. He had nothing now that was his.

Travis's own face showed less and less emotion, the

longer he looked at the blank and loose face of his son, and he hardened in accepting the irreversibility of what had happened on this ship. Nothing that could have happened to their homes or to the world could have changed them like what had happened on this ship.

"He hit Darren," Corrina was saying quietly to Gerry, but Travis could hear. She was calming her breathing, trying to hold back the crying, "Darren was there the whole time."

That was all she said. She quietly began crying again, her shoulders hunched up to her ears, coming forward and shielding her lowered-face. Her face was blotched with dried blood and wet with tears and snot.

Gerry too held her close, and she again pushed off him. She turned and hid her head in the couch. Gerry sat next to her rod still. He was trying to control his own rage. It was like being submersed, trying to swim out as a wave tossed him around and around. It was a feeling he'd not had since his teenage years when rage was all he knew. He wanted to destroy somebody's face. He was a skinny man but strong, his wiry muscles were all tensed. He was being torn to pieces, pitying his wife and longing to erase her pain, while bursting with red energy to beat somebody.

He became aware again of the presence of Travis, of Claude who had come in with him and stood well back from the scene, of the dozen or so others in the lounge who were watching, none even bothering anymore to pretend to not.

He bent his head down to hers and their foreheads touched, so that they each looked down and not into each other's eyes. She allowed it. Finally, he cried too. But the violence in his belly did not cool. He didn't want to leave her, and time seemed to just flow by without touching them, he and her, Travis and Darren. At some point, Professor Claude had disappeared from their circle.

Others came and went from the lounge.

Finally Travis picked up Darren and left. The two victims were one to him, his family, but he knew Corrina didn't need him and Darren did. He felt guilty even to be calculating that much to guide his actions, as though the proper thing would be to turn into a beast and tear off for blood. He couldn't turn it off, his calculating.

They walked a long way without much talking. Travis held him close and rubbed the back of his head and said, "It's alright. It's alright," knowing nothing better to say or truer than that lie.

They passed someone in a hallway that Travis recognized from the Atrium. Otherwise it was deathly quiet. They found a stairwell that was closed to the world and they climbed up to the Resort Deck. Then they walked further forward in a hall banked all by glass on one side. They went into the spa and Travis still held Darren as he sat down in an upright linen chair. Darren felt cold. Travis wanted to heat him up, but he felt so cold himself, like his furnace had shut down. His heart was broken, and no more heat emanated from there.

"I love you," he said. "Darren, I love you so much. I'll be here for you, always."

"Will this ever be over?" Darren said.

Travis was struck by how that beautiful voice was just as it sounded yesterday, and before any of this started. It sounded just the same but the boy was so different.

"I don't know," Travis said. "I don't know what will happen but I will never leave you and I will protect you."

He kept on that way and imagined he was speaking to Corrina. For a moment he faltered, his voice halted and he held his breath at the sadness that he couldn't even do this for her. He recovered himself and kept on, and he felt somehow stronger to be telling his son something he knew was true. He knew just how much was false, how much changed with circumstance, but he saw that love was a basic fact and immovable.

He held Darren quietly a long time. Darren was still sick and his breathing was labored. Travis looked out over the pool and realized it was different. It was clean. Someone else was using his pool, and they had found the chlorine.

He looked at Poseidon, still in the shadows, staring with milky white eyes over the room.

"You didn't," Darren whispered.

"What?" Travis said.

"You didn't protect me and mommy."

Yes, he had broken his promise to his son. The ship had done that to him as well. This ship made right action impossible. He had failed to protect his most loved ones and they were broken. He had sat back and waited to be saved, trusted in God and in other humans to keep them safe. He had the second gun on the ship, he alone, but he hadn't used it. That gun was part of the family now. But to what end? To what end did they struggle for each breath? They fought like roaches for crumbs.

The world out there had always been awful, he knew

that this had been the rule of life, and their modern American bubble, the tiny bubble of their time and place, was popped. The rule of life was pain, and it was also the rule that those that loved the most endured the most.

Since Darren had been born, Travis had understood that love brought happiness and terror. Life with his beautiful wife and their gorgeous boy was intoxicating, but nothing beautiful lasts. If he'd had a mission in life, it was to protect this fragile child from the specter as long as he could. The child was broken, Travis had failed.

Three years ago, his wife left him and his father died in the same week. He had just returned to work in New York after taking leave for his Sudan mission, so he could not take any more time off his job. When he buried his father, his wife was there, with his son. She walked by him in the line of mourners.

"I'm sorry," she said.

She gave him his son to hold and walked away, and Travis held the little boy in the car to the graveyard, putting him down only to lift a shovel and throw dirt on his father's coffin. At some point, his son and wife were gone.

The day after he buried his father, he was called to a fire scene in Williamsburg, an old warehouse converted into loft condos. The fire was put out while some people were still trapped in their rooms. Travis was part of the team finding survivors and bodies. He came upon a man alone in his room, lying on the floor, moaning. Smoke came from his body.

"You're going to be alright," Travis said.

He took the man's arms to drag him from the room,

and the skin came right off him. Travis fell, and heard the man breathe out one last time.

That had been the worst week of Travis's life, until this.

Time seemed lost to them. It became night and Travis realized it when he saw the ship's white strobe lighting like a false full moon on the bottom of a low cloud. He was struck with guilt for being away from Corrina for so long, and for keeping Darren without eating. As they walked back the hallway was dark, there was no emergency lighting along the floor here and the cloudy sky offered little solace for them through the glass wall. Travis could sense the inner wall along his left shoulder and walked straight, never stumbling. The staircase too was dark. He held the railing and they descended.

Corrina sat next to Gerry, but there was a gulf between them. Gerry sat staring, his chin on his fist, his elbow on his knee, looking absolutely frozen. Travis thought of the statue The Thinker.

Corrina was on her feet coming at them, it seemed, without even having looked up to see Darren coming. She took him gently from Travis's arms. The boy put his arms around her and patted her on the back and they seemed to just drift, as though they were blowing away altogether in a wind. The mother and son were each broken and spilling out, and only together did the leaking stop.

46

Lee's spies were refugees. A third-year student from Fordham College and a grocery store clerk from Yonkers.

They approached the Atrium walking the hallways quickly but not in any way looking suspicious. Colonel Warrant had been described to them in great detail, and they had seen photos of Hesse and Travis from Rick Dumas' cell phone. They took the long way around, finally approaching the Atrium from forward on the ship and reversing back. Here and there they ran into folks they hadn't seen in some time.

They had dismissed the idea that they'd be recognized. Before the raid, they had each spent time around the ship, they didn't feel their faces would seem new to anyone. Yet as they came from the stairs onto the Atrium floor, and the dull grey light of the skylights so far above, they felt their otherness all the same; they seemed healthier, stronger than those they passed by. There was a rotting stench in the air, like the place was dying. The mucousy coughing filled the air at all times, like crickets chirping at night. The spies were scared now, but excited.

They closely examined the first few old men they saw, imagining Colonel Warrant, but the weakness of those they met could not match the description Rick Dumas and Lee Golding had given.

There was the office, where they'd been told it would be. Inside were Hesse and the Colonel.

The student and the clerk paused in a small encampment of several groups about fifty feet from the shop front. That was as close as they dared. The silence in the room was oppressive. The grocery clerk scanned the faces and saw utter resignation. The difference to his own community in the Theater was stark. They had each passed the same amount of time on the Festival, yet those in the Theater were still alive, still spoke to each other, found ways to pass the time. These hundreds were walking dead.

The student was not watching the Atrium, but the office. This was John Hesse, who Lee Golding had railed against. That Hesse who had anointed himself to protect them all and failed, that had allowed a panic, and the loss of the food and fuel with the lifeboats, who had shortchanged the Theater just because they were out of sight and who ultimately hadn't found an answer to the big question: How would they get off the boat?

The student didn’t see it. There was something in the face of this Hesse that contradicted that history. Hesse had that look, like someone who didn’t make mistakes. Even in the positions each camp was in, the student’s side had the food and the gun, yet he wondered if he wouldn’t feel safer with this Hesse.

Hesse was speaking to Warrant but no sound escaped the office. The face turned and the student could see his eyes. This man did not look starved, scared or resigned.

The student seemed lost in the image and shocked to see Hesse out of his seat and coming through the door into the Atrium floor, their eyes still locked. He was coming towards them fast, getting bigger and more real.

The student turned and ran. The clerk saw his partner go, saw Hesse and Warrant break into a run and turned too, but too late. As he took his first steps, Hesse already was on him bringing him down.

Now there was life in the crowd, the clerk thought as he saw the feet jumping all around him and felt the weight of Hesse pressing down his chest and head into the floor.

The Colonel was after the other, up the stairs.

"Stop him!" Warrant yelled.

A man above them on the stairs reacted confusedly, stopping in his steps as the student burst past him.

Up one flight, two flights, Warrant stayed with the boy, and then without second thought, he gave up the chase. The student looked back and saw Colonel Warrant falling against the wall in exhaustion, grasping his chest. He was gone. He ran until he reached the exterior promenade. It was empty and he continued at a jog around the big bulk of the ship, home to the Theater.

He thought of that Greek guy who ran home to tell his army of some battle somewhere then dropped dead. They named the marathon after him or something. When he finally reached the backstage level and slowed to a walk he broke out in a sweat. Through the security, knocking on Lee Golding's dressing room, he was soaked. No shirt to change into. Ever.

Lee Golding emerged quickly, wearing his gun. The door was open and the spy could see Lee Golding's wife watching from inside the room, reclined on the couch but very much alert.

"They got Wells," the student said. "He knew, Hesse,

he just looked out his office and he knew, he came right after us and they got Wells."

Lee Golding's face drooped.

"Did you learn anything?" was all he could think to ask.

"No," he said. "I don't know. I don't think so."

Lee Golding's big hand came over his face and he shook his head. He was getting a sick feeling. He grabbed at the blonde beard that had grown in around the original silver goatee.

Why was there only bad luck, this stupid, useless bad luck to get in the way of everything?

47

Travis left them and went to get food. Colonel Warrant and Hesse were not around, so Travis returned quickly to feed his group. After, he would return with the gun.

Only Travis ate. Some kind of fish stew with bread. There was something wrong with the bread, he thought. They didn't have the right ingredients anymore. He couldn't guess what it might be. He didn't know bread. But it wasn't right.

He slipped back into the hallway. He found Vera's stateroom and let himself in. She was asleep on the couch. She didn't sleep in the bedroom anymore, and she was always sleeping. Travis let himself into the bedroom, finding it quietly in the dark.

When he came back out and shut the stateroom door from the hallway he again had the emergency lights along the floor to give him at least a general sense of his surroundings. Travis sensed someone else standing just by him.

He was punched in the face then thrown against the counter.

Travis had his arms and knees up in an instinctive protective posture before he even registered that someone was attacking him. He was rained on with blows in the dark. He was bent over double. The sounds were a cone of heavy breathing, grunts, clothing rubbing and fists thudding into his ribs and shoulders and cracking his face and head.

Travis drove himself into the man, getting his arms around his waist, moving towards the wall. But the angle was bad and Travis's head hit the wall along with the man's ribs. Travis went down, but he took the man with him. Travis saw him as his face came close to the emergency lighting. It was Gerry.

Gerry was on top of Travis while Travis was still dazed from the wall. Gerry frantically grabbed around Travis's waist and groin and Travis felt him retrieve the gun. Then only the metal of the gun reflected enough light to be seen, so it seemed a free-floating gun was pointed at his head.

"She's my wife!" Gerry said. "She's my wife! I'll kill him!"

He trembled violently, got up and fell back against the wall. For so many years he'd kept that ball of red violence hidden inside him, and now he had let it come up, he wanted it unleashed, he wanted satisfaction only blood could bring. When he came for the gun and found Travis there first, he knew why. He knew Travis wanted the blood that was his. The rage commanded his actions.

Travis could make out the gun as Gerry lowered it. He understood that even the right to defend the woman he loved was not his.

"OK," Travis said. "You'll kill him."

Gerry couldn't respond. He tried to wrestle back down the rage, tried to calm his breathing.

"How did you know about the gun?" Travis asked.

"I found it," Gerry said at last. "I was looking for something for Vera."

Travis came next to Gerry, both their backs against the wall.

"We're going to kill Golding," Travis said. "That's why I came for the gun. You've got three hours. Then I need it back."

Seven bullets, Travis thought. How many would they have to kill in the end?

It was a short walk back to the piano lounge. He approached Corrina and Darren. He wanted to stop time then, forget Golding and just stroke his babies. He got closer and saw that Darren was crying into his mother's shoulder. Time didn't stop quite; it slowed. It felt like a long journey to get to his family. Then he was next to Corrina, and Darren was turned to him, Travis's arm heavy across Darren's back.

"Don't, Daddy," Darren said. "Don't, Daddy."

"Don't what honey?"

"Don't leave me, Daddy."

Time stopped.

48

It was a plague upon them and they wondered why. A bacterial infection passed within hours through all Adam Melville's group, and they were all sick. First they became weak and cramped. Then, unable to move, they vomited and shit themselves in the solarium. It was a nightmare within the nightmare.

They rolled on the floor and moaned in agony, feeling a depth of depression and lowness few had experienced before. They could not focus on anything outside themselves and their pain. The sickness felt like a path to death, and many wished for that, but it did not come.

Adam felt a burning shame that he could not control his body, and show strength to his followers. He wondered that all those around him could live through this same pain. He began to see a great fireball in the center of his pain, and then visions began to spin across the flame, so quickly that he could not grasp them, only feel something.

He was grasping at these images, seeing them in familiar computer guises. He felt his point-of-view spinning in some computer data-space, with encrypted information he could see but not decode fast enough as it spun by. The data spun around his head like a cyclone. He felt he was going mad.

Hours went by, and the sickness of his mind was so great he no longer felt the sickness of his body. He lost touch with his body altogether. His brain broke into fragments, and they each spoke with different voices, over each other and unintelligible.

Hours went by, and then others began slowly to regain control of themselves.

As the flashing lights left their eyes, they saw themselves and their place, and they wept, and others began to emerge from their sickness. The cramps continued, they all cringed with the pain in turns, but they were no longer isolated within themselves. They began speaking again to their neighbors on the floor, whether they were part of their group they'd come on board with or strangers they'd come to know in the Theater or since leaving the Theater.

Adam finally stumbled to his feet, as filthy as the floor.

The visions were gone. The voices were gone, and his brain was coming back into a whole. The floor was sturdy and the room was solid again around them.

He looked around and cried at the pain he saw in these people trying to be good. He dried his eyes quickly.

"All of you who can walk, follow me," Adam said.

They helped each other, ten of them in that first group, following Adam, who carried a woman himself. Adam took them down a difficult dark flight of stairs into a hall, down the hall and to the spa. There were windows and the grey light came from outside. Adam led them through the change rooms, and to the great pool.

He stood beside the statue of Poseidon at the edge of the pool. He jumped in. From his fouled bathrobe and clothes came a diffuse cloud of his own mess.

The others followed him into the pool. All the while Adam tried so hard to focus on his people, he could not stop his mind from reaching back into his memories, searching for the visions, the voices, the data, to review them again in this new sobriety.

They took more down to the pool. Some stripped out of their outer garments and washed themselves in their underwear. Others threw out all their clothes and took bathrobes. The pool got dirtier and the people got cleaner. Over the next hours, the bug ran its course and the last of the group became able to stand and make the trip to the pool. Adam's mind began to find fragments of the things he'd seen and felt during his sickness. Biblical quotes and references, fitting together as lines of a computer program.

The dead face of the man he had shot kept appearing too, haunting him.

Over those hours of walking and carrying the sick, as ideas coalesced in Adam's mind, the unintelligible sickness visions began to have some meaning. Themes and directions emerged. Central to it all was Suffering.

He wondered if he should tell his people about the voices. They would think he were mad. But how could he make them believe if he didn't tell them? What would he tell them? He didn't understand himself, he felt a veil of reality melting away but couldn't quite see what was behind it.

As they returned, they abandoned their room under the solarium glass, and took the adjoining restaurant. There was no joy in the change in their personal cleanliness or the cleanliness of their room. The pain was too powerful. The tears and wailing flowed.

Adam stood in the restaurant, his massive body bent strangely, but his face strong.

"I remember a joke."

He tried to smile, to calm himself.

"Its weakness is that it's not very funny, as a joke. Some young fish are swimming in the ocean when an older fish swims by. 'Morning boys,' he says. 'How's the water?'

"One of the young fish turns to the other and says, 'What's water?'"

Adam looked around.

"Yeah, nobody ever laughs at that one, but I like it."

Slowly, they sat themselves up and comported themselves like people.

"God is in everything," Adam said. "Hundreds of years from now, people will look at every event on this ship and wonder what God meant by it."

"Excuse me," came a woman's voice, strange to them.

They all turned and saw two women, one old, one middle-aged.

"We heard about you," the old woman said. "We were in the Atrium. But… can we join you?"

Adam smiled. Even a few of the others smiled.

"Welcome," Adam said.

He didn't need to talk about the voices in his head. He was the voice in theirs.

49

The spy was in a chair. He was not tied. The only other person in the room was John Hesse. Hesse's knuckles were bloody. The spy's face was broken. Hesse leaned back into the breakfast bar of the suite and readied his pen and paper.

The spy spoke with broken teeth, and Hesse had a pretty good idea how the Theater was guarded.

They'd take precautions, Hesse imagined. They'd guess the spy might talk. The information might be meaningless. Everything they did might be meaningless. But there was great satisfaction here. So he beat him further, then carried him in a fireman carry up and outside to the promenade, where he tossed the spy to the deck.

The spy appeared before Lee Golding, terrified of returning, terrified of staying away. His face was unrecognizably beaten, but Lee Golding knew who it was.

"They..." the spy stammered. "They... they...they are many. And we are few. That's what he said."

50

"You have to be strong now," Jessica said to her husband in the Theater dressing room. "It is a question of strength now, which of us will win."

"Yes," Lee said. He leaned against the counter, the gun in his lap. "But smarts too. The gun's an advantage but it's not a nuclear bomb. There's still much more of them. The gun can't be everywhere. I can't be everywhere."

"That's why defense is suicide!" she said. "What are you, now? Do you choose death like Melville? For God's sake Lee, open your eyes. This world is full of cowards and children who won't see. What are you, now?"

"Their numbers are a sleeping dragon!" Lee responded. "Do I want to wake it? Do I want to give them no choice but to fight?"

Smarts had always been his secret. He was so imposing physically; he always knew that his size was a double advantage, because it made them underestimate his smarts. This was a thin line they walked, he and Jessica. To survive each day longer, for one more day's chance at rescue, he had to make every decision correctly.

She did not see it that way.

"Lee, Lee," Jessica said. "I've always believed in you."

She stood to face him, then turned and stepped away.

"I stood by you through all the mistakes you made, all the missed opportunities, because I believed that somewhere at your kernel was a strong man who could protect me. Has our life been a lie?

"You have the gun! You! Won't you use it while it can still do us some good? If you won't protect yourself, don't you have the pride to protect your wife? If we keep reacting, we'll die. We need to step outside the script. The world before was never big enough for our story, our love, Lee. This is where it should be."

They had not had sex in weeks; in the absence of bathing, the prospect had disgusted her, and Lee had given up asking. He did not ask this time, he took. Jessica responded as physically and urgently. The huge man and the thin woman everywhere at each other with their mouths and hands, clothes coming off, forming to each other's forms into the corner space between the couch and the counter, onto one and then the other. They were the last couple on earth. The rest were dead to them. It was an intoxicating commitment.

While they embraced and reached for each other they flew from the ship, from the war, from the flood. For the first time, they both were off the ship. It was such an unconscious relief that their passion soared, perhaps as a protection against that world breaking back in. They felt like titans making love, a mythic pair existing in ether with the great lovers of all time. They had transcended their fate and their worlds.

At some moment, the world broke in and they fell from the sky. They lay on the couch and moved slightly away from each other. It was impossible to ignore the smell. He dressed and she tried not to look at him, slick, discolored, slimy.

She recaptured a vision of the two of them, all alone and safe on this great empty ship, with enough food to wait as long as it would take. She felt happy. She admitted to herself that this was her happy ending: herself and Lee, alone surviving. A King and Queen of the ship.

"I'm going to save us," Lee said.

"What do you want me to do?" she asked.

"You stay here, and stay safe," he said. "I don't want you to have to see this."

"No," she said. "I want to be by your side. You'll be stronger with me."

They dressed. He picked up the gun, and pocketed the extra magazines. Had he been destined to be here? Had he been meant to be a man of instinct?

Lee had targets in his mind. He wanted to explain his thinking to Jessica but felt more powerful assuming her trust in his decisions. He wondered how that gun had come to his hands; but it hadn't come to his hands any more than the other hundreds in the Theater. Lee had taken it. There was proof of what he was.

It was exhilarating, as much as it was exhausting, nerve-wracking. Life mattered to him again, here. The stakes mattered. He wanted to be the last man to keep his wife alive and un-raped. He would protect Jessica. What was the matter with that?

But who was he going to kill? Hesse, or that Colonel? He had realized he'd have to kill someone since she'd said those words. He didn't know who, but he knew he had to kill someone. He'd killed before: the pirate he'd taken the gun from. The night of the lifeboat drill, he'd probably killed a few then, though he never knew for sure. But those were things that just happened. Instinct, again. This was different. It was planned and he was overthinking it.

Exiting their room they passed the sentry with a nod, and turned towards the Theater. Did he want to address everyone? Did he trust them? What did they need to know? To do? No, he would keep this simple. He would trust the hard things to himself.

On the stage, Jessica stayed back in the shadows. The dark, really, as the whole Theater was in shadow. Rick wasn't in the room. Jessica wondered if he were on duty somewhere.

They were all alive in this room, she thought. Men, women, children. The dead have piled up elsewhere on this ship, but those who made the right decisions — and had the right luck — were here. They were weak, sick, and dirty, but not the walking dead Lee had described of the other groups. Some had left, over time. But no one that mattered, at least since Adam Melville's group. Fewer mouths. Fewer to protect.

She shivered with an understanding. What a risk these people were! Why was Lee protecting them? This room, these people were not his army, they were his shackles. Even if Lee struck at those in the Atrium, could they ever be safe with these shackles?

Lee was watched whenever he was in the room. When he called the group to attention, the focus did not increase significantly.

"We're in lockdown. The Atrium is planning an attack. That's all we know. I'm going to find out what I can."

He held up the gun.

"I can go places no one else can. I'll find out what's

up. Jessica will watch my back. I'll go fill in Dumas. He'll be in charge of the sentries and anything that comes up. The sentries know everyone, you all know the sentries. No one else gets in. Any questions?"

There were never any questions. That's why he asked. Lee had a way of saying friendly things while holding the gun that let you know not to ask questions.

Back into the tunnel, past Jessica's dressing room and the larger dressing room that served as the bathroom, holding the porta-johns. She wondered how they went about the emptying from the Atrium? It was an undertaking in itself here, and it always required the gun. She imagined they were overflowing in their own filth by now. They weren't a group there, she thought, they were just those that weren't in the Theater.

Lee thought a few things through on the walk. It had to be Hesse. Hesse slept in the Atrium, along with so many others. But Lee knew a habit. Lee knew where he took his fresh air. Lee had seen him once, and after one of his sentries had reported it too, Lee had followed up with some snooping. Hesse was on the port-side walking deck usually a couple times a day. Rain or shine, though there had not been much shine. So he had opportunity. Then, although the Colonel might be more dangerous, Hesse was clearly the leader. So if he wanted to make a statement, there was none bigger than Hesse. So he had motive.

Motive, opportunity… I must be the killer, Lee thought. Plus, he hated Hesse.

He thought of his championship matches. The grueling night his stardom began, the pain and sweat and that big finish, lifting the 400-pound Moondaba and slamming him through the table. His arm raised, with a separated shoulder, at the center of 70,000 screaming fans at the Houston Astrodome.

When he reached the Italian restaurant, where Rick Dumas waited, there were five other men there, with several more in sentry positions nearby. When they didn't have the gun in the restaurant, they had some numbers at least. They also had a system: each next sentry was close enough to hear the one before him, all the way down to the Theater. So the gun was really always at hand.

Lee had his hand on Rick's shoulder. He had resisted Rick's forays into personal friendship for a long time, but at some point Lee found that Rick had earned his trust. Still, he kept Rick in his place. Lee did not have friends as equals.

"I'm going to make sure they stay scared," Lee said. "Keep the sentry plan we've got, I won't be long."

"Why don't I come with you?" Rick said. "You don't want to bring Jessica into this. I can help."

"There's no extra danger in coming with me, hero," Lee said. "If I go down, everyone here does too. Get some meat for dinner."

Even in the battle for their lives, there was something in Lee's words, the voice, that cut Rick. As if Lee were mocking him in front of all the sentries, the Theater, and his wife. He may not have been as strong as Lee, and sure, Lee was the leader and protector. But Rick was no coward, and Lee would have been dead a long time ago without his help.

51

After the incident with the spies, the Colonel rethought his assassination plan and decided he needed to improve the odds. Golding had a far more powerful weapon than he, but Warrant had two advantages:

Lee Golding didn't know about his gun.

They controlled the electrical grid.

He would visit Brenda and arrange a new tactic: At midnight, Brenda would kill the power everywhere around the Theater. The galley, however, would be lit up. This wouldn't require new work: they had secured power to all the galley circuits, only most were kept off to conserve energy. Brenda could turn those lights on.

Killing the other lights, in the Theater and hall, while leaving the galley powered would be a challenge, and possibly a dangerous one. Mostly, it would take time.

So Colonel Warrant didn't wait, he went unarmed to get Brenda started.

Warrant had a route that he had considered safest in evading unwanted notice, but he was always on guard. There weren't any safe routes to the aft of the ship. The lighting was dismal. Through the service corridors there was no emergency lighting, and only the low level lighting from the few stairwells broke the darkness. Warrant counted out those breaks.

As he passed one, a vision appeared in the space of the opening. Then the monster was upon him, a hand at his throat and three hundred pounds of body weight forcing him against the wall. Warrant knew who it was. He wondered why he hadn't been shot. His hand went to Lee Golding's face, but the bigger man pulled back and slammed him into the bulkhead a second time.

"Kill him!" he heard a woman's voice whisper desperately.

Warrant couldn't fight. Lee Golding was on top of him, crushing his lungs. He felt how weak he was. He grasped and struck at the monster in the dark, but to no avail. The breath escaping his mouth he knew would not come back in. The blood coming up his throat, coughing out, was life leaving him. His body had rarely failed him before. His had been such an effective machine: a body always able to manage the tasks assigned to it, a body that could be trusted to perform. He knew he could not sustain the effort he needed. He'd been starved for weeks. Now he was dead.

Lee Golding sprung back to his feet from the body, his knees unsteady. He spun and landed against the wall. He could hear his breath echoing in the space. His breath. His life. The other one gone.

"I killed the Colonel," Lee said. "I did it."

The wall seemed to lean, like he was strapped to an almost upright operating table, moving through strange angles. He regained his balance and was loose in the space. He felt weightless, bouncing.

He didn't know why he hadn't shot him. It had happened so fast. They'd heard the Colonel and stopped in the stairwell. When he saw the Colonel, the Colonel turned, and he sprung at him. Instinct, again.

"How will they know?" Jessica asked.

"Jessica, I did it," Lee said.

"I know, Lee. I know what you did. But how will they know? His people? What good is it if they don't know? Lee — you're hurting me."

He saw he was squeezing her arms.

He wiped his hands on his pants and realized they were slick with blood.

52

Gerry lowered himself down a dark stairwell in a part of the ship he hadn't been to in weeks. Funny that, they'd been here less than a month and he had routines, routes he took, places he stayed. Despite the relentless boredom, he no longer explored the ship. Now it was obviously wiser to stick to one's territory, but even before the raid on the galley, when there was no war on the ship, he had found a rut.

He had the gun in his belt, in back. He knew how to use handguns. He was in a state of bloodlust. He wanted nothing more than to kill someone. In the dark stairwell, he could not stop from seeing the back of Corrina's head, her face tucked into his shoulder.

She was shuddering as she spoke.

"He was young. He had a baby face. Big eyes, big lips. He had a red striped t-shirt and he smelled awful, like vomit."

He wasn't one of the Atrium crowd. He might be in a room, but most of them came out to the Atrium eventually. Gerry couldn't remember a red striped t-shirt on a boy like that. There were three places where he'd most likely be.

The bar. Travis had told Claude about it, Claude had told Gerry. Gerry had seen a few guys over the weeks that took their own carts of food, obviously okayed by Hesse. So Gerry figured that's where those guys went; the rest must just stay put and get the food brought to them.

Second would be the solarium. The Theater peace freaks. Gerry had asked around and learned where they were camped out.

Finally, the Theater. That would be the last place to try.

Gerry knew he was at the right deck from the stairwell. There was a smell here unlike anything else. Vile. Rotted. "He smelled awful, like vomit."

There was light in the portholes along the hallway, and there was the bar. The stench was more intense yet as he approached the yawning entrance. It was quiet, but not silent. There was noise of movement. When Gerry came around the corner to see the full bar, he saw dead and living mixed at the tables. The flesh of the living, or moving, was as discolored and rotted as the dead. There were flies. He wondered where they came from. Life feeds on life, but it thrives on death.

There were medical vials and needles on some of the tables. Hard liquor bottles.

"Hey," a man said as Gerry stepped past his table.

The man was hunched over, his head on the table, his arm flopped on the table as well.

"Hey," the man said and Gerry stepped over to him.

"Food?" the man said. "Dave is dead. We need food. Dave is dead."

Gerry stepped away and continued his tour of the place. Others reacted, raising their heads and regarding him. Some of them smiled. Others still half-asleep. But there was no crying here at least.

There was no red t-shirt.

He looked behind the bar. A young woman lay dead. All the shelves were empty.

Gerry turned and walked past the tables to the door.

"Hey," the man near the door said.

Gerry turned but did not stop.

"I'm a doctor."

Gerry stopped then. His long frame doubled over, his head dropping towards the man, staring at that near dead face, the yellow eyes and grey skin. This was the man Travis had worked with, all those weeks ago. This was that handsome, strong, assured man.

"Yes," Gerry said. His hand went on Dr. Conrad's shoulder. "Are you alright?"

"Awesome," Conrad said.

Gerry was frozen there, staring at that zombie face. Then he backed away with his feet, so that his hand fell off Conrad's shoulder. He turned and left and did not slow his pace until the stench was behind him.

The anger was still an engine within him, but he had many stairs to climb to the solarium, so his pace did slow. He saw the back of her head again in the dark.

"He was young. He had a baby face. Big eyes, big lips. He had a red t-shirt and he smelled awful, like vomit."

He walked through dark hallways, all his muscles tense, expecting anything. As he had as a boy out too late, trying to make his bedroom without disturbing his mother, passed out on the couch in front of empty wine bottles and a lipstick smeared glass. As he had as a teenager, robbing the corner grocery store with the cheap lock on the rear door. As he had as a young teacher, carrying on an in-school affair with Deirdre, the girl with the off-the-shoulder sweaters. As he had just two years ago, staying over in Corrina's apartment and sneaking past Darren's bedroom before dawn, and four weeks ago, exploring the halls of the Festival of the Waves after the pirates had smashed their engines and killed the millionaire.

When at last he arrived at the solarium, his eyes had to adjust to the light, even the grey light of this day. He saw a room covered and walled in filth. He vomited. He kept his hands to his knees, holding himself from falling into the mess. As he recovered, he heard voices.

He followed a clean path across the floor to the restaurant, where sick individuals sat haphazardly and clutched at their stomachs. They looked dirty and messed up. Many were in bathrobes or underwear.

Some of them turned and saw him. Some smiled. He knew they knew he was not one of them, but he felt welcomed. Then he saw a red striped t-shirt.

The young man was about fifty feet away, across a tangle of others and several restaurant tables. Gerry walked a wide path.

The boy was with an older woman. Gerry could see the two, see it was his mother. He had a baby face. Big eyes, big lips.

These two weren't wet or in underwear or bathrobes. They were new. The more he saw the boy, the more he hated him and wanted to kill him.

A moment behind everyone else, Gerry looked to the far side of the room. Even behind the group, Gerry had no problem seeing Adam Melville, nearly a head above everyone else. Adam Melville spoke and everyone listened.

"Things are going to start happening," Adam Melville said. "We need to talk about these things."

"Those we left have taken the food from others. Hundreds of people are starving to death in one place, while another hundred are starving more slowly in the other. One side has a gun, the other side has desperation. The conflict is inevitable, and it will be complete.

"Things are going to get very bad on this ship. And you have to ask yourself, why would God put us here in a lose-lose situation? Now, we're sick and pained, and all I can think of is a dog with an electric collar that shocks to get him to stop doing something. I think God is telling us what he wants us to do.

"'For I know the plans I have for you,' declares the LORD, 'plans to prosper you and not to harm you, plans to give you hope and a future.' Jeremiah. God does not want his servants to die in this furnace. My God is for the strong, strong enough to face the truth, not run and hide from it like rats with bloody claws. We have to see, and face, that all those things that we see and touch are unreal and temporal, and that what is invisible is all that is real and eternal."

There was an energy in the air. Gerry felt this. This giant's voice was like an electromagnetic field, attracting all it touched. Gerry wanted to dismiss him as nuts, but he couldn't deny. There was something about Adam Melville that made him seem special: touched. A conduit to something. Gerry's cynicism softened. Just enough to want Adam Melville to be special, to have a message for them. But it was a daydream ended again with the sight of the boy, and no voice outside could still the one inside that demanded life's blood.

"We had to suffer to be saved. But God doesn't want us to keep suffering. God wants us to come home," Adam Melville said.

The boy and the woman clasped hands. All he had to do was lift the gun and press it against the boy's back and shoot. His hand tensed on the gun, and he felt his whole body as a weapon. His mind was burning. The woman leaned her head on the boy's shoulder.

A great struggle took place within Gerry. In an instant, the fight was over, the gun replaced in the waist of his pants. He wiped his eyes, tensed his body one more time to rid himself of the fighting spirits, and regained his calm. He wouldn't shoot the boy now. He had him. He'd have the chance again. He didn't have to kill him in front of his mother. The rage listened to reason within him. He would have him alone soon.

Yes, God wants you to come home, Gerry thought. I can help.

53

Blue skies
Smiling at me
Nothing but blue skies
Do I see

Blue birds
Singing a song
Nothing but blue birds
All day long

Never saw the sun shining so bright
Never saw things going so right
Noticing the days, hurrying by
When you're in love, my how they fly

Travis had Darren in his lap. Corrina sat in the chair to Travis's right. Claude Bettman played piano and sang. Travis didn't know if Claude knew what had happened to Corrina. Actually, he knew Claude knew, but he didn't know if he'd been told. He once again felt warm towards Claude, as a healer, as a safe place. The song could have been sung to make it an insult. It could have been bright and happy and made Corrina quite mad. But Claude played it so that the piano was a meditation, walking above the line between happy and sad.

He sang it with the anguish in his voice of someone

who had been on this cruise ship. It was a lament of the Israelites in Babylon, a picture of beautiful Zion sung in an honest voice that told how away Zion was. To Travis, it was an embrace of Corrina that he couldn't give her. He didn't know if Professor Claude knew she loved Irving Berlin music. But he knew enough.

Travis had considered searching for Gerry, but he'd realized the futility of it quickly. Gerry wouldn't be long, and Colonel Warrant's mission could wait another hour. He had all night to get in position. Travis wondered if Gerry had gone to the Theater. They might have lost both Gerry and the gun. Or Gerry might have made Warrant's mission obsolete.

So Travis stayed with his family and waited. Nothing to do but wait and listen to the music.

Blue days
All of them gone
Nothing but blue skies
From now on.

The door from the deck crashed open and with it the sounds of the wind howling. In the grey silhouette was Lee Golding with Colonel Warrant over his shoulders. Lee Golding bent and jerked and tossed Warrant off to the ground. He stepped in over the body and his wife came in behind him. There were the usual handful of groups and solos spread around the lounge, and they reacted with one long, loud wordless exhalation

"That's your Army boy," Lee Golding said. "He wanted war. Well, he got it. For God's sake, the rest of you be smarter than Army boy."

Travis was on his feet moving in when he realized he was the only one.

"Take it easy, man," Professor Claude said.

"You're sick!" Travis said. "You're worse than the pirates! You've never felt so good about yourself, have you?"

Lee Golding held the gun up, but casually.

"Note that I could kill you. I could kill your kid and your wife. Note that I do not. Yet. It will be for all of you to decide. You can stay here, and live as best you can as long as you can, and hope. If you want to kill yourself, the ocean's out there. Don't drag everyone into your suicides."

A shot came from elsewhere in the salon, and the wall-length window behind Lee Golding exploded. Screams came from the two score refugees here who dove for the ground, or burrowed into the hidden couches in their booths.

Travis was on the floor and crawled on his belly back to his booth, wrapping himself over Darren and Corrina on the floor. Lee Golding was on his knee, looking for cover and the shooter. Jessica crouched behind him. He had his gun up. He didn't know where to fire. He began to back up out the door, pushing Jessica behind him. He switched the gun to automatic fire. He rose to his feet, one arm grabbing Jessica, the other holding the gun up behind him. He fired a burst randomly. The other gun fired again, a distinct voice in the room. Lee Golding screamed as he disappeared from sight.

Gerry sprinted across the lounge, past his wife and her

son, and Travis. He went out the door, scanning the deck.

The room was immediately colder as the wind filled it through the open window. Heads popped up between the booths. Gerry returned.

"He's gone," Gerry said. "We'd better get down to the Atrium. He could come back."

With the howling wind, the group seemed silent as they gathered themselves together and quickly made their way from the room that had changed so quickly from a shelter to a corrupt and dangerous place.

Gerry and Claude and Travis looked at each other, and turned and went back to throw Colonel Warrant's body to the sea. Claude and Travis picked him up while Gerry covered them with the gun. Darren and Corrina waited by the door. Darren did not cry now.

Lee and Jessica ran along in that wind, astern. The ship had grown much more dangerous for them. There was another gun. Lee Golding was no longer super-powered.

54

Brenda White never knew of Warrant's plan to kill Golding. She knew only her work.

Brenda had been, for weeks, a Dr. Frankenstein, working in a dim windowless lab, more and more isolated and alone. She was a tourist on the cruise, and she felt like a tourist in this lab. Communications and power generation were far from her expertise. She was writing freshman Kirchhoff diagrams trying to get the best bang for the buck from the emergency generators. It wasn't much.

She wondered if the there was a Nobel Prize in Foraging and Scavenging Unknown Technology.

After the initial epic work on power and water, she'd devoted herself these several weeks to communications. Here the equipment had been pasted together from the remnants of the original radio room. It had been painstaking, working out methods to bypass or recreate destroyed circuits had been a devil's task. After days of frustration she'd changed tactics, working out her own equipment from first principles. The ship had had two distinct physical systems for satellite communication, one for the on-board phone and data connections, one for Internet use. Brenda combined the systems, and where she found broken elements, she bridged them from scratch rather than attempting repairs.

Brenda worked long hours again. She'd begun talking

to her tools and equipment. She'd built special relationships with her multimeter and soldering gun.

She had been in this room a long time, but now she would go back to the Atrium, because she just might have a working receiver. For the first time, she felt her work might save them, might get them off the ship.

Brenda turned the cabinet of electronics on with a switch. Her headphones crackled. She felt electrified: she'd done it. She'd made a connection. No one but her, of the thousands aboard, could have done this.

The voice of the satellite was there:

THIS SERVICE IS DOWN. PLEASE TRY AGAIN LATER.

THIS SERVICE IS DOWN. PLEASE TRY AGAIN LATER.

Brenda's knees buckled and she fell to the floor, sliding the headphones off.

She was an engineer and she saw the world as problems to be solved. Now, she knew the problems were bigger than any solutions, and their rescue had never been in their hands. She sobbed, and her body quivered on the ground in front of the great wall of wires she had devoted her efforts to.

When she finally arose, she looked at that wall as she gained control of her breathing. She grabbed her chair by the backrest and swung it smashing at the electronics until the lights in the wall were dead, screaming all the while.

55

"Golding killed Warrant," Travis said.

Hesse did not speak. His eyes opened wide, then his face hardened.

They couldn't go to Hesse's office. Everyone was yelling at Hesse, if they had closed a door, someone would have knocked it down.

Travis and the others from the lounge had arrived in the quiet Atrium. The amount of time it took for Travis to reach John Hesse was the same amount of time it took for news of Warrant's death to spread around the room.

That trust in Hesse and Colonel Warrant, that combination each had of charisma and projected competence, had kept all these desperate, starving people from challenging them in any way. Now Warrant was dead. The trust in Hesse was shattered.

As the news spread, the shouting started.

"Hesse!"

"Hesse!"

"We're lost! Where are you taking us?"

"I'll kill him," Hesse said.

"No way," Travis said. "I have the gun, Hesse."

"Hesse!

"We're watching them kill us!"

"Where are you going to find him? He'll have sentries, you won't be able to get near him."

"Hesse!"

"What are we doing?"

Hesse snarled at the crowd

"Can you all be quiet? For God's sake, I need a minute to think, then I can tell you what we should do, and you all can tell me to go to Hell or we can fight back. But I need this minute."

He turned back to Travis.

"He knows about the gun now. We need to flush him out. We'll cut his power. He'll be out, and you'll hear him in the dark. He won't even be able to see you."

"If he's in the dressing room, he'll go out the back, he's got sentries right there, he'll think its safe. I'll wait there, around the corner. You get to Brenda and tell her what to do."

Hesse turned away from Travis. Travis slipped through the crowd, which had tightened around them. Hesse climbed on to his speech-bar.

"We're going to have to fight," Hesse said. "We only have a few days food left, and we can't just let him kill us as he pleases."

He didn't want to tell them about Travis and the gun, but they needed to begin preparing in case Travis failed.

The crowd was shouting back at him.

"He didn't kill one of us, he killed one of you."

"We have to fight!" Hesse said. "We have no food. And what if he finds our communications work? We could be in touch with the world in a few days."

"Why don't we just wait then?"

The crowd overtook Hesse, arguing over fighting now or waiting for satellite communications. Hesse let it play for a minute. When the level and frequency of shots slacked, he spoke.

"We can't wait for someone to save us. Every day we wait, we get weaker. Every day, he will be working to improve his own defenses."

"What do we do, Hesse?"

"We need to get ready to fight. Golding has spies. We caught one. But because he has spies, we can't just openly talk about our plans."

"THIS ONE IS! THIS ONE IS A SPY! THIS ONE IS A SPY FOR THEM!"

"What?"

Heads turned to look. The Atrium was considerably sparser of bodies than when Hesse had first climbed the bar weeks ago, so that he could easily see the speaker, and the man he was pointing at. He knew both men. Both had families.

The man being pointed out squirmed and looked around.

"I followed him! I saw him go to the Theater, talk to the sentries, then Golding. I followed him a second time and the sentries let him right in!"

The man ran, but was summarily grabbed in a number of hands and arms.

"Please! I just needed food for my family! My son is sick!"

He was enveloped in blows. More tried to join than could get into the space around the man.

"NO!" Hesse yelled.

He ran into the human shell around the man.

"Please no! NOOOO! Albert! Albert!" a woman cried.

"DADDY! DADDY!"

Travis came in after Hesse.

"Stop! For God's sake STOP!"

With each man, their peeling him off the scrum seemed to break the spell and their resistance dropped.

Albert was dead.

Hesse was stunned for a moment. He then grabbed two of the men who stood over the body still.

"Get his body out of here!"

Travis staggered. At once he understood what had happened: they had killed a father for sacrificing the group for his family. Something that they all would do themselves, to one degree or another. But you couldn't make that play and fail. The violence of the group awaited.

"There's nobody out there!"

On one of the open staircases electrical engineer Brenda White shouted at the group.

"Sorry everybody! Didn't mean to get your hopes up! No one home! No answering machine!"

The Atrium wail. It had become part of life.

Brenda stumbled like a drunk down the stairs. Her husband and girls came to her and hugged her.

Brenda White straightened up and found her way to John Hesse with her family trailing and grabbing at her.

"It's time to use my powers for evil," Brenda said.

"We've got a job for you," Hesse said.

56

Travis Cooke kneeled by his son.

"I gotta go, buddy, but I'll be back soon. You just remember Daddy loves you."

He was going to kill a man, or be killed. There were still hours before sun-up, and he was going to kill him this night, just as they'd intended with Colonel Warrant. Brenda White had been sent to her work, to disable the power in the Theater.

He remembered playing basketball with the Mighty Lee Golding, the thrill of teamwork with that larger-than-life man. If things had been different, they would probably have been friends. Only the situation revealed what Golding really was. He wondered about what friendship could mean: in a different place, a different story, you'd be trying to kill each other.

Travis stood and looked at Corrina. She met his eyes for the first time since the rape. She was sad for him.

With one look back he captured his son's face in his mind and went away holding it there. Gerry and Claude Bettman walked by his shoulders, up a dark set of stairs.

"What were you doing with the gun, Gerry?" Claude asked. "If Travis found it, and Warrant was going to use it, why were you carrying it?"

"It's a phallic extension, Professor," Gerry said. "It

makes me feel confident."

"Huh. You're funny, Gerry," Claude said. "You're a terrible shot. That man is 350 pounds, standing broadside and you couldn't get him."

"Yeah," Gerry said.

"You a killer?"

"I always thought of myself as a man of peace," Gerry said. "I'm not rash, I'm pretty patient and calm. Even keeled."

"But you lose your temper sometimes."

"Yeah."

"I don't see our friend here as a man of violence," Professor Claude said. "In fact, I think he's very poorly cast for this role."

"I'm not looking for any critic's awards," Travis said.

"You know what kind of movie this is? A tragedy. And on this Ship of a Thousand Wrongs, you're making the mistake of this whole cruise," the Professor said. "Golding doesn't want to fight. You're bringing the Reaper closer for everyone, not farther away. You have a son back there, and you're walking alone into a machine gun and three hundred haters. What is the matter with you? Look we've had a lot of yucks these last few weeks, but you're going to orphan your kid."

"Shut up, Claude," Travis said.

"Or what? You'll shoot me? Having a gun doesn't make you the hero, partner. This is not the movie you think it is. This is the one where a boy's mom gets raped, then his dad gets killed."

Travis grabbed Claude by the shoulders of his jacket and rammed him into the wall. The jacket tore, the two of them tumbled down the stairs, to a landing.

Claude and Travis disentangled from each other and stood quickly.

"I'm the one trying to protect Darren, not you," Claude said. "Go ahead and kill yourself."

Claude started down the stairs and Travis started up.

"The unbearable lightness of Darkness," Gerry said, walking a step below Travis.

"I'd rather go alone from here," Travis said.

"I'm going with you, Travis," Gerry said. "I can't let you go in there alone."

"We've got one gun. An extra set of hands isn't going to help. I need to be small, get in, and get out."

"You're not going alone," Gerry said.

"No. Gerry, if I don't make it back, Darren will need you."

Step. Step. Step. The breath of the men was their only communication.

"I'll take care of your son," Gerry said. "And I'll take care of Corrina."

"I trust you," Travis said. "You're a good man."

"The other day Claude and I went to check the lifeboats," Gerry said. "One of them needed some repairs, but we can start it now, and the davit isn't too bent. And there's another one, the boat won't start but it seems seaworthy and I think we can get the davit to work. We'd just drift. But we'll be off this boat. I wanted to talk with you about it before, but I didn't know how we'd get any food. Now, I think anything's better than staying on this boat."

Travis nodded in the dark.

"Get off this ship," Travis said. "Tell Darren how much I love him, and tell him I said to be brave no matter what, and if he wants to make me happy, to live. When he's old enough, tell him how sorry I was for what I did."

"I'll never remember all this, Travis, you'd better just survive, thank you," Gerry said.

"Forget it," Travis said. "If you get off this ship, get off this ship. Be a whole and complete dad. You don't need a ghost over you and neither does he. Just forget everything I said, and take care of him."

Travis walked off, and Gerry's breathing slipped away.

"Save a bullet," Gerry said at last.

Travis knew the halls well, which would be black and which merely twilight. He picked his way aft, then up to the Penthouse Deck, one of the top two enclosed levels still open for the whole length. He crossed over the closed-off compartment, and again disappeared down a dark stairwell. It was a long walk made very slowly, carefully rounding each corner, stooping to peer down each stairwell, listening at each closed door. He would wait at the lower Theater exits. The top exits were barred. At the lower level there was one open exit to a side hall, as well as the backstage exit to the small lower lobby. He had to be able to monitor both exits.

He gripped the pistol tightly. He knew he was getting close, knew where the sentries were supposed to be. He also knew everything might have changed since Lee Golding's killing Warrant. So Travis took his time. He had arranged for a long lead-time with Brenda. Brenda would be in danger too. The power could only be cut directly below the Theater. If Travis heard shots down below, he'd have to improvise.

He heard his own breathing, slow and controlled, the hush of his step rolling on the carpet, his shoulder brushing a corner. He sometimes imagined he could hear his heart beating as well. It was almost pounding in his chest, but he kept his breathing slow and controlled, listening for all other noises. This last hall was lit along the floor, but not well enough to see more than 20 feet ahead.

He expected sentries soon so he gently opened a door, let himself into an empty room, and waited in the dark for the lights to go out.

Twenty minutes later, he heard screaming. Panic. He put his face to the crack in the door. Brenda had done it. The hallway was completely dark now, the low-glow emergency track lighting shut off. He waited for any dangers to pass. The shouting went on, a reaction to the sudden loss of light in the Theater.

He came out and made his way forward into the heart of the dark and the dangerous.

He made his way quietly but quickly. Where he expected sentries there were still none. Then he heard two men talking:

"One of us should go in and find out what to do."

"Just let him finish and see what he says."

Travis realized how close he was to the Theater. He could hear Lee Golding's voice, loud enough to echo through the dressing rooms into the hall where Travis crouched.

"This is not an accident! They're flushing us out! If we go, we're dead. We're safe in here, we have the lower doors locked from the inside, and sentries outside to get me if they have to. We are in lockdown, and we stay in lockdown. If they want to come to us, it'll be the last mistake they make."

They don't know you don't have the only gun, Travis thought. But you do. That's why you want to stay in there. So now I have to come after you.

"FIRE!" came a shout from one of the sentries nearest Travis.

Travis saw them moving towards another corridor; he saw them because there was a glow coming from out there somewhere.

Somewhere below, Travis thought, Brenda must have touched together some wires that shouldn't have touched.

"FIRE, STAY IN THE THEATER!" a sentry yelled.

Will do, Travis thought.

As he slid behind the two sentries, he saw the fire, spreading from an open stairwell, a good twenty feet from the door backstage. He could make out the door now and found the handle. The door shook, locked from the other side.

"Who is it?" a voice said nervously.

Travis did his best Rick:

"It's Dumas you idiot, hurry," Travis said.

The door opened a crack. Travis saw eyes. Eyes saw him. Travis fired the gun, and the sentry fell inside. Travis grabbed the door and let himself in. There was renewed screaming from the Theater in reaction to the gunfire. Travis was out of the glow of the fire now, again in the dark, moving himself forward in the hallway quickly.

Now he was a killer. He didn't let himself think of the

man he stepped over, but he felt the label written on himself permanently.

"Everyone stay put," Lee Golding was shouting. He was close, in the backstage hall.

He could hear Lee Golding's footsteps, then he heard the sentries calling from out in the main hallways.

"We got the fire door closed! The fire is contained!"

Lee Golding repeated the shout back to the Theater: "The fire is contained. Everyone stay put. We have someone in here. We have someone in here who doesn't belong."

There were tense minutes. Travis had made his way towards the Theater itself. He expected Lee Golding's attack each moment.

In the dark, he felt, heard, and smelt the presence of three hundred humans and knew he'd entered the open space of the Theater. Travis moved in the dark space, keeping the gun protected in his belly as he touched bodies on each side. One of these would be Lee Golding. He was so close.

Say something again, Travis thought. Show yourself. Open that big mouth and listen to yourself sound so heroic. I'll shoot a hole right through you.

He felt the size of the man he bumped into, heard the quiet exclamation and lifted his gun. Before he could fire his arms were gripped. The gun was pointed away.

Lee Golding squeezed him tight. Golding couldn't let go, Travis thought. If he took a hand off to go for his own gun now, Travis's pistol would be quicker.

"You'll die here," Travis said.

"Maybe," Lee Golding said, "but you'll die here

today."

"LEEEEE!" came a woman's voice.

"LEEEEE! LEE HELP!"

The voice was hysterical.

Travis's head snapped back as his nose burst open, and pain shot through his brain. Lee had head-butted him. He rolled away into the protecting darkness, his world illuminated once more by red star bursts in his eyes, coloring the searing pain. Lee Golding's loud footsteps went away from him. Travis struggled to his feet.

"What's going on?"

"WHAT'S HAPPENING?"

"Stay put!" Lee Golding shouted from somewhere, "Stay put everyone!"

Travis was off after the voice. Stumbling, bouncing off others, Travis made the dressing room hall.

"LEE! HURRY!"

"I'm coming!"

Me too.

Around a corner, and they were backstage. There was light. A line of fire; a fiery tongue in the mouth of the backstage hall. Somehow the fire had beaten its containment by the sentries. There was a line of fire along one wall right out the door at the other end, and in the light there was Lee Golding's wife, halfway to the door.

"Hurry, Lee!" she cried.

"What is this? How did this happen?" Lee said.

"Just come on!"

The two rushed down the hall together. Travis raised the gun and fired at them. They kept moving, Lee fired back and Travis flattened against the wall. I'm being shot at, he thought, with a sudden feeling of how far his life had changed.

Then the door was opened and closed. He ran for it, and for a second time the door held him fast. He heard the screaming behind him. The fire had reached the Theater and it was spreading. Travis went at the door with his body. He gave it everything, and the door moved just a hair and Travis knew it had been blocked with something. The fire was filling the hall behind him. The screams had reached a new pitch from the Theater. Travis was burning. The smoke was trapped. He struggled breathing. His asthma took hold; his chest tightened. He held the door with one hand, the gun with the other and tried to stay on his feet.

The screaming behind him was hysterical now. Some were surely in the flames.

The door shook from the other side.

"Help," Travis croaked and he wondered if he could be heard.

"Hold on, I'll move this!"

He heard the clanging of heavy metal objects.

"She did it! She spread the fires!"

The door swung open and Travis tumbled out, into the hall. There was again a weak glow in the hall from the fire. The fire stretched from the backstage door across the hall to the stairwell Travis had seen it in originally, where the sentries had supposedly contained it. The fire doors were closed, and Travis wondered if White had caused a second fire.

"I saw her do it!" the man who had saved Travis yelled

at him. He was one of the sentries.

He stood by a heavy bench, and a tumbled over statue.

"I tried to stop her, but there was a wall of fire. She screamed for Golding, and I had to hide."

Travis tried to regain his balance, clear his mind. The man tried urgently to explain what he'd seen.

"She opened the fire door! She had gas or something and she spread the fire right into the Theater!"

Travis was bent over and could not see the man. He could hear the voice above him. His breathing was getting worse. He felt quickly sapped of strength, but his eyes slowly began to resolve images, and he made out the shape of the man standing over him

"Wait. Who are you?" the man said.

The man moved. Travis shot. The man screamed. He staggered back and fell to the floor on a section of wisping flames and glowing ash.

Travis staggered backwards. The man didn't move. Travis's breathing came again.

Travis fell to his side against a wall, listening to the screams in the Theater. Every once in a while they came closer as some made their attempt down the hallway, and then the pinnacle of horror as the blazing fire there penned them in.

Travis toppled as he tried to stand, then he tried again. He made it, in a crouch with his arms out for balance, like a drunken surfer. He slowly straightened his knees and gained his full height. He went looking for Lee Golding.

Back in the dark, Travis struggled upstairs quickly. The screams still came. He found the hall he wanted and turned towards the Theater rear exits. It was hot.

He heard their voices.

"I did it," she said. "When I heard of the fires I knew it was our chance to be free, really free. I ran to the kitchen and got the cooking oil. I used it to spread the fire. It was dark. No one saw it. I came around and blocked the last door with a bench. Then I saved you, Lee, just you. I knew if you heard me screaming you'd be the first one out of there."

There was a glow over them in the hallway, emanating from some small window at the back of the Theater. There was a racket like the world ending against the barricaded six double-doors. The two of them stood listening to the screams.

"We can't just let them die," Lee said.

"Why?" Jessica asked. "Why? Why? Why? Are they our children? Do we owe them anything?"

"I was protecting them," Lee said.

"You were protecting us!" Jessica said. "What did you always say our weakness was? The gun could only be in one place at a time. Now we don't need it anywhere but with us. Think about the food!"

Travis steadied himself to shoot. His breath was again constricted as smoke slowly filled the hall. His eyes clouded. He could not see them anymore. He panicked. What if they were approaching him even now? What if they were about to fire?

He was bent over, trying to steady himself against the wall. He fought for just enough breath to live at each moment. The screams never ceased, nor quieted in those minutes. It seemed like Hell.

He wanted to free them, but he knew Lee Golding

stood there with his gun. He wanted to kill Lee Golding, but he could not stand or see or breathe.

He fell to the ground. In the cacophony from the Theater, Lee and Jessica did not hear it.

Somehow one voice came out above the others. It was Rick Dumas.

"HELP ME! LEE! I'M IN HERE! HELP ME!"

Travis's eyes were shutting, two seconds, three seconds.

"I'M STILL IN HERE! LEE!"

Lee turned from the Theater and walked quickly into the dark. Jessica chased after him. The cellphone in his pocket buzzed for a text message. He knew who it was. He and Rick had learned they could send text messages directly to each other's cell phone. It had seemed a great power at first, trying to guard the Theater and galley with one gun, but they'd found the communication range too limiting for that distance. He felt that phone buzz in his pocket and knew it was from the Theater.

The doors shook mightily but the barricades held them tight. Travis heard the screams in his nightmare. That's how he knew they lasted so long. When he woke, everything was quiet. The fire was likely still burning in the Theater, but there weren't any more people.

Travis made his way back through the darkness and twilight lighting to the Grand Atrium.

Most of those in the Theater died of smoke inhalation or from crushing under the panicked mob. Rick Dumas burned for his sins. The Theater fire doors held a long time so that the fire consumed everything within it.

57

All they had been through had been about Suffering. Adam didn't take the voices during the sickness as authoritative. He knew it had been a madness. But it was a clue, and he studied on it until he knew it was the key. Suffering led to Jesus. It led to Revelations. It led to Job:

Dead things are formed from under the waters, and the inhabitants thereof.

To Abraham, Genesis chapter 22, the sacrifice of Isaac. It led Adam Melville, in his mental frenzy, bible pages flipping quickly between his fingers, finally to Judas, Jesus' betraying disciple, who suffered so much for his killing sin, as Adam suffered since killing the pirate. Matthew 27:5.

Adam's followers were starved, weak, traumatized and insulated from the old world. They had only Adam to follow and they clung to his vision and hopes for them. They parted from each other just once more, each to find where they had left their wallets and purses. They came back to the restaurant and walked together out onto the Sunrise Deck where they removed every piece, money, cards, pictures, phones, and threw them over the railings.

They returned to the solarium.

On a cruise ship, they had chairs and ladders and rope. The solarium had three metal tracks along its glass ceiling, through which rope could be looped.

"We have been chosen," Adam said. "God reached

into our lives and said, you need to be on the boat. You'll be spared from the Flood, but you'll be tested. We were attacked, so that we couldn't return to the failed world. A gun was left, to bring violence among us. Count your days! God said. Know your lifetime."

He stopped talking. He got up on his own chairs. He had two, as the chairs were small and might collapse or topple under his weight. The sun had come out at last; the clouds had parted like a curtain, revealing the great sun and the blue that had been hidden so long. Like Superman pulling open his shirt and jacket, the universe wasn't really grey; that had been only a costume to hide the magic and majesty. The universe was revealed, anew.

All that life, all that strife, all that yelling and screaming, hoping and dreaming. What a ride! What an idiot's ride his life had been. He laughed.

The others were all up on their chairs.

Life was a greater joke still, God a more honest comedian than Lenny Bruce or Bill Hicks or George Carlin. Adam had been so sure of himself all his life, the power of his mind and his form. He had believed in God, but he had only worshipped himself.

San Francisco, they'd danced naked in the park as the sun rose. He was so young, so full of energy and he felt so close to God. Perhaps that was the closest he had been to a prophet, to righteousness. Then came failed marriage, disillusionment, worship of money and technology and the power of man and mind. He had thought it was all a path, an honest consistency running from Golden Gate Park to Silicon Valley. Layers were being revealed to him now. He was learning more of his own life in these last few moments of it than he had in sixty-five years of living it. He knew there was something beautiful in it. He knew he had been special and blessed and it had guided him, off the path and back, to be here. Abraham had been asked to sacrifice his son. He felt hungry now to sacrifice himself to fill some place in God's plan. He'd been born for this, run away from it, been led to it.

When he opened his eyes he had to squint from the sun. It felt so warm on his face, the first warmth in so many weeks.

"We didn't have to wait to go to God. God came to us. God came a long way. Now he's shut all our doors, and waits just out the window. We just have to take one step to meet him."

Matthew 27:5.

And Judas cast down the pieces of silver in the temple, and departed, and went and hanged himself.

He stepped off his chairs, knocking one of them over. There was a symphony of clanging chairs going over on the tile floor, and muted grunts. A chorus of fifty righteous, willful deaths.

58

The ship was aflame.

Brenda White returned before Travis could, and warned Hesse.

After the pirate attack, fires had been contained in fire-resistant sealed sections. That time there had been an organized response led by the Festival's trained fire crew. They had now to organize something similar, with a half dead army. The indefatigable John Hesse had quickly put together a fire brigade, but they had been directed by Brenda's understanding of the fire as emanating from her electrical sabotage a level below the Theater.

When Travis came back to the Atrium he felt like a bear returning from a winter in a cave. The sun had just come up, and the light in the Atrium made him squint. Travis noticed his clothes were splashed with new vomit and blood and he wondered from whom they came. He was a killer. He felt like he should tell someone.

He saw his son and ran to him. The boy watched his father across the great floor, fixed to his spot. Finally, when his father's arms came to him and lifted him to his chest, the boy smiled. The mother watched and smiled too. She had been wasting away, draining out physically and emotionally. Her smile now was real and solid, on the face of a ghost. Her smile had been Travis's favorite thing at one time. Seeing it now seemed a final gift.

Travis stayed in that embrace with Darren, shutting his

eyes. He wished they could die this way. Finally he put his boy down to find Hesse.

Real sunlight made the Atrium beautiful again. The pillars and statues shone, the long drapes seemed bright and bold. Only the people, sick, coughing, lying down in filthy clothing, were still gray.

Travis found Hesse.

"They're all dead," Travis told him in the office.

Hesse took it in dumbly.

"That Golding, his wife set fire to the Theater. Locked them all in. They're all dead, except Golding and his wife."

How long they sat there, while the sun shone into the Atrium.

Finally Hesse said, "You couldn't kill him?"

As if the story would change and there would be a better ending.

Hesse told Travis about the firefight. Travis shook his head. The firefighters were sent to the wrong level. Even if the fire from below had been contained in the stairwell, the Theater fire would have spread. He knew at least that backstage door of the Theater had been left open. The fire would have spread from the Theater.

They were quiet a while. Then it was Travis who brought them back to the ship, and what had to be done.

"He'll be in the galley," Travis said. "It's the only place he can be, unless he wants to take whatever won't rot and move off the grid. He thinks I was in the Theater. In the fire. He thinks he has the only gun on the ship again. But he'll still be waiting. He'll be in the galley and if he's not he'll have destroyed whatever food he couldn't carry."

"Do you have any bullets?"

"Three."

"Give me the gun, I'm going to end this," Hesse said.

"No," Travis said. "Don't ask again."

They were in no rush to talk. The sun on their faces was an irresistible distraction. There were spaces between each communication.

"If he's gone from the galley," Travis said, "how will we find him? And what good will it do us?"

"If he's gone from the galley, he'll have food stashed. The perishables are irrelevant, there wasn't much left. But he'll have bread, flour, and clean water, and he'll have it hidden somewhere. It doesn't matter, it just doesn't matter what it means, what it helps, if it gains us anything. We have to kill him."

Travis agreed. Killing Golding was a need now. It gave meaning to their lives.

"I need some time with my family," Travis said. "Let's talk later."

"Wait," Hesse said. "Travis. How did we get here? What did we do wrong?"

"I don't know. There's only so much difference your choices can make when you don't control anyone else's. Maybe some games are built to lose."

Travis left Hesse; Hesse went back into his office.

Back near the grand staircase, Travis rejoined Gerry, Corrina, Darren and Claude. Claude had said nothing on Travis's return. Travis felt no animosity towards Claude. He was glad he was still around; still felt that it was more shelter for his son to have Claude there.

Gerry took Travis aside. They walked towards a closed

off staircase. In privacy, Gerry said simply, "Any bullets?"

"Three."

He handed Gerry the gun.

"Get it back fast, and with a bullet left," Travis said. "I aim to put it in Golding."

Gerry took the gun. This time he wouldn't come back without firing it. He went up the stairs; Travis went back to his group.

It was a long walk to the solarium. Gerry was in no hurry. He stopped at the first of the exterior decks, and took in the sun. Was he a violent man? Claude had asked. Yes, he was. He had lied to Professor Claude. He had always been violent. He'd hated it, shamed for it, bellowed it, rode it and used it as a threat at various points in his life, but it had always been there. There could be no greater testimony to that beast inside him than the lengths he had gone through in his life to get beyond it. Poetry. Yet in poetry was passion and violence too. It was a false cover. His life had been shaped by violence.

"If I kill, let it be for love. But let me kill."

He went back into the dark, ascending.

Professor Claude sat with Darren by his side, but felt a chasm between them.

"Flood myths are just about universal," he told Darren. "Every culture, every religion has a story of a great flood that wiped away all the earth, all humanity. No one knows if these stories are based on facts, or whether there is some deep human urge or fear of this kind of idea: wiping out everybody, even all history, and starting fresh."

"That's what God should do," Darren said.

He had no more power than the boy, the professor thought. Helpless, but to watch as whatever life had in store came right at them. He was a history professor and had at times imagined himself as a fly on the wall in some dramatic era; he'd wondered what it felt like to watch great events unfold, powerless over the direction of your own existence in the face of such forces. He was the same as the boy, now, tossed about in the sea of history, at the mercy of fate or the actions of some small handful of men.

There were hundreds of them still on this boat, and there was this bond between them, one that stretched across eons of human life; the bystanders, the victims, of history. They were the mob that lived sometimes with the illusion that they controlled their own condition.

When Gerry came into the light it was into a forest of corpses, hanging from above, swaying ever so slightly. They already smelled.

Gerry stopped at the sight. The meaning of what had happened here was obvious, but so shocking, and so overwhelming, that Gerry's brain simply stopped for a moment. Then he saw it again, and knew what had happened. He cursed their disdain for this life and this world.

He walked the rows. There was the mother. The boy in the red shirt was not there.

Perhaps he wasn't so eager to meet his judge.

"Why"

The voice was so quiet Gerry imagined he'd imagined it. But it came again.

"Why"

It came like a breath. If there were a place for ghosts, Gerry thought, this was it. He stepped softly towards where he imagined the voice to have come from. A fly buzzed around his head. He parted the bodies like curtains.

At the end of the row, the enormous, bloated body of Adam Melville hung, the fingers flexed and open to the ground.

"Why" the bloated purple face said through lips that seemed not to move at all. Two flies buzzed around his head.

The body swayed just so. Adam Melville blinked.

59

Lee Golding's galley was abandoned, not a trace of food was left, save the spills and splashes dried and scummy over the counters, floors and stoves.

In the days that followed, Hesse and Travis went together searching for him. Gerry again ventured to join them but Travis again chose to protect a father for his son.

The ship was large, even now, with more and more of it shut off to keep the fire at bay. They had always to tread quietly and with great care. It occurred to Travis that they were hunting a man with an automatic rifle, while they held one pistol with three bullets. It was suicidal. But he didn't think of stopping. When Travis was home, Hesse was hunting, so the gun never was at rest. There were no more locked cabins on the ship then.

They ate mostly fish, stretched in soup, bread and with rice.

On the second day, Travis explored some of the crew quarters that had not been flooded. In the living room there was a cell phone on a desk. It still had battery power. He turned it on. No signal. He scrolled through pictures. It showed a young woman, taking self-shots with friends in ports of call around the world. Home shots, with her parents and sister and dog.

Travis felt his knees go. He hadn't slept in days. He steadied himself and went into the bedroom. There were two bunk beds. One of the beds was still perfectly made. It was like an artifact of another planet.

Travis lay down. I'll just rest my eyes. I can hear the cabin door.

He remembered working in his dad's shop at twelve years old, the year before they lost it, cleaning the basement store room and being so tired he took a nap on the boxes until his dad knocked his head to wake him.

He held the gun, pointed at the closed bedroom door. He closed his eyes.

He dreamt of the Festival, so that when wakefulness came it seemed like a dream. His body stayed asleep and he fell back into his dream.

He heard a crack. He shot up in bed. It was dark now in the room. The sun had set and though it was still daylight out the window, the room was shadowed.

He listened and heard nothing. He swung his legs down from the bed and came to his feet. He heard nothing. He waited, with his ear against the bedroom door. Nothing. He opened the door and looked out into the living area. The cabin door was still shut. He tiptoed across the floor, and listened at that door. This time he only paused a moment before opening the door and leaping into the hallway, his gun up, his head swiveling to take in both ways. The hallway was lit by the emergency tracks and empty as far as Travis could see, as the hall melted to darkness 30 feet in either direction.

Travis returned to his group. After the incident in the piano lounge, they had moved into an abandoned suite.

"How you doing, champ?" Travis said to Darren.

"I'm bored," Darren said.

Travis's head twitched at the answer.

"You want to go swimming with me later?" he whispered.

"Yeah," Darren said.

"OK. I gotta go down to the Atrium to talk with John Hesse."

"What do you talk about?" Darren asked.

Again, Travis was taken aback. Darren had not been asking such questions, had not been exhibiting interest or hope, since long before the rape.

"How to get us out of here," Travis said.

"I want to go home," Darren said.

Travis hugged him.

"Good, honey," he said. "That's really good. We all have to really want it to make it come true."

Soon, Travis passed the gun to Hesse and returned. They never went swimming. Claude had taken a cabin on the same hall, but sat with Darren that night. The skies were clear and the night sky so bright that they opened the balcony door and looked out and the stars shone as if they were just out of reach.

"My favorite mythology is Vulcan," Professor Claude said. "You know, Star Trek. Mister Spock's people. Such a beautiful founding myth. The crowning glory of Vulcan culture is peace. Their legends tell that that peace grew out of the most violent of histories. But one Vulcan sect sacrificed their own blood to end the wars. Surak, the greatest of Spock's ancestors, sent ambassadors for peace. They were killed. He sent more, and they were killed. But he didn't give up; he didn't stop. War is a perpetual motion machine, running on blood and always making more. Surak's people sacrificed their blood for their enemies. Finally, the blood of the peaceful ran through the machine. The pump of violence lost its prime."

"I wish we could beam off this ship," Darren said.

"Well, it's all make believe," Claude said. "But it's nice to imagine."

60

The seas turned again, and the fish disappeared. Their hunger grew awful.

Each day another deck, room by room, Travis and Hesse read the remains of the ship itself: the infrastructure built by the ship's company, the detritus of the tourists and survivors, and even the dead and the living that still existed throughout. Each day they'd return to the Atrium, where those that cared to continue living came for the poor nourishment that remained, and the fresh water of Brenda White's rainwater supply. What was being eaten now would not have been food off the ship. The ventilation was out again, as were the toilets, and the air grew worse.

Death passed through the ship with a heavy hand. The last patients in the medical clinic weren't getting better anymore, and Travis and the few nurses stopped taking new ones. There were no doctors, no morphine nor whiskey left for them as they wasted away.

Corrina never told Brenda what happened, never went back to the playroom. She slowly began to speak again around her family. She fought to recover that. She had tried, for days, not to exist, but she couldn't. She and Darren had to exist for each other. She didn't leave the new room, but she could exist there.

Vera died. The baby died.

Adam stuck to himself, mostly. The open wound all

around his neck was in danger of infection, but no one was practicing medicine anymore. He hunted too, though what he looked for no one knew. His mind had broken into pieces again, and the voices returned. He wandered the ship, inside and out. He haunted the ship, and the people of the ship haunted him. The living were ghosts to him, and he walked past as though they could not harm him. Gerry wondered if he was somehow with his disciples after all. Gerry never saw the boy in the red shirt. He raged at himself. He had let the rapist go. Time went backwards, cause and effect inverted. He had let her get raped by not killing her rapist. The shame overwhelmed him so that he almost could not look at her.

The fire was spreading, they heard every day. It took out each barrier with time. Time was on the fire's side.

On the eighth day of searching, they found each other by the fire: Hesse and Travis, Lee and Jessica, each out to learn how small their ship was becoming.

Travis fired first.

Lee was quickly in front of Jessica so that Travis saw only the single silhouette at the end of the corridor.

Lee fired back, single shots, one, two, three. Hesse and Travis backed into the same stairwell they had come out from.

The Mighty Lee Golding pressed the attack, firing through the wall he knew they cowered behind. Travis and Hesse escaped up the stairs. There was a moment's respite, and they heard only their breath and heartbeats as they waited for Lee to come after them.

Two bullets left. But what chance would be better than this? Travis rolled over and sat up at the top of the stairs, completely exposed, for a clear shot when Lee opened that stairwell door.

The door never opened. Lee had retreated. By the time Travis went down the stairs and after him, they knew they wouldn't find him.

Gerry Adamson sat on the promenade deck and looked out and finished his note.

The end of the world came
And we no longer asked, who by fire and who by sword
We all died by water
In a fragile craft on a disinterested sea
We dreamed, loved, bled and hungered
For more time, when great things would occur
And then the water rose
And went over us,
And our dreams did not float, nor loves, nor blood, nor hunger

61

"Don't let them win," Jessica said.

She lay across Lee's legs, on the floor of a room they had sheltered and hidden their food stores in. She bled out her back onto his pants. He had carried her back after Travis Cooke had shot her.

Now he could not speak. Tears streamed from his tired eyes and his great frame shook with the effort to hold in his cries.

"I'm sorry," he said finally.

Her face was white, even the deep red of her lips faded.

"Don't. Don't regret," she whispered.

Her eyes were still open and she looked up into his.

"You were my hero," she said.

She died on his legs and he bent over. The tears flowed freely and he opened his mouth. For a moment nothing came, then an animal wail shook him and shook the room.

He allowed himself some minutes to cry. Then he knew he had to let her body go. He would not allow them any chance to defile her. He would not allow the indignity of them seeing her dead. He carried his broken love, he cradled her like a baby in his arms, the gun still held in his fist under her back. He was not cautious. He felt no danger, no fear this time, just a growing void, as though his universe was disappearing from inside him.

This cabin had no balcony, but a level up was the Resort Deck with its exterior promenade. He carried her up the dark stairway, then in the hallway felt his knees weaken and his shoulder bounced off the wall before he straightened himself. Tears came slowly in tracks down his cheeks, disappearing into his beard.

The air was calm, the sun bright but cool as he walked to stern with Jessica. At the rail, he looked down at her and kissed her pale lips. He kissed her eyes and forehead and her face was wet with his tears. He dropped her over the railing and there was no sound back to him as the body disappeared in a white puff far below.

Back in the room, he took out his cellphone. He had to see her again. He saw that he had four text messages, and his battery was almost dead.

The messages were from Rick. The dead man begged to be let out of the fire.

62

Travis woke late in the morning and Gerry and Darren were gone. He sat up on the couch. Corrina was up, and came over. She had a small bottle of water, and she gave him a drink and she had one. He got up from the couch and followed her out of the cabin.

They walked up the stairs to the open air of the Resort Deck and the sun. The sun, so rare they'd forgotten about it. It was warm. Travis took off his coat. They walked astern but still neither spoke. Travis took off his shirt. It clung to his skin so that he had to be slow to prevent it tearing. He wondered how he would get it back on, but he immediately felt cleaner and healthier with the warm sun and air on his skin.

There was a cushioned wood sun lounger. Corrina took Travis's hand and pulled him down with her onto the bed. They kissed. His right and her left hand mixed finger after finger. It was time, because there was no more time. She wasn't going to allow the rape to define her final days, the story of her and Travis. She could still make the choices while she breathed and moved.

He pulled her shirt up. She stopped him with her hand. He grasped her back under the shirt. Her flesh was thin and he could feel her bones. She gave him a kiss with three years in it.

Three years he'd wanted her touch, three years he'd been tortured by her presence and absence, three years he'd been in his personal hell hoping that he could have one day of life back in the paradise her love had been. He remembered the last time they'd made love. Two weeks before he'd gone to Sudan. They'd been fighting, and it was a passionate, desperate sex. They fought more afterwards, and when he left for Sudan two weeks later, that night remained the last. They were as passionate, as physically desperate, for each other now. It was the same stage play with an altogether different meaning.

They did not move a long time after. The sun made them so comfortable. Finally, she worried for Darren and stirred.

Travis sat up. The most important thing in his life had just gone right. If it meant nothing more than this moment, it was infinitely better.

"We're going to get off this ship," he said. "And you'll go back to your life with Gerry, and Darren will grow up great. And I'll be happy we had this talk."

They both smiled. Still they did not move.

"If we get through this life," Travis said, "and meet on the other side, can we be in love again?"

"Oh, Travis," she said.

Days of quiet searching followed, each day a scorecard of survivors and dead.

Hesse seemed never to rest now, between searching with Travis and maintaining somehow the structure and organization their lives depended on.

The sun stayed out mostly. It was cool and pleasant. There was a basketball game occasionally, the oppressiveness of time called for it. Never did Lee

Golding or Travis Cooke play. There were still some, like Travis and Hesse, that the flood had found in the fullest strength of their life. They could still function physically, though not well. The games were lethargic, the players weak and clumsy, but there was a joy in it, of life escaping death for the moment. Sometimes there was an audience of survivors drinking in the sun on deck, so that more and more of the sun loungers knocked over by the waterslide flood were over time set back upright.

In those days, they didn't talk much at all. They were all thirsty, their mouths sticky and the more their mouths were open, the drier their tongues and lips became. They guarded every drop of moisture in them.

Days after the gunfight in the stairwell, Claude spoke quietly to Travis's group in their new cabin.

"I found Golding's food. Some canned stuff, crackers, nuts, water. There's not much, but for us it'll be enough."

"Enough for what?" Corrina said. She sat on the couch with Darren sleeping against her shoulder.

The three men were quiet, shocked Corrina had spoken.

"To go," Claude said.

"Where was Golding?" he said.

"He was in the bathroom, I could hear him. She must have been with him. I know you got the gun. We gotta go back and get that food on the lifeboat. That lifeboat will work, Travis, ask Gerry."

"It'll work," Gerry said. "We've been working on it. It's all shot up, but the only actual damage was a gas line. We patched and stole some gas from another boat. The davit's good too. We rigged it so you can drop it right from the door, but it's gonna be a hell of a drop."

"There's just the one boat?" Travis asked.

"There's one other lifeboat with a working davit, but it won't start," Claude said.

"How many people can we get in the boat?" Corrina asked, siting up straight.

"There's not going to be any other people in that boat," Claude said. "She sails soon, and there's not enough in Golding's stash to spread around. You want to go around and pick who gets on and gets off? And try and keep that quiet?"

"You know how to get it down?" Travis said.

"Yes, we looked at the cards," Claude said.

"We can't choose our own lives over others," Gerry said. "We can have a lottery."

"I'm the only one who knows where the food is," Claude said, "and I'll tell you we aren't picking any names out of a hat. I already did it, and I picked you. Don't betray that. We've got to get the rest of the food before Golding finds out. We've played real nice since this all started, and we're either damned lucky or just damned to still be alive. This is the only chance we're gonna get, and sharing it isn't gonna work. It isn't gonna happen."

Travis looked down at the polished table. There was his reflection; a dirty, hairy old man he didn't recognize.

"I'll go back with Claude and get the food," Travis said. "I wish we could all stick together right now but it's too dangerous with Golding around. Give us a half hour head start, then come meet us at the lifeboat. Gerry, Claude — you both can find it again?"

"Yes."

"Yes."

Darren opened his eyes and looked up at Travis with a smile. Travis gave Darren a high-five. He touched Corrina's shoulder for a moment. He took a look around the Atrium. He'd risked his life for weeks for these people. Or had they been incidental all along? They were going to die and he was going to live. There was no way they could all live. If they had another rush on the last lifeboat, it would go as badly as the last one had.

Goodbye.

He and Claude Bettman ascended again into the darkness.

"Is there a piano on the lifeboat?" Travis said.

"No."

"We'll have to tell jokes then," Travis said.

63

The Mighty Lee Golding poured water over his arms, scooped from a toilet's basin. The ghost of his wife rushed to him, laying her hands forcefully on his body.

"Stop," the ghost cried.

"I have to get this off," he whispered.

"That's good water!" she said.

"I can't stand it," he said.

He rubbed at the blood on his arms, Warrant's, old and dark, smeared with Jessica's, fresh, red and vibrant.

"I'm getting crazy," he said. "I can't stand being cooped up. How could he have escaped the Theater? I tell you, it was the same one! They only have one gun, but he won't die!"

Her face scrunched as she prepared the words in reply. Lee stopped her.

"What's that?" he said.

He put up his finger to silence her.

The bathroom door was open just a crack. Lee slowly, quietly pushed it forward. The gun was ready. He stepped out onto the carpet but could not help making a sound, as the floor creaked just enough. Lee threw himself around the corner to a view of the stateroom. There was no one there. He ran to the door and peered into the hall. In the darkness he could not see anyone, but he heard footsteps, running away.

"Someone's been eating our porridge," Lee said,

regarding the pile of cans, boxes, sacks, and plastic bottles in the kitchen. Something had indeed been disturbed.

He looked at the ghost against the dim light of the drawn drapes of the big windows. He knew she was dead, that she was not here, but he spoke aloud.

"It's over," he said. "I can't keep moving all this food with me. They'll never let me sleep. They'll hunt day and night."

He looked up, where the ghost had been.

"I haven't enough bullets to kill them all, they'll win in the end."

His face went down into his hands.

"They've already won. They took you."

He looked at his hands and still saw the blood. The gun was on the floor at his feet. He stood straight and looked right at those dimly glowing drapes.

"Why fight? I don't want to stay in character anymore. The winners are picked. The moves are staged. There's no one watching us battle and scream and pound our chests, play heel and face, good and bad. I can't care any more. You're gone. They've taken everything from me, and they know it! Each moment I live is a humiliation. I'm lying on the mat, they're raising their arms above me and mocking me, and they won't let me leave. I just lie there on the mat."

He picked up the gun and studied it as if there was a secret in it to decipher.

But for that pistol, they never could come against him. They never would dare dozens of them slaughtered, even with the fire heating the air around them.

The ghost was silent, and he looked at her and ached

in his heart at the accusations in her eyes. His heartache turned to rage, as it had all his life.

"I won't let them gloat over our bodies," he said. "That can't be the end. I have enough bullets to kill your murderers. And then I'll kill the others until my last bullet and when I blow my own brains out, they'll know what I did everything for, and no one will think they beat us."

"Yes," she said.

They went into the darkness. Towards the Atrium. The fire had spread beyond their expectations. He could feel it behind closed doors.

They were close to the end.

64

Two bullets and a sudden hope, that he and Darren and Corrina might live, might see each other off this ship. That he might see Darren grow.

It was an agonizing walk to Lee Golding's hiding spot, fearful each moment of Lee and of opening the wrong door and finding the blaze. Claude led Travis to a stateroom near the top level, so that it cooled as they got closer.

It was quiet in the dark hall. No emergency lighting. They were silent. The door was closed, but the bolt had been crashed with a kick so it was not secure. Travis motioned Claude to stay back. He put his hand on the door, crouched as low as he could to the side of the door, pushed it very slowly out of the doorframe.

Travis stopped and waited. He slowly pushed the door open. He waited. He heard nothing.

They waited by the door a full two minutes. When they heard no sound, Travis walked in real low. He stayed behind the entryway wall, counted down from five, and spun around the corner, gun held high.

The room was illuminated by sunlight through the open balcony drapes. It was empty. The food was still there.

Silently, they gathered what they could. Travis used his jacket to fashion a sack, holding the bottom band out and flipped up with one arm. He added a few smaller items to his pants pockets and folded some into his elbows and arms.

They were out again. Carrying as much as they were, they could not move so delicately and quietly returning in the darkness, but they met no disaster until the last door revealed the sunlit deck.

The few remaining boats were so damaged, it seemed impossible one could still function. When Travis saw the one Claude stopped at, it seemed the more unlikely. The davits were badly bent, and bullet holes dotted the bow.

"It'll work," Claude said. "Why aren't they here yet?"

Claude opened the door and stepped up and in. He dropped his load of food and water and sat at the controls. He turned a key, and Travis saw the navigation lights switch on. The motor started with a cough as Claude tested that too for just a second before turning it off. Travis heard a mechanical clang, and the davits shook. Claude came back to the door.

"Why aren't they here yet?" he said.

Travis took of his jacket and wrapped it tight as a bundle around his food and drink. The sound of gunfire answered Claude's question. One shot, then two more. There was no screaming that could penetrate the distance from the Atrium, but Claude and Travis imagined they heard it anyways.

"We've got to go back for them," Travis said. He had already slipped several steps from the lifeboat.

"We're not going back into that," Claude said.

"I can't leave Darren," Travis said.

"I can," Claude said.

He slammed the door shut.

Travis knew his last chance was going in that boat and he leapt back to the davit, searching for a way to stop it. There was a loud clang and the davit shook. The boat dropped, but for one moment, Travis saw Claude through the window. They'd known each other thirty days, they'd seen each other every day for those thirty days, they'd seen intimately how each lived and thought and acted under the greatest pressure.

Their eyes connected, an intense final examination, and Claude was gone.

There was another gunshot and Travis's turned away without hesitation and ran back towards the Atrium, leaping several lounge chairs as he sprinted. His Darren, his Corrina; he would leave this body lifeless before he would leave them.

He raced up the walking deck. The real screams sounded in his ears as he got closer.

65

Adam saw Jessica Golding and Rick Dumas sometimes. He knew they were ghosts, and that he was in a state between worlds and could consequently see everything.

He walked through staterooms, looking for things.

Sometimes while he walked forward he walked backwards through time. He was in No Time, and everything could happen around him at the same time as all of history in the flesh and blood world.

He walked through jungles, across tundra, above mountain ranges, and watched gods and spirits, heroes and villains, and the spirits drifted in the air all about him, eagles, snakes, bears, jaguars, apes, wolves and spiders, and monsters that never roamed the Earth, but he couldn't ask them the Why that haunted him, Why he had not been allowed to go to God with the others.

He was immortal. Worse, he was immortal in all time and had to see everyone suffer.

He knew the ship was ablaze, but he didn't only walk on the ship, he walked through Rome as it burned.

He found himself in the ship's casino, as Jesus flipped the gambling tables.

Then the voices in his head all came together in a chorus, and he was called.

.

66

"Don't move," Travis could hear Lee Golding's voice above the screaming. "You move, I'll kill you."

Travis chose a closed stairway so that he could look in at the Atrium from a hidden position.

Amid the massive wood and gold columns, the cowering groups of survivors, the dead fountains and flower boxes, he couldn't see his family, nor could he see Lee. He saw that an always-open hallway was now shut off by a double fire door and he knew the fire had reached this refuge.

Then John Hesse came into sight. He walked like a titan through the refugees crouched along the floor. Lee Golding came to meet him. They were by the bar Hesse had made his first speech from. Near them was the marble statue of the great fish, diving into the water. Everything around it had deteriorated, while that statue was as Travis had first seen it.

"Where's Cooke?" Lee Golding said.

"I don't know," Hesse said.

Lee Golding pointed the gun at Hesse's middle.

Travis aimed and fired first. The Mighty Lee Golding shuddered. He spun sideways. Hesse jumped on him, as Travis ran from the stairs and others came to their feet.

The second gunshot echoed in the cavernous Atrium. The back exploded clean out of John Hesse and he fell over, against the statue, bleeding out.

Hesse's cloak of invulnerability had sheltered everyone to some extent. John Hesse had been a man of magic, made of something different than other men, something other than flesh. The flesh was destroyed and the magic was gone. Everyone stopped at the moment Hesse was killed, as though the ship itself was expected to fall in on them.

Hesse's life flashed before Travis's eyes in one beat of his heart: memories of that incredible athlete on the rugby field, saving that little girl when the pirates attacked, hopping on that bar and getting everyone to come together, organizing the medical teams, meetings in his art shop office, asking Travis to clean up the suicides, hunting Golding. Travis knew nothing of Hesse' life off the boat, but felt the contour of it: a life knowing how to behave, how to be happy. The life Travis had always wanted.

With Travis's next heartbeat, Lee Golding was back on his feet.

He lifted the rifle, steadied it with his left hand and fired at Travis, but he was hurt by Travis's shot, and the gun went off awkwardly. Travis had already crossed the Atrium to his family.

With an enormous noise, a roofed section of the Atrium near the double doors came down. Smoke filled the chamber and Travis lost sight of Lee as all were on their feet now. Travis grabbed his family and they ran with the crowd to the exits to the exterior promenade. A stairway came loose and tottered, and then just fell to pieces in the air, raining down slabs of metal and wood. He had seen Brenda White and her family below the stairway. Now, Travis could not see the people screaming in the cloud of smoke and debris.

Travis and his group came out the door and onto the deck, and now no one was sure which way to run at all.

"The boat's gone," Travis told Gerry, "Bettman's gone."

"Follow me," Gerry said. "We can lower the other one."

Fire had reached so many parts of the ship that people scrambled to escape each dead end. In the open of the deck, it was chaos. Survivors filled random disabled lifeboats, or crowded the railings waiting to jump.

Gerry led them to the one lifeboat he had found earlier that still might let them off the ship, and Travis found his jacket-food bundle where he'd left it and returned quickly to the others. One davit was bent, so one end of the boat tilted precariously. The boat looked so broken that others ignored it for the moment, sprinting past as Gerry opened the door. He came back to the davit.

"Get on," Gerry said. "I have to open the brakes here."

"How will you get on?" Travis said.

"I'll have to jump, it's the only way," Gerry said.

"No!" Corrina cried.

"I can do it! Just get Darren on the boat now!"

The fire now was prominent everywhere they could look.

Gunfire sounded and Travis saw Lee Golding far down the deck running at them. The gun was on automatic now. Travis scooped Darren up and held him at his shoulder, by the door. Now, others saw Lee cutting them off and they turned and pushed past Travis to get on the lifeboat.

Travis had one bullet left. He fired and missed.

Lee kept coming. Out of a cloud of smoke came Adam Melville, behind the Mighty Lee Golding, chasing him down.

Adam knew he had to kill the Mighty Lee Golding. He was meant to. Through Lee Golding lay peace.

Adam closed on Lee Golding as though Lee were not running at all, and then tackled him around the shoulders. The two men went down.

Flames tore through the windows and doors from the ships interior.

"Get on!" Gerry shouted. "I've almost got the brake open!"

The crowd now getting on crushed them, and Corrina was pushed away.

The two giants came back to their feet, but Lee had lost the gun. Almost engulfed in flames, the two men wrestled. They fell back into the burning wall, and through it.

The fire roared in Lee's ears, as he hit the ground. He was pinned, unable to move under Adam's weight. He'd lost, and he heard nothing but cheering.

Flames crawled upon them. They burned in each other's grasps but Adam's spirit had left the body and its pain was harmless to him.

Hands and bodies struggling to get through pierced the open space in the lifeboat doorway. Travis's arm holding Darren was trapped in with those bodies. Corrina was separated from them by other bodies.

With one arm holding Darren, Travis reached across the shoulder behind him to grab for Corrina.

Darren screamed for his mother.

Travis took her wrist and nearly snapped it as he struggled to pull her through the bodies behind him as he pushed through the bodies ahead of him, trying to get Darren through the door.

There was a shift in the Festival. Travis caught a glimpse of Gerry at the davit's controls. An explosion roared above all other noise. The ship shuddered; the lifeboat jerked. Travis lost his grip on Corrina and fell back into the lifeboat with Darren, a flash of orange light in his eyes.

"Darren, I love you!" he heard Corrina scream.

The davit released with a loud clang, the cable let itself out and the lifeboat fell away; all aboard bounced weightless for a moment as they fell. Darren and Travis screamed out for Corrina.

The lifeboat dropped three decks, hitting the sea with tremendous weight, the bow cutting into the water first, so that the open door in the boat's stern was highest. Still, water flooded in, then the boat's dive stopped and it rose again, steady with an inch of water on the floor.

Travis came to his feet first. He found Darren quickly and snatched him to his chest.

Some on the lifeboat were injured from the fall and cried out. Travis ran to the lifeboat's open door holding Darren. They looked out at the Festival, thirty feet away, looming high above them and filling their visions. It shifted, leaning further away from them. They could look up at the railings of the deck they had fallen from, but they saw only flames.

There was no sign of Corrina, no sign of Gerry. The world they'd lived on so long was crowned in flame.

They waited, and Travis watched for someone to come plunging into the water, but no one crossed the flames.

They stayed at the door watching, no one spoke. Others were at the windows. The Festival shifted again. Who knew how much time went by before it shifted a third time, toppling almost sideways.

Hours they watched. The sun ran its course and went away. They still had light, the ship still burned. No life ever emerged from the ship or the sea. The lifeboat was dead and had drifted already hundreds of feet.

Travis was never conscious of it happening, but he must have come inside with the boy and sat down, because the next thing he was aware of was waking up on one of the bench seats with Darren in his arms.

Darren had already been awake.

He was looking forward in the boat. Two men and the woman were still asleep. Near the bow was a teenage boy, with a baby face and a red-striped shirt. This was whom Darren watched.

Travis looked at Darren. Darren saw and nodded at his father.

Travis walked forward. The teenager looked up at him.

He said nothing until Travis was above him.

"What?" he said.

Travis grabbed him by the throat. He pulled him up and smashed his head into the window, which shuttered but did not crack. The others on the boat awoke. The boy grabbed Travis by the throat and each of them turned purple, starving of oxygen. Travis smashed the head again into the glass, and again. The boy did not let go of Travis's throat. Travis pressed his thumbs tighter and came up onto the bench, over the boy. Somewhere in his mind he understood Darren was watching, and he felt some satisfaction that he could show Darren that he could fight for the family, that there was someone strong to protect him. The boy was pushed down into the seat then, and Travis was on top of him until he was dead.

He stumbled to crawl back off the bench and the body, then fell backwards into another seat. He regained his feet. He went to the body of the baby-faced boy and dragged him to the stern, and dropped him out the door.

The body drifted away slowly, so that they could see it for hours, just as they moved so slowly away from the ship.

By nightfall, the fire began to burn itself out. By daybreak the fire was gone, and the hump of the ship was in the distance, and the water around them was black and shiny with oil and fuel and littered with flotsam from the ship as far as they could see.

Travis held Darren and they mourned the loss of Corrina. As dehydrated as Travis was, he still had tears, and when they were gone, he just stared down into Darren's eyes, and Darren stared up into his. The most beautiful girl in New York had loved him, and the pain of losing her again was incredible. It didn't matter if there were a God, or karma or just a cold universe, it was cruel.

It was all so random! Here were just dozens alive out

of thousands on that ship. And what qualities, what actions, what plans had determined who would be here? How were souls chosen, which to be born to live in those protected bubbles, and which to inherit the low ground?

After all that fear, pain and loss, Travis and Darren held each other and felt as lucky as they were sad. What was the nature of the world, that this felt lucky?

Travis remembered the night before the flood, when he'd taken all those sleeping pills. He wondered again if he had died, and this now was heaven, and everything else had been something he'd had to go through to get here. He hoped the real Darren might be sleeping in his bed, dreaming of his daddy.

Travis kissed Darren's head until they fell asleep. The boy and their love for each other seemed like a beautiful, shimmering flower in a wasteland.

No one spoke on the lifeboat. They floated for days, and those on the boat slept mostly. Travis relived his life with Corrina, minute by minute. He was amazed at how powerfully his memories came together, how slowly he could play them out in each detail. He reimagined the first and last nights they made love and thanked God that they had connected one more time, and that she had died with no anger between them. What had his life been about, in the end, except that one relationship and the child of it?

Darren never spoke much. He didn't seem withdrawn to Travis, but stoic and watching. He wasn't broken, Travis thought, he was fixed. He'd witnessed everything that could be. If the goal was wisdom, Darren was the winner!

How did they manage, in other places, Travis

wondered. How did they handle it?

At night Travis would wake Darren and share secrets with him.

67

A fishing boat discovered them.

The men came onto it guessing that these were some others who had been caught in the flood. As everyone had been.

"There's one alive," a man said.

He pulled Darren up. Darren woke and saw the men and said nothing. He was so weak.

The others were all dead. Their mouths and faces cracked and disfigured by dehydration.

"It's a miracle you're alive, boy," one said as he handed Darren to another man on the fishing boat.

"Look at here," another man said.

He opened Travis's jacket, which he'd pulled out from under a bench all wrapped up like a package. In it was a water bottle and crackers.

"Why didn't they drink this?" the man asked. He shook his head.

"Why?"

Give Feedback and Keep in Touch

Please **join my mailing list** for exclusive free stories, advance looks at new work, and special offers:

http://bit.ly/davidsachsnews

If your **book club** is reading The Flood, I'd be honored to join your group for any discussion, in person, by Skype, or teleconference.

For independent authors, reviews on Amazon and Goodreads are crucial. PLEASE TAKE A MOMENT TO WRITE A REVIEW. These reviews have a huge impact on how many people will get to see this work.

My review page on Amazon is here:
www.bit.ly/thefloodamazon

My review page on Goodreads is here:
www.bit.ly/thefloodgoodreads

My articles, free fiction, and other commentary on my website:

www.davidsachs.com

On Facebook, here:

http://bit.ly/davidsachsfacebook

If you would like to be a beta reader, or would just like to send me a personal message, email me at:

david@davidsachs.com

THANKS

I would like to thank, first, my wife, for more than I could ever explain, but especially for her patience living with my while I lived with a story about horrible things.

I'd like to thank Peter Whelpton, former EVP at Royal Caribbean Cruise Line, as well as Daniel Capella, cruise industry journalist and consultant, for their guidance on technical and logistical issues. They were a great help in creating the world of the Festival. Daniel even created the ship's layout at my website, **www.davidsachs.com/theflood/**. Any inaccuracies are my own fault (either for story reasons or simply out of ignorance).

I'd like to thank my beta readers (Victoria, Mary, Joe, Maureen, Jennifer, Diana, Jay, Samantha, Suzanne, Dan, Tia and CV), my brothers and many friends who did so much to help me shape this story, and to Theresa Munanga for helping me spell it correctly.

To Martin Gomez, for the excellent original artwork and Suzanne Ng for trudging in the snow for the back cover picture.

To my agent, Melissa McComas for believing in The Flood.

Lastly, to Matt Mather, a great writer and better friend, for his guidance and occasional drink through the process of bringing this to readers.

ABOUT THE AUTHOR

Award-winning author DAVID SACHS lives in Chelsea, Quebec (Canada), in the woods of Parc du la Gatineau. He is a long time feature writer for magazines and major metro newspapers, writing on politics, culture, society and the outdoors, covering everything from anti-globalization riots to Amazonian shamanism, and from homelessness to hitchhiking. He is the only writer we know of to have been featured in Penthouse and the Ottawa Jewish News.

He is a father, an avid outdoorsman and rugby old boy, and a former physicist and Canadian Forces reserves officer. David is heavily involved in political and social causes, and a deadly boogie woogie piano player.

Look for his **Short Stories Based on Themes from the Music of the Tragically Hip** and other works at David's Amazon Author's Page:

www.bit.ly/davidsachsamazonpage

or website:

http://www.davidsachs.com

david@davidsachs.com

42812529R00221

Made in the USA
Lexington, KY
06 July 2015